Reborn to Master the Blade:
From Hero-King to Extraordinary Squire ♀

3

jnc
New York

Author: Hayaken
Illustrator: Nagu

Reborn to Master the Blade:
From Hero-King to Extraordinary Squire ♀

Author: **Hayaken** Illustrator: **Nagu**

Translated by Mike Langwiser
Edited by Carly Smith

This book is a work of fiction. Names, characters, places, and incidents are the product of the author's imagination or are used fictitiously. Any resemblance to actual events, locales, or persons, living or dead, is coincidental.

EIYUOH, BU WO KIWAMERU TAME TENSEI SU.
SOSHITE, SEKAI SAIKYO NO MINARAI KISHI vol. 3
© Hayaken
Illustration by Nagu
All Rights Reserved
First published in Japan by Hobby Japan Co., Ltd.
English translation rights arranged with Hobby Japan Co., Ltd. through Tuttle-Mori Agency, Inc., Tokyo

English translation © 2021 by J-Novel Club LLC

Yen Press, LLC supports the right to free expression and the value of copyright. The purpose of copyright is to encourage writers and artists to produce the creative works that enrich our culture.

The scanning, uploading, and distribution of this book without permission is a theft of the author's intellectual property. If you would like permission to use material from the book (other than for review purposes), please contact the publisher. Thank you for your support of the author's rights.

Yen Press
150 West 30th Street, 19th Floor
New York, NY 10001

Visit us at yenpress.com
facebook.com/yenpress · twitter.com/yenpress
yenpress.tumblr.com · instagram.com/yenpress

First JNC Paperback Edition: June 2024

JNC is an imprint of Yen Press, LLC.
The JNC name and logo are trademarks of J-Novel Club LLC.

The publisher is not responsible for websites (or their content) that are not owned by the publisher.

Library of Congress Cataloging-in-Publication Data
Names: Hayaken, author. | Nagu (Mangaka), illustrator. | Langwiser, Mike , translator.
Title: Reborn to master the blade: from hero-king to extraordinary squire / author, Hayaken ; illustrator, Nagu ; translated by Mike Langwiser.
Other titles: Eiyuuou, bu wo kiwameru tame tenseisu: soshite, sekai saikyou no minarai kishi. English
Description: First JNC paperback edition. | New York : JNC, 2023.
Identifiers: LCCN 2023035595 | ISBN 9781975377915 (v. 1 ; trade paperback) | ISBN 9781975377922 (v. 2 ; trade paperback) | ISBN 9781975377939 (v. 3 ; trade paperback) | ISBN 9781975377946 (v. 4 ; trade paperback) | ISBN 9781975377953 (v. 5 ; trade paperback) | ISBN 9781975377960 (v. 6 ; trade paperback)
Subjects: CYAC: Reincarnation—Fiction. | LCGFT: Fantasy fiction. | Action and adventure fiction. | Light novels.
Classification: LCC PZ7.1.H3914 Re 2023 | DDC [Fic]—dc23
LC record available at https://lccn.loc.gov/2023035595

ISBN: 978-1-9753-7793-9 (paperback)

1 3 5 7 9 10 8 6 4 2

TPA

Printed in South Korea

Reborn to Master the Blade:
From Hero-King to
Extraordinary Squire ♀

CONTENTS

Chapter I:
Inglis, Age 15—Orders to Defend the Hieral Menace (1) — 1

Chapter II:
Inglis, Age 15—Orders to Defend the Hieral Menace (2) — 19

Chapter III:
Inglis, Age 15—Orders to Defend the Hieral Menace (3) — 41

Chapter IV:
Inglis, Age 15—Orders to Defend the Hieral Menace (4) — 61

Chapter V:
Inglis, Age 15—Orders to Defend the Hieral Menace (5) — 79

Chapter VI:
Inglis, Age 15—Orders to Defend the Hieral Menace (6) — 93

Chapter VII:
Inglis, Age 15—Orders to Defend the Hieral Menace (7) — 119

Chapter VIII:
Inglis, Age 15—Orders to Defend the Hieral Menace (8) — 153

Chapter IX:
Inglis, Age 15—Orders to Defend the Hieral Menace (9) — 181

Extra: The Artistic Count — 191

Afterword — 201

Reborn to Master the Blade:
From Hero-King to Extraordinary Squire ♀

Chapter I: Inglis, Age 15—Orders to Defend the Hieral Menace (1)

Thanks to an agreement between Principal Miriela and the new Highland ambassador, the hieral menace Ripple would be staying at the knights' academy for the time being. However, that wasn't going to put the students' regular training on hold.

Today, all of the knights and squires had headed to the Flygear dock on the shores of Lake Bolt to train together. And their return trip, as always, was a long run back to the academy.

"Ha ha ha ha! Run, run! Listen up, squire cadets! This is your chance to show off to the knight cadets who make fun of you behind your backs just because you don't have Runes! Knight cadets, if you lose to the lowly squires, you'll have no business calling yourselves knights! Everyone, show some backbone!" Instructor Marquez, who was in charge of the squires' course, led the students from a Flygear.

Rafinha panted, struggling to breathe between her objections. "I don't like how he says that... That instructor has a bad personality! We don't make fun of the squire cadets at all!"

"There's no way we could! After all...!" Leone looked at Instructor Marquez's Flygear.

Marquez's Flygear wasn't actually flying—it was being carried on top of Inglis's back. Never one to miss an opportunity for a rigorous training session, Inglis had volunteered to carry it while running. This had become a familiar sight for the squire cadets.

"Th-That's outrageous...but at least in terms of speed, I can compete!" Liselotte determinedly sped up even more. Gasping for breath, she caught up with Inglis and the Flygear.

"Oh. Hi, Liselotte. You're pretty fast," Inglis said.

"You're so nonchalant about this!"

Inglis was sweating a little but not breathing hard at all. "Yeah. I'm pretty used to this."

Liselotte was still panting. "You mean...it's tolerable...if you become...accustomed to it?"

"Right. By the way, where are Ban and Ray? I don't see them around."

Those two were Liselotte's retainers. They had both enrolled in the squire program despite having Runes in order to support Liselotte.

"They decided to withdraw from the academy and return home."

"Huh? Really? Oh, was it because Chancellor Arcia resigned?" Inglis asked.

Ray and Ban were young nobles themselves. With Liselotte no longer being the daughter of the chancellor, they didn't have a satisfactory reason to be her squires.

"Yes. You seem to have a good grasp of it. My father has resigned his post and returned to his demesne, so...there was no avoiding it. We are, at least, a landed family."

"You must feel a bit lonely without them."

"Not at all. In fact, their families instructed them to transfer to the knights' program and to abandon acting as my retainers. However, they withdrew from the academy, unwilling to make such an about-face. If they truly want to be knights, then I'll consider them my friends. Someday we may yet fight alongside each other."

Once Rafinha caught up, she gave Liselotte an encouraging pat on the back. "Exactly! Liselotte, you can use my Flygear too. I'll let you ride with me later."

"Oh, thank you..."

"All right!" Rafinha cheered. "Then let's eat something sweet at the cafeteria when we get back! My treat. In this kind of situation, it's best to eat a whole lot of sweets and change your mood. Right, Leone?"

Chapter I: Inglis, Age 15—Orders to Defend the Hieral Menace (1)

Leone had caught up too. "Yeah! I'm a bit worried about gaining weight, but today will be fine."

"Oh, right, Chris. Why don't we take the opportunity to invite Ripple too?" Rafinha suggested.

"She's busy right now," Inglis replied. "Ambassador Theodore and the principal are doing everything they can to figure out what's happening to her. When they're finished, maybe we can invite her?"

"I don't know much about the circumstances—but I think it's a great honor to be able to protect a hieral menace!" Liselotte said.

"So you'd be okay with her coming along, Liselotte?" Rafinha asked.

"Yes! A hieral menace is the kind of person every girl looks up to! Once, long ago, one protected me from a magicite beast. If I could, I'd love to befriend one!" Liselotte's admiration of hieral menaces was clear as day.

"All right, then let's hurry back! Speeeed up!" Rafinha called.

"Rafinha, wait. I'm at my limit!" Leone protested.

"Any more might be a bit much…" Liselotte agreed.

"Good idea." Inglis suddenly sped up.

"Hey, wait! Chris!" Rafinha yelled.

"Whaaat?! How can you keep up that pace?!" Leone cried.

"I… I can't believe it!" Liselotte exclaimed.

Their instructor in the Flygear hadn't expected such speed either. "Whoooa!" He fell out, shaken about from Inglis's rapid pace.

"Ah, sorry, Instructor Marquez," she said.

"P-Pay it no mind! That was some wonderful running— Gah?!" He coughed as the onrushing pack of runners trampled over him. "Ha ha ha! This feels kinda good! It's just payback for me always hazing people."

Even Lahti, at the rear leading Pullum along by her hand, stepped on him.

When the group arrived at the academy, it turned out there was no time for sweets. Inglis, Rafinha, Leone, and Liselotte had been summoned. They were going to get their orders concerning the protection of the hieral menace Ripple.

The four of them were the only first-years summoned to a room at the academy, thanks to already having experience with extracurricular work. Also present were their seniors, older academy students to whom that also seemed to apply.

"Everyone, thank you for gathering here. I have an assignment of note for you today, so please lend me your attention," Principal Miriela said.

As usual, her phrasing made the matter sound fairly low-key. The students looked underwhelmed until they saw Ambassador Theodore and Ripple appear. The situation no longer appeared to be a trifling matter.

Principal Miriela explained the situation: Ripple's physical condition was abnormal; her presence was attracting magicite beasts; Ambassador Theodore was lending his aid to analyze and resolve the issue; and finally, Ripple would be staying at the academy until a solution was found.

A boy in a third-year uniform from the knights' program was the first to speak up. "I see... So we're to escort Ripple and immediately destroy any magicite beast that appears. And, preferably, avoid damage to the surrounding area?" He had short, almost ash-gray hair, and his glasses gave him the air of a refined and attractive intellectual. From his right hand shined an upper-class Rune—no, it had a distinctly rainbow glimmer, which meant only one thing.

"That's a special-class Rune..." Inglis said.

Hieral menaces were the ultimate Artifacts. Their true power could be manifested only when transformed into a weapon, which was said to be the one power that could defeat a Prismer, the strongest type of magicite beast. The only people who could control a transformed hieral menace were holy knights with a special-class Rune. This young man was likely a future holy knight, then. He would be a hero tasked with preserving the country, and he would presumably be following in Rafael's footsteps.

"That's Silva Ayren, the younger brother of the Royal Guard's captain, Reddas Ayren. Silva is the only student here with a special-class Rune," Liselotte explained quietly.

"That would make him the strongest student at the academy, right?" Inglis asked.

Chapter I: Inglis, Age 15—Orders to Defend the Hieral Menace (1)

"I suppose so."

"Nice... He seems strong. I hope I can fight him sometime."

"Is that all you think about?" Liselotte gave her a dismayed stare.

Principal Miriela continued. "Silva is correct. You're the select members of the first-, second-, and third-years we're tasking with this. I'd like you to form teams and take turns guarding Ripple. You're permitted to seek assistance from other students at your discretion. If an emergency occurs and a magicite beast appears, please use the Artifacts we'll be providing you to immediately ward the area. You must both eliminate the magicite beast and avoid collateral damage."

The chosen students answered as one. "Understood."

"And these are those Artifacts," the principal said. "Each of you, take one. I'd like you to make sure that there is always someone by Lady Ripple's side to immediately respond to any emergency and set up a ward."

Ambassador Theodore presented the many Artifacts. There were various types—swords, spears, staffs, and so on.

After some examination of the offerings, Rafinha said, "No bow. There's nothing I can use."

"Then I shall take a spear," Liselotte announced.

"And I'll take a sword," Leone said.

The gathered students were each given an Artifact, and yet there were still some left over.

"I guess I should take one too." Inglis didn't have a Rune, but a Rune was just something that channeled the flow of mana in a certain way. If she converted aether into mana and let it be channeled, she should be able to use one. And furthermore, if she studied the effect the Artifact created, she could recreate it directly. It would be difficult if it was complex, but she wanted to try.

Inglis stepped forward and reached for an Artifact.

Silva stopped her. "Wait. Cease this foolishness. What are you going to do with one of those?"

"Hmm? Is something the matter?" Inglis asked.

"You know exactly what I'm getting at. There's no point to you carrying one of those. It's nothing a Runeless squire cadet could handle. Keep your hands off it," Silva insisted.

"Understood. I apologize." Inglis bowed her head politely and quietly stepped back.

"Hey, hold on! That's rude!" At times like this, Rafinha always spoke her mind.

"It's okay, Rani. Don't worry about it. You don't have to be angry." Inglis giggled to herself, confusing Rafinha.

"Wh-What are you grinning for, Chris?"

"It's fine. Let's let it go. Okay?" Inglis, on the other hand, seemed quite pleased.

It seemed Silva took a dim view of squire cadets. He was short-tempered and rather high-strung. He looked sophisticated, but on the inside, he was emotionally immature. A person like that could be easily provoked into a fight. A holy knight or hieral menace couldn't be goaded into such emotional displays unless it was already a hostile relationship. But she might just be able to instigate a duel with this boy.

"Now, now, Silva. There are extras, so it should be fine for her to take one," Principal Miriela said.

Silva protested, "I must disagree, Principal Miriela! If that's the case, we should keep them in a safe place and use them as spares if any are destroyed. There's no such thing as an Artifact we can afford to waste."

"Well, that's true, but Inglis... Well, Inglis probably won't waste it. Aha ha ha ha! ♪"

"This is no joking matter! What's a squire cadet even doing here in the first place? Are you sure there wasn't a mistake in selecting personnel? This is an important mission, isn't it? That's all the more reason to have the most suitable people for it. A Runeless could become a liability. I want her out of here now!"

The room went silent.

This was becoming inconvenient. As Inglis wondered how she could talk him out of it, a girl with shoulder-length hair the color of cherry blossoms raised her hand.

"Yes. Understood." Judging by her uniform, she was a second-year student. She was extremely cute, but she also had an extremely cold air about her. Her right hand, which she'd raised, had no Rune inscribed on

Chapter I: Inglis, Age 15—Orders to Defend the Hieral Menace (1)

it. It seemed that she too was Runeless. "Thank you. Now, if you'll excuse me." She quickly made for the exit.

"Ahh, hold on a minute! Wait, Yua!" Principal Miriela, flustered, stopped her.

"What is it? I'm tired. I want to sleep." Yua didn't even bat an eye.

Even though the situation was an emergency, Yua didn't seem to have any interest. That in particular made Inglis think this girl wasn't ordinary.

"Aha ha, well, ah, you heard my explanation, right? We need everyone's strength," Principal Miriela insisted—albeit gently.

"Tee hee." Yua stuck out her tongue, but her expression was otherwise blank.

"Aha ha ha ha…" Miriela was in the habit of covering up inconvenient situations with a giggle, but Yua proved even more elusive, and the principal found herself in a quandary. "Anyway! This is a big deal, and we need your help. You're the star of the second-years. It would be troublesome without you."

"But Four-Eyes over there told me to leave… Wait, did I dream that?"

"That's right! It must have been a daydream! No one said that, right?"

"Then I guess I have to," Yua said after a pause.

As Yua returned to her seat, Silva raised his voice. "No, I did indeed say that! Cadet squires aren't up to this task. Stay out of this."

"Understood. Thank you," Yua replied simply.

"Ahhhhh, wait! Silva, don't take us back to square one!" Principal Miriela said.

Liselotte watched them, muttering to her classmates, "I'd always thought the principal was awfully accepting of oddballs like you bunch… but if the senior students are like this, I can see why she acts the way she does."

"Huh? What do you mean by 'you bunch'? You're one of us, and we're all friends," Rafinha said.

"F-For better or worse, I suppose," Liselotte added.

"Aha ha. I think it's better we're all friends," Leone remarked.

"Well, if Leone's fine with it, I don't mind," Liselotte said.

Silva continued his protest. "And not just cadet squires, but a relative of the traitor! She's the sister of that traitor—Leon! I'll never trust her!"

"Now hold it right there! Leone isn't like him! You shouldn't talk about her that way!" Rafinha insisted.

Liselotte agreed. "Indeed! That's a shallow, simplistic view. When you get to know her better, you'll understand!"

The situation was getting complicated, so Inglis tried to push through her demands as if she were an arbitrator. "Now, now. Silva, would you be willing to test our skills to see if we're worthy of the mission? I don't see any other way for us to address your concerns, so…"

Silva pondered over that. "Hmm…"

"Hey." Yua raised her hand.

"Ah, yes, Yua. What is it?" Inglis asked.

"Sounds like a hassle. I don't wanna."

Inglis had nothing to say in response.

What was going on? Rafinha, Leone, and Liselotte all had their own personalities, but they were all serious at heart. This Yua girl had a seriously unique temperament. There was something fundamentally different about Yua—different from Inglis too, of course. She'd never call the chance to fight a "hassle."

Another second-year student said, "But without you, Yua, I don't know if we'll be able to do this. We're supposed to split up by academic year, right? We need your strength."

There were only three second-years there, one fewer than the first-years.

"Understood. I'll do it," Yua agreed.

"Then, Yua, shall we test our skills against Silva?"

Yua shot her down without a moment's hesitation. "Don't wanna. It's the principal who gave the orders, so if someone has a problem with them, they should leave." She was oddly straightforward now.

"Well, that's true, but I was going to leave, like Silva said…" Inglis said, suddenly taking on a softer tone.

"Heh heh… Don't have the guts to face me, huh?" Silva stared the second-year down.

Chapter I: Inglis, Age 15—Orders to Defend the Hieral Menace (1)

Yua took a moment to choose her words. "We know who would win. I don't like bullying."

"What?!" Silva yelled, indignant.

Inglis wondered if Yua and Silva had fought before. Perhaps Yua had won? In that case, Inglis found her extremely fascinating. It wasn't hard to imagine Silva, with a special-class Rune, having power like a holy knight's. If Yua was beyond that, Inglis could expect a considerable fight.

"Principal..." she began to stealthily ask.

"Yes, Inglis, it's as you assume. During a mock battle, just once. Since then, those two haven't gotten along... If you could somehow patch things up between them, I'd be grateful. After all, you are the star of the first-years," Principal Miriela said.

"I think Rani's better at interpersonal matters, but if you want me to give them both a beating, I'd be glad to."

In the first place, it seemed like Silva was trying to pick a fight with Yua. Meanwhile, Yua wasn't paying him any heed.

"Well...I suppose strength frequently comes to those with a less delicate touch..." Principal Miriela sighed.

Suddenly, everyone heard a loud thud.

"Lady Ripple! Pull yourself together!" Ambassador Theodore responded first. Ripple was seated directly next to him and had collapsed. Her consciousness was already gone, and she was wrapped in a black sphere. Inglis had seen this happen before, back at the palace.

"Theodore! Get away from her—it's dangerous! I'll create a ward. Everyone, be on guard!" Principal Miriela waved her Artifact staff, creating a broad barrier covering the area. There was a translucent wall of light that Inglis could see through the window.

A moment later, a spot high on the wall twisted, and magicite beast after magicite beast poured out through the space. They were humanoid, just like at the palace—demihumans, the same as Ripple.

"H-Here they come!" a student yelled. Tension among those gathered rose quickly, but none screamed or tried to flee.

"Principal, which class is on duty today?!" Silva asked in a hurry.

"Huh?" Principal Miriela replied.

9

"The three teams, split by class year, were supposed to trade off daily, right? Do you mind if we're the first?"

"No, not at all…"

"All right! Then, no one other than us lay a hand on—"

Bammmmmm!

Inglis had already sent a trio of the magicite beasts flying with one kick. The impact caused the wall to cave in, and the entire room creaked slightly.

"Wh—?! Hey, you! I told you not to lay a hand on them!" Silva snapped.

"Yes. So I used my feet instead," Inglis answered back, a smile drifting to her face.

The senior students were all amazed.

"Huh?! That girl's a cadet squire, but she's crazy strong!"

"Well, if she was called here, that's to be expected!"

"Sh-She's like Yua! This is like watching Yua!"

"And she's absolutely adorable!"

She didn't mind the compliments, but hearing them shout that last part in unison was a little off-putting.

"This isn't the time to discuss that! Third-years, give battle! No matter how much of a beating you inflict on it, that won't do anything to a magicite beast!" As Silva barked orders, he leveled his own Artifact, which took the form of a unique long cylinder—a gun. Highland had developed it as an anti-personnel weapon. It was rare to see them on the surface, but Inglis and Rafinha had seen one in Ymir; Duke Bilford had one.

Gun Artifacts were quite rare. They were a weapon not many on the surface used. Silva, with his rainbow-colored special-class Rune, could use any Artifact. For him to have chosen this one, it must have had an exceptional Gift. A bright-red pattern floated on the gun's barrel, indicating that it used the fire element.

Let's see what you've got, Inglis thought.

* * *

Chapter I: Inglis, Age 15—Orders to Defend the Hieral Menace (1)

Whoosh!

But before Silva could move, bright white arrows of light had shot past his face. They had been let loose by Rafinha's bow Artifact. They pierced through the magicite beasts that Inglis had embedded in the wall. Not one, not two, but three arrows. They completely silenced the magicite beasts.

"Rani? He might get mad," Inglis said.

"Huh? I didn't use my hands. I used my bow," Rafinha replied.

"Doesn't seem like it'll be a problem, then."

"Yep, agreed."

"That's garbage logic!" Silva yelled, enraged. "I don't care if you're Holy Knight Rafael's little sister, you can't selfishly—"

"Just who's being selfish here?!" Rafinha didn't back down. "Ripple doesn't want to see anyone here get hurt! So we need to do everything we can to stay safe! We don't need to fight over who does it! We need to work together. You're going to be a holy knight, right, Silva? So you should be the one most concerned with Ripple's feelings! You're going to be the one fighting alongside a hieral menace!"

"Wh—?! What are you— You don't even have a special-class Rune, who are you to—"

"I may not have a special-class Rune, but I've seen someone who does up close!"

She meant Rafael, of course. Comparing Rafael and Silva, it was impossible not to see Silva as immature. Rafael was older, to begin with, and he had been a well-mannered person even as a child. This was only speaking of this point in time, and Inglis couldn't deny Silva's future potential. The qualities of a special-class Rune were well-known. One could develop into whatever one wanted, depending on one's mindset.

But Inglis knew one thing: she liked Rafinha when she stood up for her ideals and sense of justice. She didn't usually look so serious, and her effort in keeping her expression stern was cute and very like her.

"Ah?! I swung my spear and hit one!" Liselotte called.

"And I hit one with a sword! Sorry!" Leone followed.

They had also attacked the magicite beasts, hoping to take some of Silva's ire.

"Yua! You heard him, right?! Be sure not to make him mad! For Ripple's sake!" Rafinha called out.

"O-Okay! Sorry!" Yua was surprised by Rafinha's intensity.

Inglis glanced over at Yua, who rushed toward another magicite beast that had just manifested. She resembled a small animal, as if she would be in need of protection. However, with a puff of air, Yua seemed to disappear. She popped back into view in front of the magicite beast that Inglis was rushing toward. She had slipped in between them somehow! Inglis had been able to see the whole thing, but Yua was still absurdly fast.

Thwap!

Yua struck the magicite beast with an ever-so-light karate chop. And yet...

Rrrip-crackkk!

That delicate move brought forth loud destruction. Yua had left marks that dug into the body of the magicite beast.

"Wow! Amazing!" Inglis said with a gasp.

That kind of power from a light attack was impressive. Furthermore, she had approached the magicite beast even faster than Inglis had—though Inglis *was* under increased gravity.

However, magicite beasts were invulnerable to purely physical attacks, so that attack had been pointless...but not in terms of getting Yua into the fight.

Yua was powerful. Inglis could find nothing to criticize. She'd absolutely have to ask for a sparring match sometime.

"There." Leaning forward, Yua kicked the magicite beast with her heel.

Whaaack!

* * *

Chapter I: Inglis, Age 15—Orders to Defend the Hieral Menace (1)

The magicite beast flew right in front of Inglis with the force of a bullet.

"Ah, sorry," Yua apologized.

Inglis reassured her. "It's fine! Haaaah!"

Baaam!

Inglis delivered a kick directly up. The magicite beast gained even more momentum and plunged headfirst into the ceiling.

"Oh. Not bad." Yua's normally blank expression contained just a little bit of awe.

"Thank you. Shall we have a match sometime?"

"I don't wanna. I don't want a trial of strength or anything." As Yua spoke, she kept blows flying at the magicite beasts.

"I insist! Please!"

As Yua and Inglis conversed, they kept the blows coming, matching each other's same speed.

"Nah."

"Is there any way to persuade you?"

As they continued their negotiations, Inglis and Yua used their blows to lock down the magicite beasts.

"Amazing, you two! This'll be easy!" The other students only had to move to finish them off.

"Ugh… Does no one listen to me?!" Silva complained.

"Now, now! Silva! Then, I order everyone, as your principal, to respond! So no one will be doing anything wrong! Keep it up, everyone!" Principal Miriela ordered, flustered.

Even after that, the battle situation wasn't much different. As new magicite beasts appeared, first Inglis or Yua sent them flying, and then the other students finished them off.

Only elemental attacks affected the magicite beasts; even if their bodies were twisted from physical blows, they would recover. But if Inglis and Yua could create a small opening, that was all the time Rafinha and the others needed.

Furthermore, there was a reason Inglis could take the initiative: she could detect the signs of a magicite beast appearing by the change in the flow of mana. Thus, she could act a step or two ahead of the others.

And Yua was moving in the same way, so she likely sensed the same things. Just what *was* she? The impression she gave off was different from that of a hieral menace.

A Highlander, maybe? But she had no stigmata.

Was Yua a divine knight like Inglis herself was? Or was her perception more like that of the Steelblood Front's black-masked man? Inglis sensed no aether from her, but she could be hiding it.

So far, Inglis couldn't say anything definitive. She simply knew that she didn't have the answers. That was fascinating, though. She was glad she'd left rural Ymir to come to the capital. There were so many fascinating opponents she wanted to have the pleasure of fighting.

"Everyone, I think it's fine. The phenomenon has stopped for now," Ambassador Theodore announced. He had been watching Ripple. The black hemisphere covering her had returned to normal.

"Ripple!" Rafinha was the first to her side.

"If it's the same as before, she should awaken after a little while..." Leone sounded worried.

"I see. We know what we have to do now. This much should be no problem, Principal Miriela. We third-years, at least, will complete the mission without casualties," Silva said with confidence.

"Yes. However, this is only a method to prevent any harm to our surroundings, not an ultimate resolution. There is a possibility something else may happen, so please be careful," Miriela warned.

"Will you have a solution soon?" Silva asked.

"I'm sorry. That will take some time, but we're hurrying as much as possible. I understand the burden on you, but please bear with us," Ambassador Theodore replied.

"Yes, that would be quite helpful." Principal Miriela sighed deeply, her gaze on the room's ceiling. The harsh impacts of the magicite beasts had left it warped and beaten in places. "If we don't do something about this soon, it doesn't seem like there'll be any trace left of the school building..."

"It's the fault of these brutes." Silva looked at Inglis and Yua in turn. The two tilted their heads in confusion.

"Don't play dumb! It's because you were indiscriminately sending the enemies flying!" Silva accused.

Yua replied, "We were still holding back, right? Uhh…"

"My name is Inglis."

"Umm… Inkle? Inli?"

"Inglis."

"Hmm…" Yua frowned.

"Yua has a hard time with names," one of the older students noted.

"Beanpole's right," Yua said.

Well, that senior student *was* slender, but he did also have a full-fledged upper-class Rune.

He playfully faked a sob. "Ahhh… See? A whole year and she's still like this. By the way, I'm Morris. Pleased to meet you."

"You too." Then Inglis turned back to Yua. "Anyway, you can call me whatever you'd like."

"Hmm… Boobies. You were holding back, weren't you?" Yua asked.

"Huhhh?! That's a bit…" Inglis protested.

But Yua didn't seem to be listening—she had turned to face Silva. "In the first place, if you had been working harder, we wouldn't have had to go on such a rampage."

"I was just holding back because I didn't want to burn the school building down with my Artifact! Think harder when you fight, you two!" Silva barked back.

"Now, now. It's better than worrying about that and getting hurt," Principal Miriela stated with a wry smile.

Ambassador Theodore had a similar expression. "Ha ha… Maybe Artifacts that transport you to another dimension, rather than those which cover the area with a ward, would be better."

"Like the magical spaces created by Highlanders, you mean?" Inglis recalled when the Highlander Fars had sealed her in another dimension. She didn't know if *every* Highlander could do that, but it seemed some could. Meaning, he had been quite a powerful magician.

"Correct," Ambassador Theodore said.

Chapter I: Inglis, Age 15—Orders to Defend the Hieral Menace (1)

Principal Miriela continued, "The closest is the Labyrinth of Ordeals that you entered the other day. That's an Artifact based on the Highlanders' dimensional magic."

"Ahh, I see…" Inglis replied.

"However, the dimension-shifted can't be seen by those around them. It would be difficult to know whether to send in reinforcements, making it more dangerous. And I believe there are fewer people who can use that than a warding-type Artifact," the principal said.

"But it's true that having both would be good. I'll prepare those as well," Theodore offered.

"Well, yes. It depends on the situation. If you'd be so kind, Theodore."

"Understood."

Thus, the operation to defend the hieral menace Ripple began in earnest.

Chapter II: Inglis, Age 15—Orders to Defend the Hieral Menace (2)

"Aha ha ha. She picked *that* for your nickname, Inglis?" Ripple laughed as she listened to the first-years' recounting of the events with Yua and everyone else.

She seemed to be doing well enough today, but she was probably still suffering inside. Everyone knew that from the expression on her face when she awakened from the spells of unconsciousness or when her expression clouded. She was trying to act cheerful, though. She didn't want to worry everyone.

As Principal Miriela had ordered, each team would take turns guarding Ripple, rotating daily. Today was the first time Inglis's team—the first-years—would be on duty. Ripple had free access to the grounds of the academy, but even while acting as her bodyguards, the students still had to avoid missing class if possible. Thus, Ripple would be attending their classes with them. Inglis had heard that Ripple had done the same for the older students. It was as if a hieral menace, a guardian of the country, was sitting in on their classes. Her presence raised the morale of their classmates.

Thinking back on Yua's nickname for her, Inglis said, "Yes. It was a little embarrassing..."

Inglis still felt her spirit was that of a hero-king. She'd gotten used to having a woman's body—she even enjoyed it. But for the day to come where her nickname was Boobies... Fate was strange.

"Yua's kinda odd. She couldn't remember my name either," Ripple replied. Not remembering even a great hieral menace's name was certainly daring.

"So what does she call you?"

"Lady Dog Ears."

Inglis just stared.

Well, Ripple *did* have dog ears. And "Lady" *did* attempt to show some respect.

"Well, whatever. What did she call Rafinha?"

"Little Demon." Yua hadn't taken kindly to being shouted at. Rafinha had scared her a bit.

"And Leone?"

Leone gestured toward her chest, where Rin was burrowed and relaxing. "Also Boobies... Probably because of..."

"Yeah, that must be why... And Liselotte?"

"S-Spike..." Seemingly because her curls were pointy at the ends.

"Ha ha ha. She got you good," Ripple chuckled.

After a pause in the conversation, Rafinha got everyone back on track. "Well, Yua is almost as strange as Chris, but I think we managed to understand one another. The problem is probably Silva. Ripple, did he ever say or do anything rude to you?"

"Hm? Not really. I feel like he's a little overzealous, but I get along well with him."

While Inglis listened to them, she moved one of the chess pieces in front of her. Across the board, Leone frowned. As one of their lessons in the classroom today, they'd played chess, and the group had stayed in the classroom a little bit longer to finish their matches.

"Ugh... I give up..." Leone's shoulders slumped. "This is no good. No matter how many times I try, I can't win! Sheesh, Inglis, you're the kind of person who can only think of charging in and beating enemies up when they appear, and yet..."

"Most people would be offended by that description," Inglis replied.

Chess and reality were different. Real "pieces" grew. With that growth eventually came the strength to smash through all the enemy's "pieces." Her behavior in actual battles was simply what she considered

Chapter II: Inglis, Age 15—Orders to Defend the Hieral Menace (2)

to be the most effective way to maximize her growth. That was why she so frequently slammed full-speed into a thoughtfully prepared enemy.

Rafinha and Liselotte were sitting next to them at their own board.

"Well, Chris is good at chess—she always has been."

"I'd never have expected that based on how she normally acts," Liselotte said.

"On the contrary, even from the first few times she played, her own father, Rafael, and my father couldn't beat her."

"And what about you, Rafinha?"

"Me? There's no way I can win!" Rafinha said, a bit ashamed. "You can tell from this, right?" Liselotte's position on the board was extremely favorable.

"I suppose... Perhaps you need to put in a bit more effort?"

Rafinha was not suited to tests of subterfuge or tactics. Chess was exactly that sort of game, so Rafinha was not surprised by her own poor performance.

"Well, there's no actual reason for me to be good at it. If I'm in trouble, I can leave it to Chris. Right?"

"Well, as a full-fledged, independent knight—"

"Yeah. I can just leave it all to her."

"Isn't that a bit naive?! Inglis, I think you've been going a bit too easy on her."

"Really? But it's fine, as long as I always stay Rani's squire," Inglis said.

"W-Well..." Liselotte said, taking a moment to figure out how to respond. "Are *you* fine with that? With your strength, I'm sure your exploits will give you both rank and honor."

"I have no interest in those sorts of things." In fact, Inglis was worried about accidentally getting too much responsibility. She wouldn't be able to stand on the front lines, then. Even if she was pressured into becoming a leader, she planned on taking advantage of her status as a Runeless squire to firmly reject it.

"Ha ha ha. You're a strange one." Liselotte didn't understand, but she smiled in a lightly teasing manner. In the meantime, she advanced a piece on the board, ending her game against Rafinha.

"Ugh! I lost again...!"

"And would you like to play, Lady Ripple? I'd simply love to see how you perform," Liselotte said.

"Naw. I'm just like Rafinha, I'd rather leave that kind of thing to Eris. She's the brains and I'm the brawn."

Inglis nimbly offered a suggestion. "Then why don't we spar? It'd be good to loosen up after just sitting around so long. After all, exercise is good for your mental health. Letting loose is great stress relief."

Inglis really wanted a match against Ripple, and she couldn't let this chance for a fight with a hieral menace get away.

"Hey, Chriiis?" Rafinha glared at Inglis.

"Not now, Inglis. What would we do if something happened to her?" Leone chastised.

"Indeed. We absolutely can't risk that," Liselotte said, nonplussed.

"Hey, hey—wait. I'm not necessarily the only one who wants to fight. Maybe it would be good for Ripple too! Right, Rani?"

Inglis's attempt to defend herself did not persuade Rafinha. "Absolutely not. Don't be selfish. We have enough on our hands with the magicite beasts."

However, Ripple unexpectedly nodded toward Inglis. "Hmm, I'm okay with it. Why not?"

"R-Really?! Thank you so much, Ripple!" Inglis's excitement was plain as day.

"Miriela and Theodore did say they wanted to see what would happen if I got in a fight. I've wanted to experience your power anyway. Plus, you seem reeeaaal happy about it. Ha ha ha!"

"Yes! I love you, Ripple!" Inglis's eyes were sparkling like shiny gems. Ripple found the girl's bliss a little frightening.

The group visited Ambassador Theodore and Principal Miriela in the principal's office. Ripple had said she was fine with the bout, but she needed their permission first.

Chapter II: Inglis, Age 15—Orders to Defend the Hieral Menace (2)

"You two want to spar? Well, Inglis being Inglis, I expected she might ask. I can't say I'm surprised," Miriela said.

"You know your students well, Principal," Theodore remarked with a smile.

"I *am* a proper principal, after all."

"I think Chris is a lot easier to understand than a normal girl," Rafinha said.

Leone and Liselotte both agreed.

"Yes. She only thinks about one thing."

"Indeed."

Miriela laughed. "Looks like they've described you to a T, Inglis."

"Whatever, I want to hurry up and fight! It's okay, right, Principal Miriela? C'mon, c'mon, c'mon…!" Inglis's eyes were still sparkling.

"Aha ha ha… Well, it would be a shame to keep you waiting, so let's get to it." Miriela turned to her colleague. "Theodore, if you would?"

"Certainly. Leone, this is for you."

Ambassador Theodore held out Leone's original dark greatsword Artifact. Its Gift extended the blade at the wielder's will. When smashing the falling flying ship away from the palace, Inglis had put too much force into the swing, and the blade had shattered.

"Ah, is this my—?!"

"Yes. The base is the same as the one you had used, Leone," Principal Miriela explained.

"The base?"

"Yes. It looks the same, but it's upgraded. Where before it had one Gift, now it has another—it's an exceptional Artifact with two Gifts! Isn't cutting-edge technology a marvel? ♪"

Leone stared in amazement. "Huh…"

"Wow! Isn't that great, Leone?" Rafinha cheered.

"What is the other Gift?"

"It's an effect that separates nearby people off into another dimension!" Miriela answered. "It's the safety measure we were talking about earlier. This dimension-jumping ability will prevent damage to the school building! Based on the elemental affinity of your Rune, you're the most suited to use it out of everyone, Leone."

"It was created on short notice, so we'd like you to test the strength of the dimension and the duration of the effect. Please hold Inglis and Ripple's sparring match within the effect of the Artifact. If there are no problems with the results, I'll distribute them to the other groups as well," Theodore explained.

"When a Highlander trapped us in another dimension, our Artifacts didn't work inside. What about with this?" Leone asked.

"That won't happen, of course! No worries there, Leone," Ambassador Theodore reassured her.

"Understood. I'll give it a try!"

"Go right ahead, Leone! There's no time like the present!" Principal Miriela encouraged.

"What?! Here and now?!"

"Do not worry. We'd like to enter it with you and observe the Artifact's operation," Theodore said.

"Understood. Then—" Leone gripped the hilt of the sword with both hands and focused. "Ugh... Grrr... It feels different from what I'm used to...!"

"You don't have to rush it. It's a Gift you haven't used before. Take a deep breath, and let yourself be carried away on the flows the Rune creates."

"Okay." Leone inhaled deeply at Principal Miriela's instruction.

As she calmed and felt a rhythm, she controlled both her breathing and the flow of mana. The dark blade of the sword began to distort— to be precise, space itself distorted, making it seem as if the blade had.

"That's it, Leone. Keep going."

"Yes!"

The distortion spread farther and farther until it reached its peak. The world had gone completely blank around them. As their vision adjusted, they realized they were in a space with no walls or horizon.

"I did it!"

Leone was right. The seven people from the room had been transported to another dimension.

"Wow! It worked! It's just like the Labyrinth of Ordeals or the Highlanders' magic!" Rafinha looked all around, comparing this dimension

Chapter II: Inglis, Age 15—Orders to Defend the Hieral Menace (2)

to the other similar experiences they'd had recently. It didn't seem like any illusions would appear, nor were their Artifacts sealed. This Gift only transported people inside of it. "Leone, are you okay? It wasn't too hard on you?"

Leone was definitely tired, probably because the ability was so new to her.

"I'm fine. I just have to get used to it. You can start the match."

"Understood. Thanks, Leone. If you would, Ripple…" Inglis prompted.

"Sure thing! Let's give everyone some space. And Miriela, can you keep an eye out for stray shots?"

"Of course. We'd like to check the strength of this space, so could you start off lightly and then gradually increase your strength?"

"Of course," Inglis said.

In that case, they would begin bare-handed without weapons or projectiles. Inglis clapped a fist into her other palm and shifted into her stance.

"No probs, Miriela! Okay, Inglis, let's go!"

Ripple was a good person. She got right down to the fight. Inglis was glad she'd broached the idea of inviting her to the academy.

"Right! Here I come!" Inglis sprinted straight ahead, her fists at the ready. It was a head-to-head fight, no tricks.

Smack!

"Nice punch!" Ripple remarked. A crack rang out as she caught Inglis's fist, loud enough to make the surrounding air tremble. "Fast *and* strong!" Ripple added as her own punch flew at Inglis.

Smack!

"You're strong as well!" This time, Inglis had stopped Ripple's attack.

And so, a grappling contest had begun. This was still just a warm-up, but the hieral menace was as impressive as Inglis had expected.

Their overwhelming power had stopped each other in place as they grappled.

"Heh heh…!" Ripple grinned.

Inglis frowned, confused. She saw Ripple's fluffy tail wagging like an animal's. It was quite long. Unexpectedly, Ripple used her tail to tickle the armpit of Inglis's outstretched arm.

"Eek?!" Inglis reflexively cowered, and in the moment where her strength wavered, Ripple twisted, building up her momentum.

"Gotcha!" The whiplike high kick was already before Inglis's eyes. At this rate, it would strike her. That was a bit unfair, but it was everything Inglis had hoped for!

"Release!" Inglis typically kept herself under increased gravity to train. Naturally, she had done so during this fight until now. Whenever she released herself from added gravity, she could react to even the impossible! She suddenly sped up, moving herself out of the kick's arc.

"No way!" Ripple, who'd expected her kick to strike true, gasped in surprise.

And Inglis quickly went back on the offensive. This time, she let loose a flurry of punches.

"Haaah!"

"Yahhhhh!"

Rrrumble!

Inglis and Ripple's fists met, and a heavy sound shook the air.

"Amazing! I've never seen anyone fight like that!" Liselotte involuntarily gasped, overwhelmed.

"But they're not done yet. They're still only fighting bare-handed," Rafinha remarked.

Miriela had been watching closely and quietly. She remarked to herself, "I'll have to take a closer look at what Inglis is doing—for future reference."

With her increased gravity released, Inglis gradually took the upper hand in the high-speed clash of fists. "Oomph!" Pushing through Ripple's loose defense, Inglis's fist caught her on top of the shoulder.

Chapter II: Inglis, Age 15—Orders to Defend the Hieral Menace (2)

"Ah—ow!" Ripple was blown backwards and fell on her butt. But she quickly clambered back to her feet, practically leaping back up. "Not bad, Inglis!"

"You too!" Inglis's fists were still numb—proof that Ripple was no ordinary opponent.

"Now that we've warmed up… Let's do this for real! I'm not really the fistfightin' type, y'know?" Ripple extended her hand toward Inglis. In it, a golden cylinder appeared.

"A gun?!"

With a cheeky grin, Ripple replied, "Sure is. ♪"

"Interesting…!"

Ripple had said she got along well with Silva. Inglis hadn't understood before, but now she wondered if it was because they shared a weapon.

"All right, here goes!" Ripple said.

A shining bullet, seemingly condensed from light, shot forth from the gun in Ripple's right hand with a *fwoosh*. It left a shimmering trail in the darkness of the dimension as it raced toward Inglis.

That's even faster than the arrows of light from Rafinha's Artifact! Inglis thought.

She flipped sideways to avoid it—a moment later, she realized that may have been a mistake. The next round had already left Ripple's gun, aimed for where Inglis would land.

"Wh—?!"

If she'd dodged more precisely, she wouldn't have left that opening. The hero-king hadn't needed to contend with guns before. This was her first occasion in both of her lifetimes facing one. She had been overly cautious on her previous approach. She still had more to learn.

But that won't pose a problem!

Clink!

Inglis converted her aether into mana and magically created a blade of ice in her right hand. Although it required the tedious process of converting divine aether into the less powerful mana and then manipulating it, the ice sword itself was quite user-friendly. Between daily practice and regular use in actual combat, she could now activate it almost instantly. She quickly swatted away Ripple's bullets of light.

Ping!

With a clear, dry sound, Inglis repelled the bullet.

"Hm? Didn't hit? I knew you'd be a toughie! Then how about this?" Ripple fired a three-shot burst. The guns she had seen so far normally required notable time to be reloaded between shots. However, Ripple could fire a volley with no such effort.

"You won't touch me!"

Ping, ping, ping!

Inglis had repelled all three of the bullets. Ripple's line of vision, the angle of the gun's barrel, and the movement of Ripple's fingers—by observing them closely, Inglis could predict the trajectory of a bullet.

Ripple gasped. "Ah?! Crap!" Now the bullets were flying toward the others.

However, a faintly glowing wall of light blocked them, and they fell to the ground. Some kind of protective barrier must have been erected.

"We can handle this much. As long as it's *this* much." Principal Miriela's bitter laugh may have been in anticipation of how much more intense the fight would become.

"Thank you. Then we'll give it our all!"

"Were you even listening to what I said?!"

Inglis advanced. If she didn't close the distance and go on the attack, she had no chance of winning—well, she *could* counterattack with something like Aether Strike, but that would be a waste. Ripple was perfectly controlling the space between herself and her opponent with a near-impenetrable hail of gunfire. Evading Ripple's ranged attacks and challenging her with melee attacks would be the best for Inglis's experience and growth.

Chapter II: Inglis, Age 15—Orders to Defend the Hieral Menace (2)

Taking on an opponent at their best and winning despite their strong points—that was how Inglis Eucus fought.

Dodging gunfire by a hair's breadth, she advanced forth, using her sword to bat away any bullets that seemed like they might hit. Inglis made snap judgments on when to evade, step in, or swipe at the bullets.

Ripple grinned. "Heh heh heh... But I'm not stopping either!"

"I'll catch up with you!"

The distance between Inglis and Ripple slowly closed.

"You sure do have a nice bright smile on your face! If you're enjoying it this much, it's fun for me too!"

Despite her words, Ripple still remained calm and analytical. *Inglis still has something up her sleeve*, she thought. *The question's when she'll bring it out... Just this much is impressive. Her predictions are precise, and her movements are incredibly agile. Every movement she makes flows with a sense of beauty. She's maybe even faster than Eris and Rafael. From what Eris said, she can make herself even faster, but Eris didn't completely understand how. This girl is unfathomable. She's so cute, though.*

Yet, even with Inglis's ineffability, even with the big words about wanting to take down a Prismer, Ripple welcomed her. Someone she couldn't understand just might be the person who could break through problems not even she or Eris could handle.

More than anything, I want to see her give her all...

And then, Inglis—having avoided the attacks from the gun in Ripple's right hand—was on her. She swiftly circled around to Ripple's left side so that it would take Ripple a moment to readjust her aim. One more step forward, and Inglis would be close enough to strike Ripple with her sword.

From Inglis's perspective, this must be the best chance to attack. She's gonna step in... And then blam, *right in the nose!*

As Inglis moved in, Ripple thrust her empty left hand at her. In it, a golden gun quickly appeared.

Inglis gasped. "Another?!"

"Sure is! I can dual-wield!"

* * *

Fwoosh!

"Guh?!" Inglis barely managed to avoid a direct hit by twisting her body just in time, but the bullet grazed her shoulder. Her clothing was torn, a severed scrap sent flying, and her whole body was pushed by the momentum of the bullet.

"Gotcha! Right there!"

"I'm not done yet!" Even being blown away, Inglis tried to somehow recover her footing. As she fell back, she used her sword of ice to repel the relentless gunfire. By the time she was fully back on her feet, Ripple was even farther away than when they'd begun.

"The tables are turned! Can you still close in?"

"Ugh..." There were no gaps in the barrage of fire! With Ripple's guns not running out of bullets, even indirect shots kept Inglis from closing in. She was too busy being on the defensive.

If this keeps up, will Ripple's guns run out of ammunition sometime? Or will my strength ebb first? Inglis asked herself.

She was weighing options in her head when she saw the move she needed to make. "No!" Even though Ripple was on the offensive, Inglis took the initiative. Ripple had stopped in her tracks.

So I'll...! Inglis deliberately bent her back leg and half-crouched. Gripping ice swords in both hands, she held them at her waist to swiftly and efficiently counterattack. Three strong puffs of air sounded as Ripple fired her burst of shots. Their trajectory matched Inglis's low-to-the-ground stance.

Inglis's eyes gleamed like those of a bird of prey observing its target. "I saw that coming! Haaaah!" Inglis whipped her ice swords forth in a flash!

Ping, ping, ping!

The sounds were crystal clear. Taken aback, Ripple watched the scene unfold: Inglis had reflected her bullets of light. And they were headed straight back for her.

"Huhhhhhh?!" she exclaimed in surprise. Ripple had been a hieral

Chapter II: Inglis, Age 15—Orders to Defend the Hieral Menace (2)

menace for a long time, but this was the first time someone had not just deflected her gunfire with a sword, but sent it back *at her*. Ripple hadn't been moving around, so Inglis had aimed to return her fire.

Such a fearsome ability! Ripple thought. *This isn't just a matter of power—it's a masterful technique! Why is this little cutie so skilled?!*

"Ugh…! Dammit!" Ripple tried to shoot down the incoming bullets. *I managed two… But the third's coming straight for me!*

"Mmph—!" She had to jump back to avoid it. For that moment, her fire stopped. She hadn't wanted to take her eyes off Inglis, but she'd been preoccupied. "Huh?! Where'd she go?!"

She practically disappeared!

No sooner did Ripple think that than a beautiful silver thread danced on the edge of her vision. It was the sight of Inglis's long, platinum-blonde hair swinging in the air.

She was close—too close.

She's right here! Ripple thought in a panic.

"Haaaah!" Inglis yelled.

Bam!

Inglis used the momentum of her lunge to smash her shoulder into Ripple's back.

"Aaaaaah!" Ripple, light of frame, was sent flying by the force of the blow. She flew in the direction of Principal Miriela, who was setting up a barrier. Ripple expected to slam into the ground but made an unexpectedly soft landing. Perhaps Principal Miriela had manipulated the barrier.

"Owwww…" Ripple groaned. "That was one heckuva body slam. Amazing. And shooting my own bullets back at me? You're twisted, Inglis. No one's done that before."

"I'm actually more of a sword fighter than a fist fighter, so…" Inglis said. Truthfully, she had wanted to break through a two-gun curtain of fire up close. She was a bit unsatisfied about having relied on projectiles.

I guess hieral menaces really are strong enough not to let me get my way, Inglis thought. *Anyway, back to the battle. It isn't over yet. I don't want it to end yet.*

"So, Ripple, shall we?"

First, Ripple looked at Miriela behind her. "Thanks, Miriela, that barrier stopped me. Only one ouchie today."

"Oh…" Miriela stared in confusion. "I didn't do anything. I thought you were going to slam into the ground, but something brushed over you, and the barrier disappeared as if sucked away." She tilted her neck as she stared at her ring.

That must be the Artifact that created the barrier, Inglis assumed.

"What do you mean by the mana being sucked away? Miriela, you didn't do that intentionally, right?" Theodore asked.

"No, I didn't."

This seemed to have dredged up a memory from the ambassador.

This doesn't bode well, Inglis thought. "Um, about that fight…" But no one was listening. The flow naturally continued as if the fight had ended, even though no one had said it was over.

"I'd like another one of you to try a different Artifact. It will be dangerous, so ideally one whose function isn't an attack," Principal Miriela requested.

Liselotte raised her hand. "Then, I shall." Her Artifact's Gift created bright-white wings which gave her the power of flight, rather than being for straightforward attacks.

"Go ahead."

"Yes… How's this?"

"Thank you. Now, Lady Ripple, please touch her wing."

"Okay, got it." Ripple patted one of the wings which had appeared on Liselotte's back.

Inglis began to object. "Um…! The fight isn't ov— Mmph?!"

"Now, now. Quiet down, Chris. This is a serious conversation." Rafinha placed a hand over her cousin's mouth as the weighty discussion continued.

"Do you two notice anything different?" Theodore asked.

"Not at all," Liselotte replied.

"All normal," Ripple said.

Chapter II: Inglis, Age 15—Orders to Defend the Hieral Menace (2)

"In that case, Miriela, could you try using Liselotte's Artifact?" Theodore suggested.

"Th-The angel wings? I don't really think that's appropriate for a lady my age..."

Ripple quickly took the chance for some playful jabs. "Yeah, wings like that are only for when you're young and cute. Maybe until your early twenties?"

"Ugh..."

Liselotte chuckled. "Here. Go right ahead, Principal."

"Laugh while you can, young lady! One day, time will make its mark on you too!" Miriela warned, much to Liselotte's confusion.

"Err...?"

"Miriela, this is no time to be troubling your students," Theodore said.

"Of course. Then... Here goes!" Bright white wings sprouted from Miriela's back.

"So I touch them like I did before?" As Ripple did so, the wings disappeared with a *swoosh*, as if sucked away.

Theodore understood right away. "So it *is* absorbing mana...but only Miriela's!"

"Perhaps because a hieral menace can only receive the power of a holy knight's special-class Rune," Miriela said.

"Precisely. Lady Ripple's existing ability to transform into a weapon, which occurs through both her intent and the power of a special-class Rune, seems to be distorted in a strange way. Without meaning to, Ripple is taking in mana from Miriela, who has a special-class Rune. And when enough of that mana accumulates..."

"Ah...?!" Ripple gasped.

Vwoom!

A dark sphere covered Ripple's body. Magicite beasts would be appearing soon.

Ambassador Theodore's expression became stern. "As expected, this phenomenon seems to be what's summoning the magicite beasts!"

"M-My bad, Inglis," Ripple said, struggling to hold on to consciousness. "Take care of the rest for me...!" Then she collapsed, but Inglis fortunately caught her before she hit the ground.

Having been maintaining the dimension this whole time, Leone was struggling. "S-Sorry! I'm at my limit!" She was sweating quite a bit; the burden on her had been significant.

The scenery around them shifted into the familiar surroundings of the principal's office from earlier. And as they arrived back at the school, a magicite beast dropped in from above.

Crassshhh!

The creature smashed into the desk in Miriela's office, breaking it into pieces. "Ahhhhh! My desk!" she exclaimed with a mournful cry.

Inglis's attention was focused solely on the magicite beast. This time, only one had appeared. Like the previous occurrences, the creature had ears and a tail, characteristic of demihumans—but something was odd.

"It... It's huge! What the heck?!" Rafinha exclaimed.

It was enormous—more than twice the size of the previous ones. The various colored stones that studded its body were harder and more akin to ore. Its eyes were like jet-black jewels, implying it had dark-elemental power. This magicite beast was certainly stronger than the previous ones. Inglis inferred that was due to Ripple having drawn more mana from Principal Miriela.

"Be careful, Rani. This one's probably about as strong as Rahl or Cyrene were as magicite beasts," Inglis warned.

Ripple's condition seemed to be a trap prepared to punish surface-dwelling forces who did not align with Highland. Inglis deemed it a rather half-hearted Highland plot. The might of the summoned magicite beasts was not that different from that of those produced by the Prism Flow, despite the latter being more common. However, Highland likely had more up its sleeves. Moving Ripple to the knights' academy had been a wise decision.

"I appreciate you looking out for me, but your warning doesn't match your expression, Chris!" Rafinha quipped.

Chapter II: Inglis, Age 15—Orders to Defend the Hieral Menace (2)

"Oh, whoops! We're on a mission, so it would behoove me to at least appear serious."

"That is not the issue here! Beat that thing—with haste!" Principal Miriela waved her Artifact to create barriers in a hurry. The light of the barrier covered the world outside the window. "Please stop trying to get enemies to show you everything they've got before you do anything!"

Miriela knew Inglis too well by now. The squire tried a different approach. "Perhaps…it's because I prefer to keep an open mind about people?"

Principal Miriela ignored her excuse. "Prevent as much damage in here as you can! And I'm not saying this just because I have my things here. I'm not!"

The students stared in silence.

Regardless, the barrier Artifacts they now had could cover a wide area centered on their position, confining the battle inside; everything within the confines of the barrier could be destroyed.

"Leone, can you create that dimension again?" Inglis asked.

"Not right away! Sorry!"

"Everyone, take care! It's attempting something!" Liselotte cried out.

"Gwoooooohhhh!"

The magicite beast let out a great roar, and sparks of darkness began to condense around it. Even though its coloring was different, the flow of power that Inglis sensed reminded her of Cyrene's heat rays. She anticipated the creature would probably shoot some sort of beam.

"It's preparing to launch light-based attacks at us!" Inglis exclaimed. If it was to fire off wildly inside this building, that would pose a problem.

That got Principal Miriela's attention. "Ehh?! S-Stop it!"

Well, stopping it would probably be good, yes, Inglis thought.

Rafinha shouted, "Chris! We've gotta do something now!"

"You're right, Rani. I'm on it!"

Inglis and Rafinha had their minds on one thing: that the principal's office was on the floor above the cafeteria. If the magicite beast unleashed its attack here, the cafeteria would be caught in the blasts as well—Inglis absolutely had to stop that from happening!

"Principal Miriela, please drop your barrier for a moment! I have a plan."

"O-Okay! Go for it, Inglis!" Miriela dropped her barrier.

"Yes...!"

No holding back now!

Inglis swiftly activated Aether Shell. Clad in the bluish-white light of aether, she sprinted toward the magicite beast in a flash. She kicked with a twist of her hips. "Even if I can't stop it in time..."

...I can smash it away to somewhere where its beams won't cause any problems!

Blammmmmm!

Inglis's kick sent the gigantic magicite beast soaring at an incredible speed. It smashed straight through the ceiling far into the sky; in the blink of an eye, it looked no larger than a pea. There, it scattered dark light, but it didn't hit anything.

Most importantly, the cafeteria was safe. That was good.

"Good job, Chris! You protected our cafeteria!" Rafinha cheered.

"As always, Inglis has very Inglis-like solutions," Leone said.

Principal Miriela was shocked. "Wh-Whoa! It's flying off really, really fast!"

"Such incredible brute force...!" Liselotte gasped.

"Your strength... It's incredible. Just what *are* you?" Ambassador Theodore asked.

"I apologize for the damage. I seem to have put a hole in your ceiling and roof." Inglis gave a polite, apologetic bow to the principal.

"W-Well, pay it no mind. I would consider that minimal."

Liselotte brought up an important point, though. "B-But it's going to fall! Furthermore, physical attacks are not sufficient to deal with magicite beasts, so it hasn't been defeated yet!"

Inglis agreed. "First, let's make sure it isn't going to fall on the school building."

Chapter II: Inglis, Age 15—Orders to Defend the Hieral Menace (2)

Truthfully, a kick delivered with Aether Shell active would likely have been enough to take down a magicite beast, but Inglis understood the importance of confirming a victory. Plus, she needed to make sure it wouldn't land on the school building somewhere. With a yell, Inglis leaped through the hole in the ceiling and landed on the roof. Behind her, Rafinha and the others followed, and they gauged the trajectory of the falling magicite beast.

"It doesn't look like it's going to crash into the building," Rafinha said.

"Yes, it's headed for the school courtyard!" Leone said.

"I propose we finish it off quickly as soon as it lands!" Liselotte suggested.

The magicite beast was approaching the ground, but a new problem had arisen. "Ah...! Someone's there!" Leone cried.

"Yua?!" Rafinha exclaimed. The second-year student was wandering by.

"Yuaaa! Look up, look uuup! Watch ouuut!" Principal Miriela warned loudly.

Yua did as instructed and noticed the falling magicite beast, but she did not get out of the way. "Oh no. Someone save me." Her karate chop sprang forth swiftly, clashing with the listlessness in her tone of voice.

Slash!

With that, the falling magicite beast was cleaved in two.

"Wow! Yua, you're amazing!" Rafinha said.

Even if Inglis had already critically weakened the magicite beast, none of them had expected Yua to be able to cut it in half with a karate chop.

That was fantastic. Yua really is a gem. I absolutely must fight her someday, Inglis thought.

The bisected magicite beast dissolved into the air. Meanwhile, Yua ambled casually back into the dorms as if nothing had happened at all.

After watching her depart, Ambassador Theodore took a deep breath and spoke. "The dark light has disappeared. I sense no more disturbance in Lady Ripple's mana. She should come to shortly." He paused to reflect for a moment. "We've learned quite a bit today. And not only does the dimension-displacement Artifact seem to be working fine, I don't anticipate a recurrence of this phenomenon for a while. Thank you, everyone."

"Sir Theodore, why do you say that?" Leone asked.

"Because we've established that the phenomenon only takes place when Lady Ripple's body can absorb mana from the bearer of a special-class Rune," he answered.

"Is that because summoning that magicite beast drained that mana, meaning it will take time for Ripple to reach that same level again?" Inglis asked.

"Yes, that's correct. It's as Inglis says." He turned to her. "You understand well."

The warmth of his smile reminded Inglis of his sister, Cyrene. They really were siblings.

"Sir Theodore, there's something I don't understand," Rafinha said.

"Yes, what is it?"

"Why are these magicite beasts always former demihumans?"

"Hmm, if I had to put forth a theory, I'd say it's because Ripple herself is a demihuman. Demihumans seem to have a superior sixth sense, one which even allows them to communicate telepathically. It appears that she's able to call out to others of her kind through this connection."

Inglis found that explanation convincing. Even when Ripple had inadvertently called forth a magicite beast more powerful than usual through Miriela's mana, it had been a demihuman. Her summoning ability was likely limited to demihumans.

"So it's something that could only be done through Ripple..." Miriela remarked.

"Indeed. In fact, it's even possible that they specifically made a demihuman into a hieral menace for this purpose," Theodore said to his old friend.

"So they're using the demihumans, who were wiped out by the Prism Flow..." Even Principal Miriela's expression became stern and overcast.

Chapter II: Inglis, Age 15—Orders to Defend the Hieral Menace (2)

"Many Highlanders do not see surface-dwellers as equals. I believe they're willing to do anything, attempt any measure... And thus, I believe they have arranged this. As a Highlander myself, it shames me to admit it, but..."

"Poor Ripple... Using her friends like that..." Rafinha remarked.

"It seems like we, along with everything else, are just tools to Highland..." Leone said.

Liselotte didn't like it either. "This really is dreadful! And after all Lady Ripple's done to defend our country..."

Another voice suddenly reached their ears. "Calm down, everyone. It all depends on your perspective." Ripple was sitting up now; her consciousness had returned. "Thinking about it the other way around, it's a chance to lay to rest my peers who have become magicite beasts. I don't want them to be stuck like that. And I'm sure they'd be happy to be stopped from hurting anyone."

"Ripple... You're right. And we'll make totally sure nothing serious happens!" Rafinha said.

"Thanks. I'm gonna be out cold, so I won't be able to help. Give it your all. Don't hold back against them."

Inglis tentatively raised her hand. "One potential countermeasure has occurred to me. If I may?"

"Yes. Let us hear it, Inglis," Ambassador Theodore prompted.

"With aid from the principal, Silva, and Rafael, we allow Ripple to absorb large amounts of mana. As such, she'll summon vast numbers of powerful magicite beasts. And if we beat 'em, and beat 'em, and beat 'em, and beat 'em all..."

Judging by what Ripple and the others had said, the demihuman population had already been turned into magicite beasts and there was no hope of saving them. If Ripple only ever brought forth demihuman-type magicite beasts, then she had a finite number to call.

Inglis continued, "I propose we neutralize that phenomenon by having Ripple run out of summoned creatures."

"That's, uh, very like you, Chris. The 'Beat Them All Up! ♪' strategy?" Rafinha remarked.

"Yeah. Don't you think it's a good idea?" It would let Inglis fight to her heart's content. In addition, it would provide opportunities for her to see Rafael, Principal Miriela, and Silva at their best, as well as Yua and Eris. It would be a very interesting battlefield to watch; just imagining it made her excited.

"I...don't quite think that's wise," Leone said haltingly. "But I think it could work if handled well, and it's very much like you, Inglis. Very much so..."

"The ultimate in brute force... But to be quite honest, I don't believe it's an awful idea," Liselotte said.

Ripple agreed and gave a laugh. "Ha ha ha! If you can handle it, I think you can pull it off."

Even though the students were willing to take risks, the adults had their reservations about Inglis's suggestion. Miriela objected, "Weeell, the problem is that it's total war... We can only do that if we're prepared to endanger ourselves in a significant fashion. That would be a last resort. Wouldn't you agree, Theodore?"

"Correct. I'd like a bit more time to find alternatives—" A rapid knock at the door of the principal's office cut off the rest of the ambassador's sentence.

"Yes? Is there something urgent?" Principal Miriela answered as she opened the door for them to see Rafael and Eris.

"Rafael!" Rafinha called out to her brother.

"Eris!" Ripple did the same to her friend.

"Hey, Rani, Chris. Sorry, but something important came up," Rafael said.

"Ripple, I've been so worried about you! Let's talk later. We have an emergency on our hands," Eris pressed.

"What's happened?" Theodore asked.

"We've come to summon you, Sir Theodore. Prince Wayne requests your presence at the palace immediately!"

"Did something happen?" the ambassador asked.

"Venefic's armies have crossed the border and are invading!" Rafael exclaimed. "Prince Wayne requests you. He'd like to discuss our response."

Theodore's expression turned grave with a stiff intake of breath. "I see. I'll be there immediately!"

Chapter III: Inglis, Age 15—Orders to Defend the Hieral Menace (3)

On the outskirts of the capital, a flying battleship made by Highland hovered low in the sky. The hangars on its lower hull were open, with many Flygears and Flygear Ports inside. The knights who would be using them were preparing to deploy to Venefic's frontier.

Inglis and her friends had also been recruited to help. Right now, they were aboard a Flygear Port piloted by Rafinha. Their objective was to bring not just the Flygear Port itself but also supplies like rations and its array of Flygears to the hangars of the flying battleship. While the first-year students had trained for a significant amount of time with Flygears at the academy, they had only a passing familiarity with Flygear Ports. Inglis thought this would be good on-the-job practice for Rafinha.

"Phew. This is pretty exhausting." Rafinha wiped sweat from her brow.

Flygears could dock with a Flygear Port and connect to provide added thrust. However, the Flygear Port itself needed to be powered with mana just like an Artifact. While it was possible to pre-charge it with power, Rafinha was supplying it directly, which took a lot of energy out of the pilot. If the Flygear Port wasn't powered from the pilot or recharged when its reserves depleted, it and its Flygears would malfunction.

Therefore, it was necessary to entrust each Flygear Port to a knight—preferably one with a middle-class or better Rune. A lower-class Rune did not provide enough power to move the Flygear Port. The strength of the knight's Rune affected the Flygear Port's charge capacity and speed, so a knight like Rafinha with her upper-class Rune was highly sought after.

Under the knights' current organization, a Flygear Port, its complement of Flygears, and their pilots were treated as a single element. People like Rafinha, Leone, and Liselotte would typically become captains of such a unit the moment they became full knights upon graduating from the academy. Their training was preparation for such duties.

"Shall I take over for now? I'd like some practice as well," Liselotte said.

"Yeah. Thanks, Liselotte." Rafinha passed the controls to her before lining up next to Inglis, who was standing at the railing.

"Good work, Rani. Want something to drink?"

"Yeah. Thanks, Chris." Rafinha gulped down water from the canteen Inglis passed her, then sighed in relief. "There's still plenty to haul, and a long way to go."

"I'll fly when Liselotte needs a break," Leone offered.

"Guess I'm in charge of the canteens for today." Inglis jangled the clump of canteens for everyone, which was hanging from her neck.

"I kinda feel like you're slacking off, since there aren't going to be any fights today, Chris..."

"Isn't it better if I leave the Flygear Port to you and the others?" Inglis replied.

"Just saying, Inglis, you usually put your all into something when it's a fight," Leone said.

"That's okay. Chris acts that way because she likes fighting; it's what she lives for."

"Yeah. No room to argue with that," Inglis said.

"Ha ha ha... I think I'd be more worried if that wasn't your answer." Leone laughed wryly.

"But really, the ship's so big that it's tough to get it loaded up swiftly. That's why they mobilized us too," Rafinha added.

"There isn't much time until they deploy," Inglis noted.

This ship, which was Ambassador Theodore's personal vessel, was even bigger than the Highland one which had nearly crashed into the

Chapter III: Inglis, Age 15—Orders to Defend the Hieral Menace (3)

palace during the offering. Both its armor and armaments had been reinforced, making it quite imposing.

"Lord Theodore is doing so much for us... Even supplying such a grand ship..." Rafinha said.

"I wonder whether he's crossing a dangerous line with Highland by doing this," Inglis pondered.

Highland had not yet approved large flying ships besides Flygear Ports to be given to the surface, so Theodore had a cover story in mind: the positioning happened to coincide with the ambassador's inspection of the kingdom's knights. It was a flimsy excuse, but Theodore was willing to make a risky move in this circumstance.

"I'm bringing it in!" Liselotte, a nervous note in her voice, guided the Flygear Port into the flying battleship's hangar. Inside the hangar, there was already a line of Flygear Ports accompanied by a large force of knights. The murmur of their conversations carried an uneasy tone, perhaps because they were new to the battleship as well.

"I'll land it in an empty bay." Liselotte cautiously brought the Flygear Port deeper into the hangar.

"Sorry! Can you land it here?!" Rafael's voice called out from below. He'd taken direct command, Inglis assumed. Eris was also there, watching over the work from a short distance.

"Yeah. Rafael's the dedicated type. He doesn't like to leave things like this to others." Rafinha sounded both pleased and satisfied.

"Understood!" Liselotte nervously responded and brought the Flygear Port close to the specified point.

A proper landing had to avoid collisions with the walls or any other Flygear Ports—a simple but daunting task. As Inglis stared at the designated landing point, she saw another Flygear Port suddenly cut across their path. It was very low, almost low enough to scrape the floor. As Inglis squinted, she realized that someone was carrying it on their own.

Various knights had taken notice as well. "Wow! Such incredible strength!"

"Amazing! She must be an academy student..."

"And in the squire program, to boot!"

They weren't referring to Inglis either. She was waiting, holding canteens for Rafinha and the others.

Then she recognized who it was. "Yua...?"

Silva and the other third-years were guarding Ripple today; the first- and second-years were aiding in the knights' mobilization. Inglis watched Yua carry an entire Flygear Port deeper within the hangar, presumably to free up space near the entrance. Now there was a commotion inside the hangar as more people were amazed by Yua's strength.

Inglis barely stifled a chuckle. "Ha ha... Rani, I'm gonna get to work too!"

"Ah...! Chris!"

Inglis leaped down from the Flygear Port and approached the older squire. "Yua, allow me!"

"Okay...? Then help me bring this one all the way in back." Yua heaved the Flygear Port over to Inglis.

"Huh?!"

Thump!

It wasn't only the Flygear Port in Inglis's arms—it still had many Flygears inside as well, making it tremendously heavy.

"Oof!" Inglis wobbled before recovering by releasing the enhanced gravity on herself. "Phew." Without that added weight, she could carry it normally. *So Yua has at least this much strength when nothing's affecting her.*

"You okay?"

"Yes. I'll be fine!"

Inglis and Yua energetically packed the Flygear Port in line deep within the hangar as nearby knights gaped at their strength.

"That girl's amazing too!"

"*Another* squire girl? Just what's going on with the squire program?!"

Then came the loudest comment of all, voiced by a crowd: "And she's so cute!" Well, Inglis didn't pay it much mind.

"Mm. Should be all of 'em. Thanks, Boobies."

Chapter III: Inglis, Age 15—Orders to Defend the Hieral Menace (3)

Yua still didn't remember her name. It was a bit embarrassing to be called "Boobies" every time, but Inglis wasn't going to let it get her down—not until they'd had their fight.

"You're welcome, Yua. By the way, feel like getting some more exercise in?"

"Nah. I hate working."

"Well, I saw before when you karate-chopped straight through that falling magicite beast. It was amazing. Would you mind teaching me how?"

Yua didn't refuse to answer, but her replies didn't get to the point. After a pause, she said, "I just put my strength into it..."

"I'd be really happy if you could show me some practical examples."

"That wouldn't make me all that happy, though."

"Hmm... Then, can we work out some kind of exchange? I'll do something in return for your own satisfaction."

Yua's interest piqued. "Well, there's something I'd like to learn from you."

"Oh? What is it? Anything, just ask!"

"How did you get your chest that big?"

"Huh? Um... All I can say is it grew naturally."

Yua shook her head at the response. "That doesn't help at all. I want big boobs so I'll be hot." Yua tried to flounce her chest at Inglis, but there was very little there. She was lithe and slender; she probably had a chest even smaller than Rafinha's.

But this was the first time Inglis had heard anything like that at the knights' academy. Yua really was a bit off-kilter.

Inglis sighed. "Well, they're heavy, they make my shoulders sore, and everyone stares at them. It's not all fun and games." Inglis suddenly became embarrassed as she realized she really sounded like a girl. What she'd said had no trace of the old Hero-King Inglis. Habit was a frightening thing. Just how much more accustomed to this life would she get?

"I don't mind. I want cleavage to show off like yours, Boobies."

"Th-That's not my intention at all!" *What a terrible thing to say.*

45

I might enjoy it myself in front of a mirror, but that's for me. *Not anyone else.*

"Anyway, if you teach me how to make my breasts bigger, I'll fight you anytime."

"W-Well... All right..." Inglis herself had gotten big before she even noticed, so she had no real ideas. She'd have to ask among her friends later if they had any ideas.

"That's our deal." Expressionless, Yua left quickly.

After watching her depart, Inglis returned to where Rafinha and the others were. Liselotte had already brought the Flygear Port down safely. They were standing in a circle, watching Inglis's approach.

Rafael, in the center of the circle, called out to her. "Thanks, Chris. Opening up a space up front made it easier to land."

"It was no trouble. It gave me a chance to talk to Yua too."

"What did you talk about? Does she still not want to fight?" Rafinha asked.

"Well, she agreed to it, but I have to teach her something in exchange."

"What?"

"How to make her breasts bigger."

Rafinha giggled. "Well, well. She and I have got something in common."

"*That's* what she's intent on...?" Leone said. "Mine hurt my shoulders, and everyone stares at them. It's not all fun and games having large breasts."

The way Leone voiced the same complaints as Inglis had made the reborn hero-king stop. If Inglis thought the same as Leone did, that meant that her own sensibilities had become those of a normal girl. Inglis didn't really mind, but it was a little bit embarrassing.

What she really couldn't agree with, though, was Yua's line about "wanting big boobs so she'd be hot." *What's so good about making guys interested, anyway?* Inglis thought.

That part of herself was still completely unchanged. Even if she did appreciate to a degree how her body filled out a dress or how she looked to herself in the mirror, she wasn't interested in what men thought of her appearance.

Chapter III: Inglis, Age 15—Orders to Defend the Hieral Menace (3)

Rafinha pouted. "I really envy you. Girls who got big without any effort don't understand the feeling of those not so blessed."

"Rani, you've probably tried a lot of things, right?"

"Yeah, I'm trying hard, but nothing is working!"

"Can you tell me all the methods you've tried later? They obviously didn't work, so I'll avoid recommending them to Yua."

"Boo...! Why don't you just shut up!"

Liselotte tried to butt in. "Now, now. Let's not embarrass ourselves in front of Lord Rafael and Lady Eris."

"Liselotte, you're just saying that because yours are bigger!" Rafinha protested.

"Not big enough to make her shoulders stiff either. She got the best of both worlds, in a way," Leone said.

Liselotte let out a sigh. She had intervened to cool things down, but now she was caught between the jealous stares of Rafinha and Leone.

"And you don't have to worry about Rin squirming around your chest either," Inglis noted.

"That's right. Liselotte needs to experience that for once," Leone added.

"All right, Rin! You're allowed to go inside Liselotte's clothes!" Rafinha tossed Rin at Liselotte.

"Eeek! Ah, no, that tickles! Eeep!" Liselotte shrieked as Rin squirmed around.

Once she was satisfied, Rin returned to Inglis's cleavage. With a sigh, Inglis said, "But she always comes back." She poked Rin and felt more wild squirming at her chest, almost as if in revenge. "Sheesh, Rin...!"

"It really is great to see big ones swaying, isn't it? I understand how Yua feels." Rafinha nodded in comprehension.

With a touch of disappointment, Eris sighed. "Rafael, should a commander stand for this sort of a lack of discipline?"

"Ah, right. Sorry, Lady Eris..." Rafael said.

"You can't blame him, Eris. Whenever Rafael's around Chris, he only has eyes for her."

"C'mon, Rani...!" Rafael complained.

Rafinha gloated, "Aha ha, Rafael's maaad. ♪"

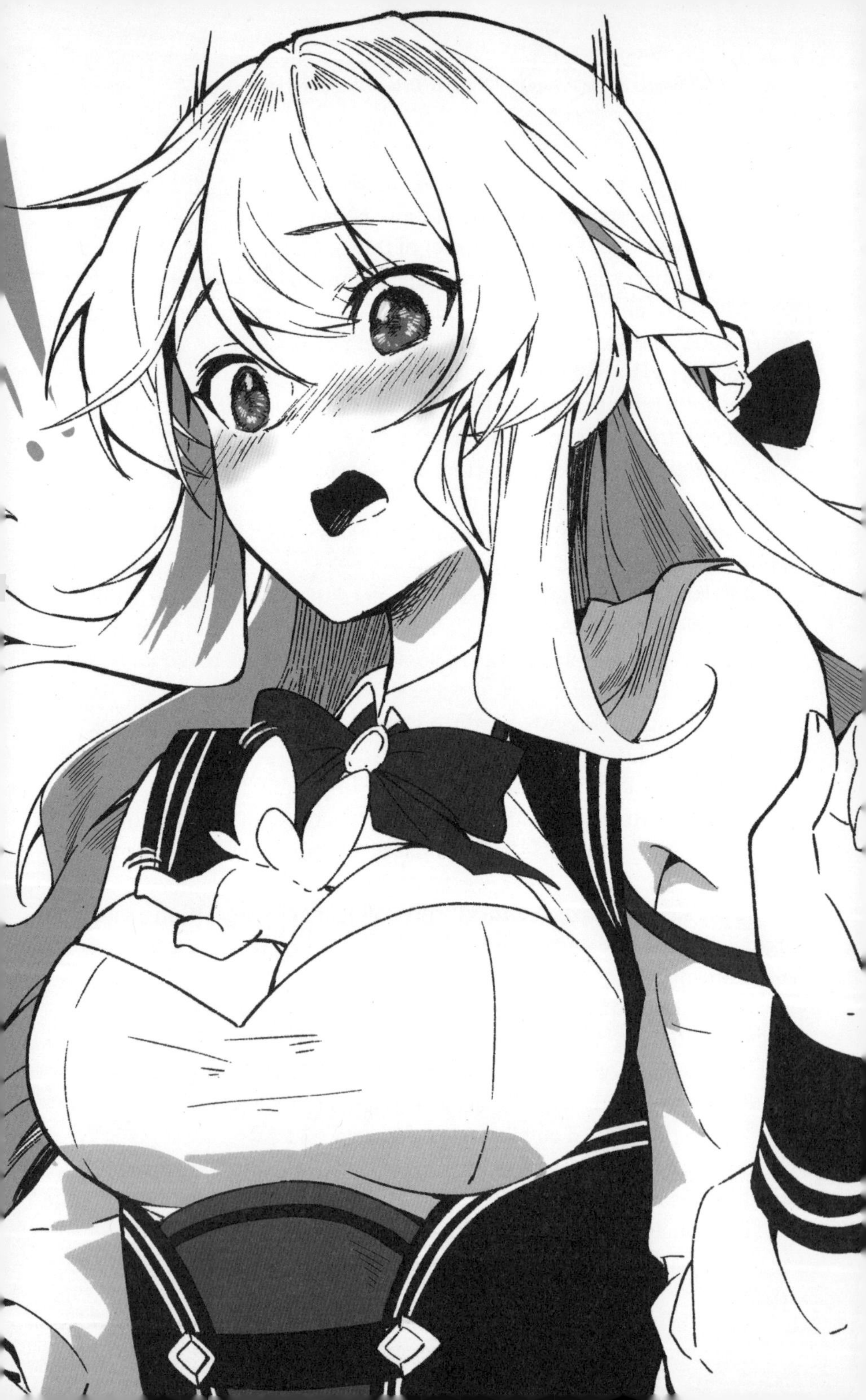

Chapter III: Inglis, Age 15—Orders to Defend the Hieral Menace (3)

Eris sighed again. "It's noisy over here too…"

Inglis turned to her. "By the way, Eris. Do you have any ideas?"

"About what?"

"How to make your breasts bigger."

"You're the first person I've ever heard ask a hieral menace such a vulgar question."

"This is a matter of life and death for me!" She had to do this; it was all for the sake of her duel with Yua. Eris would be leaving soon to the border with Venefic, so this was Inglis's only chance to ask.

"I don't know, and I don't really care. When we become hieral menaces, we don't age or grow further."

"How about before you became a hieral menace?"

"That was so long ago I don't remember. And I didn't have the kind of peaceful life where I could just sit around and think about unimportant matters."

"Meaning there was some kind of fearsome foe?! Was it a magicite beast? Has anyone taken it down yet? If it's still alive, can you set me up to fight it?"

Eris stared long and hard at Inglis. "You *really* do think of nothing else, do you?" Eris let out a deep, deep sigh and shook her head. "Anyway, how's Ripple doing?"

"No real changes. The phenomenon where she summons magicite beasts persists, but we've prevented any further harm. Sir Theodore will be going with you this time, so I presume the status quo will be maintained until he returns."

Eris hesitated a bit. "I see. Take good care of Ripple."

"Yes. Leave it to us."

From the side, Rafinha peeked her face in. "We'll be working hard, so don't lose to Venefic either, Eris! It's not nice to attack someone's country when we're busy protecting ourselves from magicite beasts! So knock them back!"

"Well, honestly, I think Sir Theodore is with them for an entirely different purpose," Inglis said.

"Huh? What do you mean, Chris?"

"With a Highland ambassador present, no one will be making any rash moves. Because Venefic's Highland ambassador is from a different faction, if the situation isn't handled carefully, it could trigger conflict between forces in Highland as well, right? If Sir Theodore is there, Venefic will have to keep that in mind in case we're willing to go that far."

Theodore, who had appeared from nowhere, chuckled. "That's correct, Inglis. You have a very good grasp of the situation."

"Ah, Sir Theodore!" Rafinha's eyes gleamed.

"I'm terribly sorry to leave Lady Ripple in such a state, but as Inglis observed, I simply must be present. Until I return, please take good care of Lady Ripple and Cyrene. You have my gratitude."

"I pray that no armed conflict occurs and that the situation is resolved peacefully." As Inglis spoke, astonished looks appeared on Rafinha and Leone's faces.

"Huh? What's wrong, Rani?" asked Inglis.

"I can't believe what I'm hearing. Did you eat something bad?"

"I'm fine. It'd be a waste for a fight to happen where I can't join in. That's all."

If Inglis were on the field, she'd be hoping for things to come to blows. However, it'd be unfortunate for the forces of both countries to whittle each other down while she wasn't present; it would mean fewer foes for her.

Rafinha laughed. "Ha ha ha... So that's what you meant."

"Now it all makes sense. Inglis is still the Inglis we know," Leone said.

Theodore smiled wryly as he cleared his throat. "Anyway, I leave the matter in your hands. Oh, and Rafinha."

"Yes?"

"I'd like to speak with you. Come this way, please." He beckoned her toward the lower decks.

"On my way." Rafinha, completely unguarded, smiled innocently.

Conversely, Inglis's sense of danger was exceptional. "I'll come as well. I'm Rani's squire, so I should be at her side."

Any kinds of vermin lurking in wait for Rafinha had to be exterminated. When potential threats were around, her guard had to be thorough.

Chapter III: Inglis, Age 15—Orders to Defend the Hieral Menace (3)

"Yes, of course. Leone, Liselotte, you're welcome as well." Theodore proceeded as if he didn't even notice.

Is he adept at hiding his true self, or is he really not that interested in Rafinha? He did seem to be struck by Rafinha's honesty and sense of justice, just like his sister Cyrene had been. Either way, I must be prepared for anything. Rafinha has absolutely no need for a lover just yet. I don't want to see that happen.

"Then we'll keep working. Rani, Chris, everyone—handle things while we're gone," Rafael requested.

"Take care of Ripple for me, please?" Eris added.

Everyone nodded and bid their farewell to Rafael and Eris. Inglis, Rafinha, Leone, and Liselotte followed Ambassador Theodore into the ship's lower decks. The room he led them to was filled with unfamiliar research equipment. However, while crowded, it was neatly organized. Inglis thought this room perfectly reflected his personality.

Theodore pulled an Artifact from the many contents around them and handed it to Rafinha. "I thought I'd at least give you something helpful, so I prepared this. Please, take it."

It was an Artifact in the form of a bow. Its appearance, white with winglike decorations, was very similar to Rafinha's favorite bow, Shiny Flow.

"This is the same as my Shiny Flow...?"

"Yes, the base is the same. Furthermore, it's an upgrade; it has a second Gift."

"Wow! Thank you! The second Gift—is it the same as Leone's?"

"No, this one is different. This Artifact can also heal wounds."

"Wow! Incredible! I've never heard of an Artifact like that!"

Rafinha was right. This was the first Inglis had heard of such an effect. Even during the age of Hero-King Inglis, healing magic had been exceptionally rare.

"Yes. They're quite rare and not something that can be made in any great number... I want you to have it. I feel this Gift suits your pure heart."

"Ha ha ha... You are too kind..."

"There's no need to be so modest. There are few people like you,

51

particularly among Highlanders, so I can see your shining heart clearly. I'm absolutely sure Cyrene felt the same way."

Rafinha tried to figure out how to respond to that. "Maybe? What do you think, Rin?"

Rin lay down on top of her head, feigning ignorance.

"If anyone happens to be wounded while defending Ripple, use that Artifact to heal them," Theodore said, getting back to serious issues.

"Understood! Thanks for giving us so much." Rafinha gave a polite, precise bow.

"Yes. Use it well. Of course, I hope a situation won't arise in which you need to use it, but I think it's necessary to be prepared. I didn't have time to tell Miriela, so please inform her for me."

"Yes! I'll get right to practicing so I can use it well when I get back!"

Rafinha was determined—but as soon as she returned to the academy, she'd have to use the power of her new Gift for real.

◆◇◆

After they'd finished assisting the knights and had seen them off, Inglis and the others returned to the knights' academy. It was already evening, and they were rather hungry.

"I'm starving! Let's hurry to the cafeteria and have dinner!" Rafinha rubbed her stomach.

"Yeah. Rani, there's supposed to be a new menu starting today."

"Ah! You're right! I'm looking forward to it. ♪"

"Hmm? What's on it? I'm hoping for a new salad or a vegetable soup," Leone said. That was so like Leone, who was choosy about her food thanks to her slow metabolism.

"I'd rather enjoy more options for dessert. The lack of variety is so stifling." Liselotte's request was fitting too.

"Nope, neither of those!" Inglis and Rafinha shook their heads in unison.

"You know? What is it?" Leone asked.

"The super-sized bone-in meaty cheese melt, the super-sized supreme Alfredo pasta, the super-sized supreme blazin' hot pasta, and—"

Chapter III: Inglis, Age 15—Orders to Defend the Hieral Menace (3)

"Now hold it right there! Those all have 'super-sized' in their names! Why's that?!" Leone protested.

Inglis and Rafinha answered in unison. "It's what got requested!"

The cafeteria had solicited ideas for an updated menu, but didn't get much of a response, either because people weren't interested or were satisfied with the current selection. But Inglis and Rafinha had proactively offered their suggestions. In these cases, the loudest voices prevailed. Those who didn't speak up were to blame.

"What does the 'supreme' part entail?" Liselotte asked.

"They've got beef, pork, chicken, fish, everything!" Inglis and Rafinha replied together.

"Ugh... Just thinking about it gives me heartburn..." Liselotte grimaced.

"Do they even taste any good?" asked Leone.

"Yeah. They may not be the prettiest dishes, but that doesn't matter when it's in your stomach," Inglis answered.

"Yeah. We're going to eat it all anyway, so we may as well have it on one plate," Rafinha added.

That would be less work for the lunch ladies too.

"Alfredo and blazin' hot are new flavors too," Inglis added.

"With new flavors, it's so hard to pick a protein, so throw 'em all on there! That's our strategy," Rafinha said.

"I'm really looking forward to it, Rani."

"Me too, Chris." Inglis's and Rafinha's eyes gleamed as they nodded to each other.

"Ha ha ha..." Leone and Liselotte, watching them, could only laugh dryly.

Then—

Smassshhh!

A roaring sound echoed from the direction of the courtyard. Smoke was rising from there.

Inglis turned at the sudden noise.

"Wh-What?!" Rafinha yelped in surprise.

"There's smoke!" Leone exclaimed.

"It's coming from the courtyard!" Liselotte said.

Immediately, the conversation started buzzing. The girls couldn't see the courtyard from where they were near the front gate, but they could sense the confusion.

"Let's go take a look!"

At Rafinha's order, they all headed to the courtyard. A portion of the school building's walls were crumbling; they were even about to burst into flames. In front of the crumbling walls, they could see the scattered, crumpled remains of a defeated magicite beast. It was of the larger, more powerful type that had recently begun to show itself. The fight itself seemed to be over already.

"Let's put out the fire!"

"Don't worry, we'll have it out soon!"

The third-years who were there had already begun addressing the fire emergency. No one had a reason to worry about that problem now. Instead, their concern was focused on a particular person.

"More importantly, is Silva okay?!"

"Silva! Are you all right?!"

"Hold on!"

Surrounded by a ring of third-years, Silva lay flat on the ground. His body was covered in wounds, as if he had taken many hits. He was barely holding on to consciousness. He couldn't stand on his own, and needed to be helped up by other students.

"Silva...?!" Inglis gasped.

"Th-Those wounds are terrible!" Rafinha said.

The magicite beast must have been quite strong to badly wound Silva, possessor of a special-class Rune. Or perhaps he had simply been overwhelmed by many of them at once? In either case, an unusual situation must have occurred.

"This isn't enough...to take me down... More importantly, take Lady Ripple somewhere else before she awakens. I can't let her see me like this. It would give her cause for worry."

"Got it!" The students, ordered by Silva, prepared to move Ripple.

Just then, Principal Miriela arrived, having heard the commotion.

Chapter III: Inglis, Age 15—Orders to Defend the Hieral Menace (3)

"What's going on?! Silva, are you all right?! What in the world happened to you?"

"Principal... I have no excuse to offer. This was my fault. I'm sorry."

The other third-years, however, had different opinions. "No! It wasn't Silva's fault at all!"

"That's right! It's because this guy screwed up!" a third-year said, grabbing another student. Inglis recognized him.

"Lahti?" He was a first-year in the squire program, just like her. As usual, he was with Pullum from the knight program.

"Sorry, you guys are right—it's my fault this happened." Lahti's face paled as he slumped toward the ground.

With tears in her eyes, Pullum bowed her head over and over. "I'm sorry, I'm sorry, I'm sorry! Lahti tried to protect me! So it's my fault! Really, I'm really sorry!"

"Lahti, Pullum, did something happen?" Inglis asked.

"Ah, Inglis... H-He covered me when a magicite beast was about to get me... That's how he got so hurt..." Pullum pointed toward Silva.

One of Silva's classmates yelled, "That's right! It's your fault! It's your fault this happened to him!"

"St-Stop it, guys...!" Silva stopped the third-years as they began to grow more heated.

"But Silva—"

"To begin with, it was our mistake to catch those two in the slip to the other dimension. Beyond that, it's only natural for someone like myself, with power, to protect the weak Runeless." Then Silva turned to Lahti. "You there, are you hurt?"

"Huh, me? Nope."

"I see... Good..."

Silva passed out shortly afterward.

Principal Miriela gave orders in a flustered hurry. "Silva, you mustn't! You're heavily wounded! If you're not careful, your life could be in danger! Get him to the nurse's office!"

The time for Rafinha to test her new Artifact had come quite suddenly. This was an opportune moment to practice.

"Wait! I'll do something! There's something I want to try!" Rafinha had already stepped forward.

"Rafinha? What is it?" Principal Miriela asked.

"I just received a new Artifact from Sir Theodore! It looks the same, but this one has a second Gift. And that Gift is the power to heal wounds…!"

"What?! That Theodore… How'd he have that much spare time…? But thank you, Rafinha. That'll be of vital assistance!" Principal Miriela's face lit up.

"I haven't ever done this before…but I'm going to try anyway! I'd like to give it a shot!"

Rafinha took the initiative in situations like this before Inglis could even say anything. She followed the goodness in her heart without fearing or flinching at the consequences. As Inglis looked at Rafinha with the gaze a grandparent had for a grandchild, she was pleased. Seeing Rafinha be so serious inspired her to follow suit.

"Yes, of course! Go right ahead! I'll help too!" Principal Miriela encouraged. "Don't worry, Rafinha! I've used an Artifact like your new one, so I know you can do it!"

"Hurry, Rafinha!" Inglis urged.

"I'm going for it! Watch this, Chris!"

"Yeah. It'll be fine. You can do this, Rani." Inglis nodded, and with that, Rafinha began to focus and take in deep, steady breaths.

"Mm… It's different from normal!"

"That's because the power is flowing to a different Gift. Keep going," Principal Miriela said.

"O-Okay!"

Generally, using the various Gifts of an Artifact required familiarity, which was certainly true in Rafinha's and Leone's cases. At first, one couldn't help but be a bit confused by a new one, but once that had been overcome—even if the help of a Rune was necessary—the wielder could manage the wavelengths of two types of mana.

And if one could control mana… Well, that control was linked to the ability to use magic on one's own. It would likely increase Rafinha's and Leone's power. But on the other hand, Highland would be unhappy

Chapter III: Inglis, Age 15—Orders to Defend the Hieral Menace (3)

to see people of the surface using magic on their own. If that technique spread from people inspired by Rafinha and Leone, the balance of power between Highland and the surface would collapse.

In order to protect themselves from magicite beasts, the people of the surface had no choice but to accept Artifacts from Highland. If surface-dwellers could use magic, that had the potential to disrupt Highland's dealings. Presumably, Ambassador Theodore and Principal Miriela had to have some sense that Rafinha and Leone had been handed the key to realizing the true nature of mana. However, even if they did know, they weren't saying anything about it.

As with the flying battleship, Inglis thought that Ambassador Theodore was intending to close the gap between the surface and Highland. And what results would that bring? She didn't know, but right now it seemed to be linked to saving Silva.

As if guided by Principal Miriela's advice, a gentle light washed over Rafinha. "Is this light what heals people…?" she asked.

"Not yet. Focus on the tips of your hands…" Miriela prompted.

"All right…!" The light coating Rafinha coalesced around her left hand. The smaller it shrunk, the brighter it shone.

So this was the power of a healing Gift. The flow of the mana which made up its light was complex, unable to be easily replicated.

"That's it, Rafinha! Now shine that light on Silva!" Miriela announced.

"Of course!" Following the principal's instructions, Rafinha knelt beside Silva and extended the light in her left hand. The wounds covering Silva's body began to recover.

Principal Miriela gasped. "Wow! Silva's injuries…"

"They're healing!" Inglis said.

"All right! It's working!" Beads of sweat broke out on Rafinha's brow. New Gift or no, healing seemed to be quite a strain. "Ugh… Ngh!"

"Rani, are you okay?"

"I… I'm fine…!" Sweat ran down Rafinha's face and fell to the ground. Silva's wounds were healing, slowly, but at this rate Rafinha's limit would be reached first.

Then, here— "Rani. Let me help." Inglis's hand softly covered Rafinha's as she grasped the new Shiny Flow Artifact.

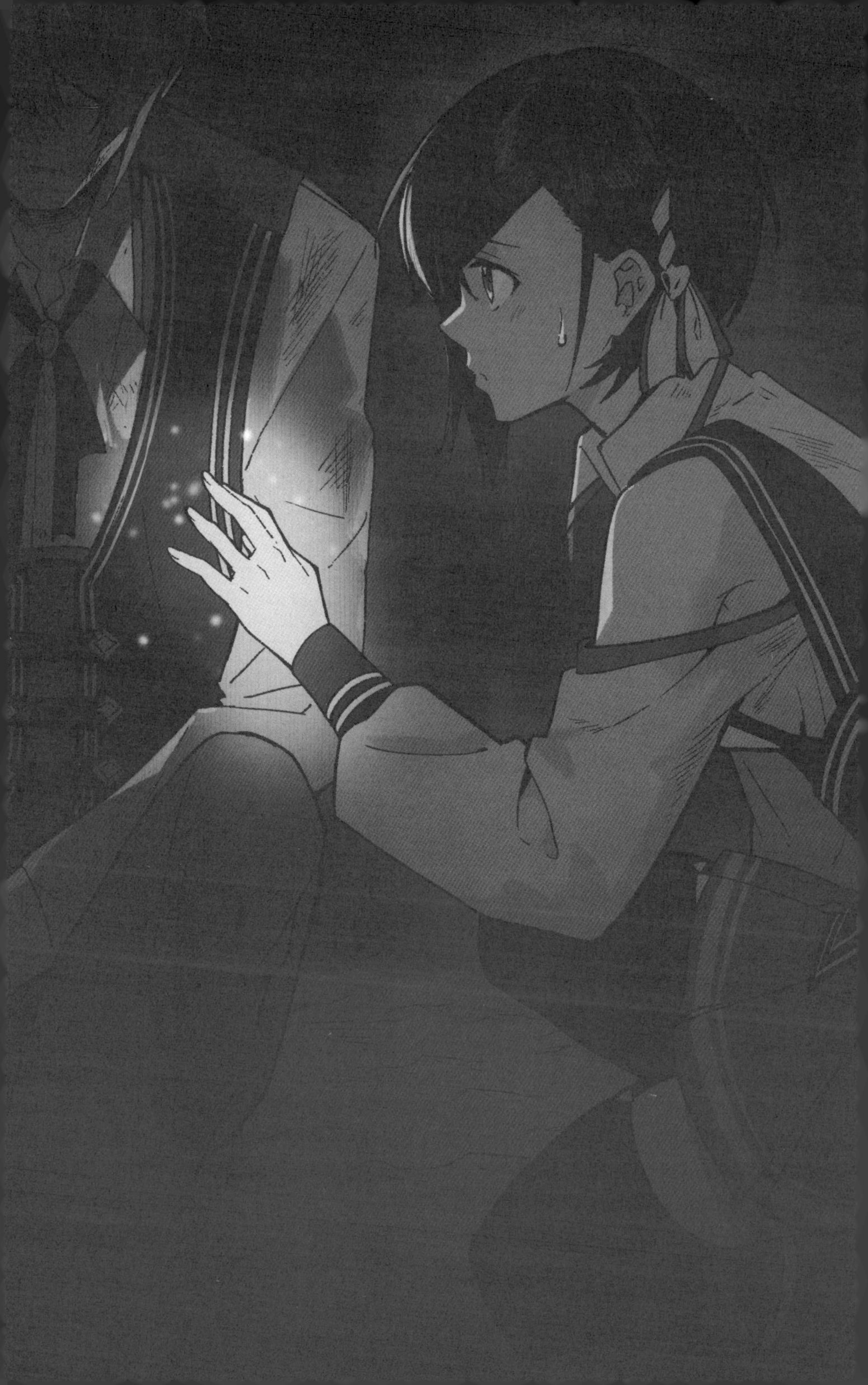

Chapter III: Inglis, Age 15—Orders to Defend the Hieral Menace (3)

It may have been difficult to duplicate the Gift itself by manipulating mana, but Inglis could still bring her own mana onto the same wavelength as Rafinha's and feed it into the Artifact. And then the Artifact would transform it into the phenomenon called a Gift. Inglis tried to recreate the flow before it was transformed.

"Chris?! Yeah, this helps a lot!"

The glow around Rafinha's left hand increased—proof that the healing power had been strengthened. The speed at which Silva's wounds were recovering increased dramatically.

As they watched, the wounds disappeared.

Principal Miriela congratulated Rafinha. "Yes, he's fine now! Thanks, both of you! Now, let's get him to the nurse's office—his wounds are already healed, so he should wake soon."

"Of course!"

The third-year students turned to Inglis and Rafinha before carrying Silva off. He was a popular guy.

"Thank you both!"

"Thank you for helping Silva!"

"No, it was a given," Rafinha replied with a brisk smile.

"I echo her sentiments." Inglis grinned.

Then, after seeing off the third-years, Rafinha smiled at Inglis. "Thanks, Chris! That helped!" It was a much cuter smile than she'd given to the third-years, so Inglis was satisfied.

Chapter IV: Inglis, Age 15—Orders to Defend the Hieral Menace (4)

Heavy breathing. Gasping. Panting.

Beads of sweat appeared on Inglis's forehead. Her cheeks flushed cherry red. The sweat trickled down them to her neck, before dripping down to her chest and absorbing into her clothing. To onlookers, she seemed even more alluring than usual. Inglis was always the center of attention, but the focus on her at that moment was more intense than usual. The boys snuck quick stares at her blushing face. She, however, was completely unconcerned, focusing her attention on what lay in front of her. Rafinha, beside her, was also sweating.

"Uh... Rafinha? Inglis? You both okay?" Leone asked.

"We're fine!" the two replied in unison.

"I-I sure hope so..."

"That certainly does have an impressive color to it. It's blazing red," Liselotte said.

"Because it's blazin' hot!" Rafinha said.

The super-sized supreme blazin' hot pasta—it was one of the new dishes Inglis and Rafinha had requested for the cafeteria. For the entire day, they were taking the blazin' hot challenge.

"That doesn't look all that edible..." Leone said, overwhelmed by the sight of the spicy dishes.

"But it is! It's delicious!" Rafinha insisted.

"It tastes so exciting!" Inglis added.

Pullum chimed in, "Honestly, I think it looks good too."

"Huh?!" Leone gasped, realizing she was alone in the mild camp. "You do?!"

"Yes, quite delicious, actually."

"We're from Alcard to the north. It's cold up there, so we eat spicy things to keep warm. We're used to it," Lahti explained.

"He's right. It reminds us of home."

"Pullum, why don't you order one?" Rafinha suggested.

"Well... I don't think I can eat something that huge..."

"Then let's split mine!" Rafinha moved some of the red pasta to Pullum's plate.

"Wow, thank you!"

"Oh. Gimme some too, Inglis," Lahti said.

"Sure. Here." Inglis offered her share.

Pullum wasn't going to have that, though. "No! None for you, Lahti!" she insisted.

"What?! Why?"

"No indirect kisses allowed!"

Lahti looked at her for a while before saying anything, but he eventually acquiesced. "Fine, fine, okay."

"Wow! You—listening to Pullum? That's a surprise," Inglis said. Lahti didn't usually go along with Pullum clinging to him.

"Well, after my screwup yesterday... I feel like I have to make it up somehow." Lahti scratched his cheek.

"That wasn't your fault, Lahti! You were just trying to help me, so I don't blame you at all," Pullum insisted. "But an indirect kiss is still not allowed!"

After a brief pause, Lahti grumbled, "Okay, okay. I can't even talk frankly when you're around."

"Hey, if you keep saying things like that, Pullum's going to get sick of you," Rafinha warned. "And believe it or not, she's pretty popular with the guys. She even got a love letter recently. Don't expect a girl's feelings to stay the same forever."

Lahti's chair clattered to the floor as he jumped to his feet. "Wh—?! Hey, Pullum, seriously?! Who was it from?!"

Chapter IV: Inglis, Age 15—Orders to Defend the Hieral Menace (4)

"Oh, look who's interested now!" Rafinha teased. "You're so easy to read. I was just kidding. If that bothered you so much, why don't you just get your act together to begin with?"

"Ughhh…!" Lahti winced.

"That's right! That's right!" Partly hidden in Rafinha's shadow, Pullum shook her fist. But Lahti's glare made her duck back into full cover.

"Stop that, Rafinha. It's not nice to lie," Leone said, but she found the whole thing amusing nonetheless.

Inglis added, "That's right, Rani. Little boys are never honest with girls they like. When he grows up a little, he'll start lavishing her with attention."

"Really, Inglis?!"

"Yeah. That's just how guys are."

"What makes you all experts on this?!" Lahti howled in anguish.

Rafinha cast a suspicious glance at Inglis. "That coming from someone who isn't interested in boys doesn't make you sound very convincing, Chris."

"Oh, right. When we asked her which boy she thought was the coolest, she said the Prismer, didn't she?" Leone added.

"That's a different story," Inglis nimbly responded, but Rafinha and Leone tilted their heads quizzically, wanting to ask, *How?* Inglis had no inclination to explain, though.

Rafinha got back to the topic at hand. "Anyway, you were about to get hit by that magicite beast trying to protect Pullum, right?"

"Yeah. And that's when that upperclassman—Silva—covered me and took the blow instead," Lahti said. "It's good you were able to help him, but I still messed up. When I see him again, I've gotta apologize."

Leone shook her head. "He didn't seem that angry with you, though. The way he's treated Inglis and Yua makes me think he has something against squires, but…"

"Oh! I get it!" Rafinha exclaimed.

"Get what, Rani?" Inglis asked.

"He must be a guy who likes guys! Maybe that's why he's so gentle with Lahti."

"Seriously? You've got to be kidding me," Lahti remarked.

A new voice cut into the conversation. "Indeed. Could you refrain from making baseless assumptions about people?"

The sudden new entrant to the conversation was the very person of discussion.

Lahti bowed deeply and forcefully to Silva. "Um...sorry about yesterday! You got hurt because I screwed up!"

"Don't worry about it. It was my mistake for getting you caught in our dimension shift. And more importantly, you all helped me as well. I'd like to apologize for my rudeness and to express my gratitude as well. Thank you." This time, it was Silva bowing—to Inglis and Rafinha.

Rafinha took Inglis's hand, rose abruptly, and bowed once. She silently urged Inglis to do the same. "No, if anything we should apologize for being rude! Anyway, we've all apologized, so we're even now, right?" Rafinha grinned, and thrust her hand toward Silva.

Rafinha's charm was in her pleasant, friendly manner. She was easygoing and didn't hold onto grudges. In her mind, bygones were bygones.

"Of course. I'm amenable to that." Silva shook Rafinha's hand. Their newfound allyship was a welcome sight—but not for everyone.

"Yes, yes, that's enough, Rani. I still have to give my own thanks," Inglis quickly interrupted, ending Rafinha's handshake with Silva.

Inglis could not abide any man outside the family having physical contact with Rafinha. *There's no such thing as too much caution*, she thought.

◆ ◇ ◆

A week later, Ripple's condition was still unchanged, and Inglis and the others continued taking turns on guard duty. That day was the first-year students' shift. When Ripple lost consciousness and a magicite beast appeared, Leone immediately used her new Artifact to draw them into another dimension, allowing Inglis and the others to take care of it. The magicite beast that had appeared that day was one of the stronger ones they had encountered recently.

"Leave it to me!" Inglis stood at the front, both index fingers extended

Chapter IV: Inglis, Age 15—Orders to Defend the Hieral Menace (4)

and pointed at the magicite beast. The pale blue light of Aether Pierce erupted from both her hands, making a humming sound.

Vvvssshhhhhh!

Her attack pierced countless holes into her enemy's face, then its neck, shoulders, chest, gut, legs, and feet. The magicite beast collapsed and then disappeared before it could take a step.

"Huh?" Rafinha tilted her neck at Inglis.

"There's more coming! Be careful!" Leone warned.

"Sure! Leave it to me!" Ignoring Rafinha, Inglis turned to the new magicite beast.

Vvvssshhhhhh!

And again, without saying a word, Inglis fired a wild burst of Aether Pierces. Riddled with holes, the magicite beast had no way to respond.

"Chris...?" Rafinha tilted her head even farther.

"They're still coming... One more!" Inglis focused on an empty space as she spoke.

"Eh...? I don't see anything?" Leone said, but Inglis sensed the approach of the magicite beast. She could feel the flow of mana as space twisted.

"Mm... I can tell—there you are!" Inglis extended a palm toward a point above her head.

Aether Strike!

Bammmmmm!

A gigantic burst of aether shot upward.

"Hey... Hey, hey, hey! Chris, what's gotten into you?" Rafinha asked.

Inglis let out a loud battle cry. "Haaah!"

She leaped up as if to follow the Aether Strike. In that space above her, a magicite beast suddenly appeared in the path of her attack. Her prediction was correct; her Aether Strike swallowed the creature whole and obliterated it.

"Oh..." Inglis let out a disappointed sigh and stood in place. The light from her Aether Strike continued to rise.

Crshshshhh!

With a great sound reminiscent of shattering glass, the dimension created by Leone's Artifact was destroyed.

"That's amazing! You destroyed the dimension like it was nothing..." Rafinha said.

Inglis had broken through the Labyrinth of Ordeals created by Principal Miriela before. This wasn't that out of the ordinary.

As the dimension collapsed, the scenery around them was replaced with the school courtyard where they'd begun. The Aether Strike rose higher and higher through the sunset sky, eventually disappearing from sight.

Liselotte let out a quiet laugh, partially from shock. "Ha ha ha... This reminds me of a beautiful fireworks display." Liselotte had been looking after Ripple the whole time.

"Well..." Inglis's face remained sullen.

"What's up, Chris? Usually when you've got an opponent knocked down, you try your hardest to get them up and continue the fight... But now you're just finishing them off quickly," Rafinha noted.

"Was I *that* brutal?"

"Pretty close, if you ask me," Leone said.

Liselotte nodded to Leone. "As usual, Rafinha understands Inglis well."

Rafinha thought for a moment, then suddenly clapped her hands. "Ah! I know! You want to sneak off and eat something tasty without us! That's why you wanted to get back quickly!"

"Nope. I was just doing some research."

"What kind?"

"Mm. A new technique."

All of her friends exclaimed, "A new technique?!"

Chapter IV: Inglis, Age 15—Orders to Defend the Hieral Menace (4)

"Yeah! You and Leone got new ones, right?"

"Well, I wouldn't really call that a technique..." Rafinha said.

"Just a Gift for the Artifact," Leone added.

"Yeah, that's it. I was a bit jealous, so I thought I'd come up with something new as well." A glittering smile floated to Inglis's face. "I decided to try something more powerful than I've ever used before!"

That meant she needed to use aether. Inglis's control of it had increased, as she had recently become able to fire Aether Pierces from both hands. As a result, she'd thought of a new possibility—but for now, she was testing it through trial and error.

Rafinha laughed wanly. "I feel like something terrible might happen..."

"Agreed," Leone followed.

"I think you're quite powerful enough already," Liselotte said.

Inglis silently shook her head. "It's not about how I compare with others; it's whether I'm satisfied with myself. And since I'm trying for a strong, new technique, I need to practice harder. But if I fight seriously, my foe goes down immediately... Ah, I wish a truly powerful enemy would appear..."

"In the end, Chris reaches her usual conclusion. You're always so *you*," Rafinha said.

Leone laughed. "We need to make sure we don't get left behind, then."

"Anyway, let's return to the principal's office when Lady Ripple awakens. It's time for the next shift to begin," Liselotte reminded them.

Next up were Silva and the third-years. At the principal's office, they could report on their events and escort Ripple to them.

As soon as Ripple regained consciousness, they headed there and heard Principal Miriela speaking loudly as they approached. "Now hold on a moment! That's nothing but tyranny! We've avoided major damage so far. The plan has presented no problems!"

Something slammed onto a desk. Whatever debate was occurring on the other side of the doors sounded like a passionate one.

"Huh? Is Miriela angry about something? That's weird," Ripple said, confused.

"Oh? She's usually rather mad around me…" Inglis said.

"Well, duh! Inglis, you're a handful. Ah well, let's go."

They had business in the principal's office, so they had no choice but to enter. They knocked on the door, and a voice full of semi-concealed anger invited them in.

"Pardon us," the group said as they entered.

They saw an unfamiliar man inside the room. He was a tall knight with long, gray hair, and he looked to be in his late twenties or early thirties. From his right hand shone an upper-class Rune. From that, Inglis assumed he was a high-ranking knight. His uniform was slightly different from what Rafael and the others wore, which indicated he was from a different branch.

He must have been from the Royal Guard, under the king's direct command. The students had already learned about them at the academy. Rafael's knights were officially called the Paladins. Together, the two were the Grand Orders. They possessed the numbers and the brute strength necessary to be the kingdom's primary forces.

Having already arrived to take over guard duty, Silva and the other third-years must have been privy to the conversation between the Royal Guard and Principal Miriela. None of them looked cheerful; Inglis could see the surprise, frustration, and awkwardness on their faces.

Silva in particular seemed the most confused. "B-Brother! Please rethink this! Principal Miriela is correct; we've done well. This isn't necessary."

"But Silva, you were wounded. I was so worried about you! When I heard, my heart nearly burst forth from my chest!" the knight said.

"I… I just messed up a little bit! But there are other talented students here who made up for it! Our end result was a success."

"Did he say 'brother'…?" Inglis asked.

"That man is Reddas Ayren, the captain of the Royal Guard. He is Silva's older brother," Liselotte explained.

The boys' hair, while kept in different styles, did seem to be similar colors. Their eyes were similar as well.

Reddas turned to the new arrivals at the principal's office. More

Chapter IV: Inglis, Age 15—Orders to Defend the Hieral Menace (4)

precisely, to Ripple, as a relieved grin washed over his face. "Good evening, Lady Ripple."

"Er, ah... Good evening?"

"I was just speaking with Lady Miriela—I have something to tell you today."

"Yes, what?"

"The king has requested that you leave the knights' academy."

"Huh...?! And then what?"

"For a time, you'll be under the protection of the Royal Guard."

"What exactly does 'for a time' mean...?"

"At the risk of sounding rude, I must be clear—you will return to Highland, and His Majesty intends to welcome a new hieral menace."

Ripple gasped in surprise, and her eyes sprang open. "I see..."

So that's the crown's plan, Inglis thought. She couldn't deny that it was one solution. Ripple had suggested something similar earlier, but Prince Wayne and Ambassador Theodore had chosen not to take that route.

Theodore was the country's line of communication with Highland. In other words, the ambassador's will could be thought of as the will of Highland. If the crown took the opposite course of action, that suggested the problem went beyond Ripple herself; this concerned statecraft as well.

Regardless, Rafinha's face flushed with anger. "What?! Why would you do such a terrible thing?! Ripple's helped us for so long! You can't just throw her away because she's inconvenient! Ripple isn't just a thing to be replaced! She's in trouble now. We should be repaying her for her help!"

It was a naive, childish response. It was pure, immature—and adorable all the same. Inglis knew that Rafinha would of course have this response. If she hadn't, Inglis would have been worried that she was seriously ill.

"Yeah... This isn't right!" Leone quietly, but forcefully, agreed.

As did Liselotte. "Indeed!"

Reddas examined Rafinha, recognizing her. "Sir Rafael's sister, I presume? It would do you good not to speak to me of justice. This is His Majesty's word," Reddas said.

"Then bring me before him so I can speak to him myself!" Rafinha insisted.

It seems like she intends to go yell at the king. I should probably stop her before she actually makes them angry, Inglis concluded.

Unexpectedly, someone else came to her aid. Silva clapped a hand on Rafinha's shoulder and stepped forward as if to shield her. "Her words carry truth, brother! It may be His Majesty's orders, but that doesn't mean it's something to be proud of! As the captain of the Royal Guard, you should persuade him to reconsider!"

Rafinha and Silva shared a nod.

Well, that's still in the forgivable zone, but... Maybe he could stop putting his hand on Rafinha's shoulder? I imagine he's probably worked up and not realizing that he's being impolite, but it bothers me. Really bothers me, Inglis thought.

"I have no intention of conveying that to His Majesty," Reddas stated.

"But why?! Don't you care what happens to Ripple?!" Silva asked.

"I do...but I have a different set of priorities. I'm not personally opposed to His Majesty's will either," Reddas said.

He was likely considering the risks to the nearby people and surroundings. From the perspective of a normal person, it was safest to value those highly.

"Why, brother?!" Silva demanded.

"Because I'm afraid of you getting hurt! If Lady Ripple stays here, the same might happen again! I'm worried about you!" Reddas declared, his eyes wide and his expression extremely serious.

Rafinha and Silva both were taken aback by the unexpected response. They stood in silence.

Inglis understood Reddas's position, though. *Silva must be to Reddas how Rafinha is to me. Reddas adores him and can't help feeling concerned about him.* She felt a slight sense of familiarity.

Inglis broke the silence to move the conversation forward. "But even if His Majesty goes forth with this plan, will Highland accept?" She also casually slipped Silva's hand off Rafinha's shoulder.

"What is it? Do you have something else to add?" Reddas at least had the magnanimity to listen to the words of a first-year squire trainee.

Chapter IV: Inglis, Age 15—Orders to Defend the Hieral Menace (4)

At his prompting, Inglis continued. "Ripple's presence at the academy has been the will of Ambassador Theodore—that is to say, the will of Highland. To stray from that path—then the Highland you speak of must belong to a different faction... It must be the Altar faction."

The Altar—or properly, the Papal League. They opposed the Triumvirate, also known as the Throne faction. They were the two great forces in Highland. The current ambassador was on the side of the Throne, but in the past, Karelia had accepted Throne and Altar ambassadors in turn, striking a balance between the two in their relationship with Highland. During this back-and-forth period, the Throne had granted Eris and the Altar had granted Ripple as hieral menaces to Karelia.

"Hmm... What you say is true," Reddas conceded.

"And what is Ripple's condition but punishment from the Altar? I believe they're indignant, displeased that the balance has tipped in the Throne's favor," Inglis stated.

Reddas hesitated before admitting, "We were not aware of that. We believed it to be merely a change in Lady Ripple herself," Reddas admitted.

"Ambassador Theodore's assessment differs," Principal Miriela said.

"Ambassador Theodore is of the Throne. As their opponent, sometimes his guesses will be wrong," Reddas countered.

"Have you received any assurance that Highland will provide a replacement hieral menace?" Inglis asked.

"No—I've heard it's still being negotiated."

Inglis continued, "Then, bearing in mind that the negotiations may take some time, I believe we should only take Ripple to them when well prepared. So far, we've had no major problems for both the students and the surrounding city during her stay at the academy. If Ripple's condition were to result in greater collateral damage after her transfer to the Royal Guard, you would be unable to deny comparisons that the academy's students fared better."

"You can't say there have been no problems. A child as important as Silva was injured, was he not?" Reddas, the doting brother, seeming all too like an overprotective father, was unconvinced.

Inglis had expected this reaction from him and turned his own logic on him. "Yes, even someone as talented as Silva was vulnerable. That's how immense this threat is. Thus, you must be prepared."

"Prepared...in what way?"

"Ambassador Theodore prepared new Artifacts for us. It's thanks to them that we've prevented harm as much as we have."

That wasn't the entire truth, but that wasn't Inglis's concern. Now was the time to convince Reddas of the students' value; they could postpone matters under the guise of a transitional period. They needed to avoid having Ripple taken away today, leaving them unable to get involved. Delaying the matter would give them time to plan their next move.

Such an idea had already formed in Inglis's head, but she would have to ask what the others thought later.

"Hm. Then as to Lord Theodore..." Reddas began.

"I believe it would be safest to first transfer the Artifacts, select suited wielders, and train them in their use," Inglis said.

"Hmm..." Reddas appeared to be swayed. He needed to complete his mission safely; he would probably accept a period of a few days to arrange the transfer.

Finally, Inglis fired the decisive shot. "And I believe it would be best to ask Silva to set up the handover. As a replacement for guard duty, of course."

"Mm... Yes, that would be good. I agree."

If Silva was transferred off of guard duty, Silva's safety was instantly guaranteed. Given Reddas's personality, that must have been the Royal Knight's priority.

Inglis turned to face Miriela. "And as I have no authority to make this decision, Principal Miriela, do you approve?"

It took less than a second for Inglis's vision to be filled with Rafinha's face, her fingers tugging on Inglis's cheeks. "Well, *I* don't! What are you thinking?! Do you want to abandon Ripple?! No, absolutely not! Even if it's you, Chris, I'm not gonna back down on this!"

With her cheeks stretched out, Inglis couldn't speak properly. "Au-au. Ifnaw rychem hrantau fumhen vav. (Now, now. It's not like I'm trying to do something bad.)"

"Huh...? What do you mean?"

Chapter IV: Inglis, Age 15—Orders to Defend the Hieral Menace (4)

"Vulow vuhai orvee feefin ev, rhy? (You know what I'm always thinking of, right?)"

Rafinha took a moment. "You want to fight strong foes, eat tasty food, and wear cute clothes?"

"Enh olvay vi ahn aurh fai. (And always be on your side.)"

"Can I trust you? Because I do. Is that okay?"

"Vef! (Yes!)" At Inglis's nod, Rafinha finally let go of her cheeks.

"They seem to have had a conversation, but I didn't understand a word of what Inglis said," Liselotte whispered to Leone.

"For some reason, those two always understand each other... It's some kind of special power," Leone whispered back.

"I-I see... Well, let's go with the proposal from Inglis and Reddas." Principal Miriela had seemed angry before, but she was calmly nodding along now. Inglis assumed the principal must have realized what she was planning.

"Lady Ripple, are you satisfied with that?" Reddas prompted.

"Yes... I'm fine. If everyone says so..." Ripple gave a small nod.

"Then, it's decided. We'll move ahead by beginning the transfer process to the Royal Guard tomorrow. Is that acceptable, Lady Miriela?"

"Yes, that will be fine."

Reddas turned to Silva. "And you're good with this, Silva? I have high expectations."

"Understood, brother." Silva nodded, holding back his emotions.

Lastly, Reddas turned his gaze to Inglis. "Inglis, was it? Are you in the squire program?"

"Yes. First-year student, Inglis Eucus of the squire program."

"Hm... Your speech, your nerve, and your wit—quite impressive for one your age. Thank you for saving me from Lady Miriela's fury. For a while, I looked entirely in the wrong."

"Well, of course you did," Principal Miriela grumbled. She was in charge of directing Ripple's guard. Inglis understood her lack of enthusiasm for criticism.

"You flatter me," Inglis said to Reddas, bowing to him.

"I'll remember you. When you graduate from the academy, you

should join the Royal Guard. Runes and brains are different things, and the era where squires would be treated as inferiors has passed. We'll prepare a path for you in our staff where your talents can be used to their fullest."

Inglis refused immediately. "I hope to be posted to the front lines. I appreciate the offer, but I'll have to pass on any opportunities that would put me behind a desk."

The last thing she wanted to do was engage in scheming and brainstorming as general staff. She'd already done that in a position of more responsibility, as king. She was *done* with that.

"What?! Very well, but..." Inglis's response had clearly thrown Reddas off. He must have thought she'd be pleased by the offer. Meanwhile, Rafinha giggled.

"Then, if you'll excuse me. I'll send over the officer overseeing the transfer later." With that, Reddas left the principal's office.

Rafinha giggled again. "He didn't get you at all, Chris."

"He really didn't. Don't join the Royal Guard after you graduate from the academy, Rani." Inglis was going to follow Rafinha, but she certainly didn't want to be with the Royal Guard, likely to be transferred to the rear.

"If you want me to promise you that, you're going to have to give me an explanation for earlier, okay? What's going on?"

"First, we prevented them from taking Ripple outright. Those were royal orders. Even if we disagree, serious resistance would make us traitors on the spot. Now, if you're okay with that, then I am too, but..."

Principal Miriela gasped. "A-Absolutely not! Please try to keep your ideas to sensible ones...!"

Ripple was surprised as well. "Th-That's a pretty bold thing to say, Inglis..."

"There's no way we could do *that*!" Rafinha said. "Rafael would be our enemy! And we don't know what would happen to Ymir..."

"I agree. So, rather than that, we can pretend to cooperate while extending the schedule—and use that time to settle on a plan," Inglis explained.

"Oh! Great idea!" Rafinha nodded, her expression very earnest.

Chapter IV: Inglis, Age 15—Orders to Defend the Hieral Menace (4)

"Principal Miriela, I apologize for overstepping," Inglis said.

"No, I don't mind. I understood your intentions... And I wasn't thinking with a cool head. If I had been too aggressive with Reddas and made him angry, we may not have even had this respite."

"But what shall we do now, Principal Miriela? There isn't much time. We have to hurry." Silva's impatience was plain in both his words and his expression. He seemed desperate.

Is there something else he's feeling? Rebellion against his brother, maybe? Inglis pondered.

"Hm... There's one thing that comes to mind right now..." Principal Miriela began.

"What do you propose?!" Silva impatiently asked.

"We allow Ripple to absorb the mana from me and Silva, as we have special-class Runes... That power is then used to summon magicite beasts. Until that stops, we keep defeating the magicite beasts. Only demihuman-type magicite beasts appear, and the number of those is limited. If we wipe them out, we'll effectively neutralize the danger that Ripple brings..."

Principal Miriela's suggestion sounded familiar somehow...

"What...?! That's nothing but brute force!" Silva replied.

"Indeed it is. And if we proceed with that plan in the time we have left..." She danced around the idea reluctantly. It was obvious that this wasn't her preferred choice.

"Miriela?! Isn't that what Inglis suggested earlier?!" Ripple asked.

"Y-Yes..."

It sure was. If the group wanted to solve this problem quickly, they needed to resort to forceful measures. Plus, it wasn't *technically* disobeying royal orders. They could justify their activity as a coincidental increase in Ripple's drawing of magicite beasts.

Leone's eyes widened. "I-Inglis... Did you..."

"Did you actually..." Liselotte began.

"Chris, is *that* why you said that to Reddas?!" Rafinha and the others looked at her suspiciously.

Inglis evaded their questions with a smile. "Let's do our best!"

Ripple raised her voice. "That's no good! It's too dangerous! Eris isn't here, Rafael isn't here, Wayne isn't here, Lord Theodore isn't here—everyone's gone! I won't let you expose everyone here at the academy to that level of danger!"

Inglis understood where Ripple was coming from. Ripple normally exhibited a cheerful personality and a lack of deep thinking, but she was a hieral menace who valued her mission. She valued herself in how well she could protect the people of the land.

"I'd rather just go along to Highland than have that happen!" Ripple yelled.

She didn't want to expose the students at the academy to a desperate all-out fight. She thought the best course of action would be to give herself up quietly.

"Ripple, consider this," Inglis said. "I don't think that's the best way to keep the surface safe."

"Huh...? What do you mean?"

"Reddas may not have realized, but Ambassador Theodore thinks this is punishment from the Altar, and I agree. That implies we wouldn't have a simple rotation of hieral menaces. If you wanted to make someone subservient, would you help them when they said they needed it? Now, if we were to bow and scrape and offer something much more..."

"Offer...what, Chris?"

"Surface land, probably. Or more precisely, a city and its inhabitants. Remember what happened in Nova where Cyrene was, Rani. I think they may want to take a whole city with the Floating Circle."

Ripple's face tensed. "No! Th-They can't..."

"That's even worse! Cyrene said she wouldn't let such a thing happen, but other Highlanders won't do the same!" Rafinha exclaimed.

"That's right, Rani."

After careful consideration, Miriela said, "I must agree with Inglis on this one. No matter what Reddas says, people far above us are scheming something."

"If not, negotiations would be much slower going, and the Royal Guard would suffer significant losses. Maybe even the capital too, if they did poorly," Inglis noted.

"That would be bad enough, but also, command of hieral menaces is in theory entrusted to the Paladins—to Prince Wayne. If the matter

Chapter IV: Inglis, Age 15—Orders to Defend the Hieral Menace (4)

with Ripple were to paint the Paladins in a bad light, the prince could be held responsible and lose his duties. If so, what would happen to the academy?"

"Worst of all, couldn't it spiral into a civil war? If the trade were for land, Prince Wayne might not keep silent when he hears of it—and if the crown predicts a backlash, they can preemptively position the Royal Guard and the new hieral menace to attack him from the rear. Caught between that and Venefic's army, the Paladins would be torn to pieces."

The ambassador with Venefic's army belonged to the Altar faction. If the Karelian king's men held the same allegiance, they could coordinate to attack Prince Wayne and Ambassador Theodore.

"That's ridiculous! My brother would never attack an ally from behind! He's not a bad person like that!" Silva shouted.

"Then things will become even more dangerous. They'll just find someone who will. To countries, people are like pawns. Easily replaced," Inglis replied coldly.

Silva stared at her, surprised. "You get so excited in battle, but you're frighteningly calm and ruthless in situations like this. How can you stay so detached?"

"Well, life experience, I guess?" Inglis said with a smile, but Silva only responded with a confused look. There was no reason he'd know of Inglis's experiences in her past life.

"I'd... I'd *like* to say that that would be unthinkable..." Miriela said, "but it's true that relations between His Majesty and Prince Wayne are anything but good. We must keep the possibility of that worst-case scenario in mind."

Inglis nodded. "So at this rate, the worst case is civil war, and the best case is... Hmm. If negotiations stretch out, Prince Wayne and Ambassador Theodore resolve the situation with Venefic without great losses and return, and as a result, nothing happens. Something like that would be our best outcome. If the situation worsens, I believe the forceful solution from before would be effective," she suggested.

"In conclusion, we need to carefully assess how things turn out before we take decisive action."

"I suppose." Inglis chuckled to herself. She would, of course, prefer to see a situation where she had to use force, and she expected it to turn out that way. *Isn't it so exciting, imagining just how strong the foes called forth may get?* she thought.

From the feel of her own practice, she could tell that the new technique she was developing required a foe of a certain strength to be viable.

I hope an opponent comes through that's sufficient enough to use it.

"C'mon, Chris. Your thoughts are clear as day on your face. Stop smirking like that," Rafinha chided.

"Oh, right. How embarrassing." Inglis dropped her delight and assumed a serious expression once more.

Leone sighed. "Well, Inglis is as usual, and I have a feeling we'll pull through as usual too."

"Indeed. That broke the tension right at the end," Liselotte said.

"Anyway, Silva, for that reason, try to postpone our handoff of Ripple for as long as possible," Miriela said.

"Understood. I'll do what I can."

The principal continued, "Also, Prince Wayne and Ambassador Theodore need to be informed of this. We should send a messenger right away. After that, as I said, we'll carefully watch the situation. I'm going to lean on all the connections I can to find out how the negotiations are going. Furthermore, Ripple—please don't think your sacrifice is a better option. Believe in us."

"Okay… I'm really sorry, everyone…" Ripple stared at the floor, her voice weak.

"Don't worry about it. If anything, I thank you for the opportunity," Inglis remarked.

"Chris! Everyone's being serious, stop joking around!" Rafinha scolded and yanked on Inglis's cheeks again.

"Mmh, ah fewhuh! (No, I'm serious!)"

"About fighting, you mean?"

"Vef! (Yes!)"

Ripple chuckled as she watched Inglis and Rafinha. "Sheesh. They're good girls—brazen, but in the right way." After a rough day, a faint smile had finally crept to her face.

Chapter V: Inglis, Age 15—Orders to Defend the Hieral Menace (5)

Five days had passed since the Royal Guard Captain Reddas had visited the knights' academy. Ripple was still at the knights' academy. Silva had done well in postponing her transfer to the Royal Guard. Every knight in the Royal Guard knew that Silva was Captain Reddas's little brother. Even though many felt Silva's progress was lacking, as if he was taking his time, no one would publicly take an issue up with him. Because the king's advisors hadn't finished their negotiations with Highland yet, there was no pressure for Silva to hand over Ripple immediately.

Meanwhile, the Chiral Knights' Academy had sent Lahti and Pullum as messengers to the deployed knights near Venefic. Lahti was one of the most skilled pilots at the academy and could push the Flygear past its normal speed limits. Pullum was accompanying him at her own request; she wanted to protect Lahti. Also, if the Flygear was to run out of power, she could charge it directly with mana from her Rune.

Now, the students and Miriela could only wait for their return. Their cover story was unchanged. However, among those who knew the situation, the tension increased day by day.

But they didn't just sit around with their anxiety; the volatility of nature wouldn't let them rest. That night, the Prism Flow fell. A glittering, rainbow-colored mist danced across the night sky.

And through that fantastic yet terrifying scene flew Leone and Liselotte, using the white wings created by Liselotte's Artifact. A magicite beast in the form of a gigantic crow clawed and pecked at the roof of a house.

"Hurry, Liselotte! That magicite beast's on the attack!" Leone called out.

"Yes, here we go!" Liselotte rapidly picked up speed.

Today Inglis and Rafinha were, in place of Silva, helping the third-years guard Ripple, leaving Leone and Liselotte on their own. Local knights were on the scene as well, trying to clear away the monsters.

The academy had a curfew for students to be in their dorms, but there were some exceptions to this rule; Principal Miriela had allowed some students to leave that night for practice in fighting off the magicite beasts.

That said, Leone already had a habit of occasionally leaving the dorms at night to make the rounds. She'd started sneaking out when Inglis and Rafinha had mentioned they saw Leon in the city. She was well aware it was against school rules, but she couldn't sit idly by if Leon could be in the capital.

Leone's roommate, Liselotte, tacitly approved and accompanied her on her patrols sometimes. However, as she cared more about following the rules, she was always nervous the next day that they'd be caught. But with the Prism Flow falling tonight, they could act with impunity and have no such worries.

"I'm closing in!" Liselotte called out to Leone as she approached the targeted magicite beast.

"Off I go!" Leone let go of her hand and sailed through the air on her own. As she fell, she extended her dark greatsword Artifact. "Yaaaaaa!" Using the momentum of her fall, she took a fierce swing at the magicite beast.

That was her intention, at least. Just before she made contact, a shining four-legged animal leapt in from the side and smashed into the magicite beast.

Thud!

* * *

Chapter V: Inglis, Age 15—Orders to Defend the Hieral Menace (5)

Its body exploded into an intense flash of light.

Leone gasped as the incredible force of the explosion pushed her sword away; her hands were tingling. Of course, the magicite beast caught in the explosion couldn't withstand it either, and it was blown to bits.

"What?!" The explosion wasn't what took her most by surprise, though. "This... This is one of the lightning beasts from Leon's Artifact!"

She used to watch him show them off to her over and over. She'd never forget what they looked like. She was absolutely certain. That meant Leon was here! She'd finally caught him!

Leone's eyes lit up with rage as she scanned her surroundings, tense. "Leon?! Where are you?! I know you're around here! Come out!"

Liselotte landed nearby. "Leone! What's gotten into you?!"

"You saw that, right? That lightning beast! That's the power of the Artifact Leon likes to use! He's got to be around here somewhere!"

Liselotte drew in a sharp breath.

"Ah! There, over there!" Around a turn in a narrow alley behind Liselotte, Leone glimpsed a lightning beast. "I won't let you get away!" Leone took off at full speed toward it.

"Ah...! Leone! You mustn't rush in alone!" Liselotte followed her closely.

The lightning beast vanished as soon as they turned the corner, only to appear at the next corner as if beckoning them on. Then it disappeared again as they approached. As they chased, Leone and Liselotte gradually lost their bearings.

"Leone! It's obviously just leading us on, isn't it?!"

"I know! But I can't let it get away! If you want to leave, go ahead!"

"No, I'm with you! If worst comes to worst, we can use my wings to retreat!"

"Thanks!"

As they chased the lightning beast, they turned a corner that led to a straight segment of road terminating in an underground passage. The lightning beast descended into it and disappeared.

"Up ahead...!"

"It might be a trap. Be careful."

"Yes. Here we go!"

The two shared a nod to each other and followed the path below ground.

Ahead of them was a large empty space that seemed to be some kind of warehouse. They walked on for a while, their own footsteps cutting through the silence, until a lightning beast suddenly appeared. Its glow illuminated the surroundings, and a shadow emerged.

"Yo. Long time no see, Leone." Leon's tone was cheerful, but he looked uncomfortable.

"Brother...! And—"

Leon was not alone. There was also the black-masked leader of the Steelblood Front, as well as their hieral menace, Sistia.

"Leone, do you know them?" Liselotte asked.

"Liselotte, be careful! That's the Steelbloods' leader and their hieral menace!" Liselotte may have seen the former holy knight Leon before, but she was unlikely to have seen the other two. Even when they had appeared at the assassination of Ambassador Muenthe, Liselotte had just missed them.

"Why—! If it isn't the evil boss!" Liselotte said.

"That is not our intent," the man in the black mask said. "Terms like 'justice' and 'evil' have a change in meaning depending on one's position."

"For us, this country's future knights, you're obviously the evil ones!" Liselotte declared, brandishing her halberd Artifact.

"Hmph. That's brave of you."

Sistia took a defensive position in front of the masked man. "Pay her no heed. She only says that because she knows nothing."

As she watched them, Liselotte thought, *Just who is this man?* Leone had said before that Leon himself might be the leader of the Steelblood Front, but that didn't seem to be the case. Seeing him here along with the masked man debunked that theory. If a person with a special-class Rune—like Leon—was the leader, the presence of a hieral menace in their organization would make sense, but there was something else going on here.

Who could command the loyalty of both a holy knight and a hieral menace? Why did he hide his face? If he wanted to gather supporters and

Chapter V: Inglis, Age 15—Orders to Defend the Hieral Menace (5)

lead people, he'd be more effective by showing his face and giving his name. Did he have some reason to hide them? Perhaps this was a second identity, separate from his first? What was the first, then?

"Hey, Sistia. Don't just go and attack her on your own," Leon chided.

"I know!"

"Really, do you? You're the most bloodthirsty hieral menace I know. But we didn't come here to fight tonight."

Leone's sword slashed through their exchange. "I don't care what you have planned!" The extended blade of the dark greatsword swung down toward Leon.

Clang!

Sparks flew and a loud sound rang out as Leon's gauntlet blocked Leone's sword.

"Leone...! Stop! This isn't the time for such things!" her brother cried.

But Leone was in no mood to hold back. "What are you saying?! For me... For me there's nothing more important than this!" Leone withdrew her sword to its original length and then thrust again from a distance. It rocketed forward, using her own strength behind a full-force thrust plus the speed of her Artifact extending ahead. Combined, the two brought more speed than Leon expected. The thrust grazed Leon's shoulder lightly as he tried to dodge, taking him by surprise.

"I see you've improved!" he said.

"I won't let you get away!" Unfortunately for her, Leon leaped out of the path of her follow-up sweeping strike. Moreover, the lightning beast remained in place to take the blow for Leon, and her sword struck it. The beast immediately exploded, and the shock jerked her sword around in her hands. "Ugh...!" she grunted.

"Leone! Please, listen!"

"I will not! Not to someone who betrayed his country, his family, his hometown, even his own aspirations!" Leone recovered, and again slashed at Leon.

"Hmph. She's more bloodthirsty than I am," Sistia commented.

"It's beyond us. This is between two who share blood. It isn't our place to interfere. Let us watch," the black-masked man ordered, watching the siblings fight. Sistia looked astounded. "And you, the Arcia girl. Please refrain from interfering. If you move to join her, we'll be forced to protect Comrade Leon."

"Indeed we will," Sistia said after a brief pause.

With Leone's fighting style being made up of strong, all-in-one aggressive pushes, it would be difficult for Liselotte to make a move to assist, for sure. But the masked man seemed to know about her. Liselotte may have been the daughter of the former Chancellor Arcia, but she was still only a first-year student at the academy. The Steelblood Front would need insiders and collaborators to gather that kind of information about her. She wondered if perhaps such people were hidden among the Arcia family's servants or inside the knights' academy.

Sparks flew again. With a clang, Leon had caught Leone's sword between his gauntlets. They were standing close together now.

"Father and mother are gone! But for the sake of those who remain in Ahlemin, I won't forgive you!"

"None of that will matter if the city itself is gone! That's how drastic things have become!"

"Huh...?!"

The instant that Leone's brow furrowed, the black-masked man spoke. "The royal court has decided to give up land on the surface in order to improve its relations with Highland's Altar faction. The regions in question...are Ahlemin and Charot."

Leone and Liselotte both yelled, "What?!" in shock. Ahlemin was Leone's hometown, and Charot was Liselotte's.

"They're just offering them up?!" Leone gasped.

"Why?! Why would they do that?!" Liselotte asked.

The black-masked man continued in a gentle voice. "There's nothing strange about it. With Ahlemin no longer fulfilling the role of observing the frozen Prismer, and Charot's lord retiring from his role as chancellor, they're distanced from both the king's and prince's factions. Meaning, they're of no further use to either side. Losing them will have the least possible impact."

Chapter V: Inglis, Age 15—Orders to Defend the Hieral Menace (5)

The two girls pointed fierce questions at him in a fury.

"That's not the point!" Leone insisted.

"Why must they resort to such extreme measures? Where is the justice in that?!" Liselotte protested.

"I agree. We're here because we can't accept it either," he said.

Sistia raised her voice as she addressed the pair. "That's right! Don't be misled! If you're going to vent your anger, let it out at your foolish king who's willing to sell his own subjects for Highland's favor!"

Leone and Liselotte tensed. Neither had a counter to Sistia's accurate criticism.

"Hmph. This country is in a petty squabble between the king's and prince's factions, unable to see what is most important. And that blindness will kill innocents," Sistia said, pausing to turn toward Leon. "I don't like this man, but I think he's a lot smarter than those foolish royals."

"That's going a bit far," Leon protested. "My choices brought misfortune to the city of Ahlemin, my parents, even my little sister—I'm a fool to the end. I'm a fool who couldn't live up to their expectations. In the end, I only cared about myself."

The masked man chided, "Sistia, no matter how Leon appears, he's a kind man. His heart aches when he considers the path untaken, caught between his ideals and the people closest to him. So let him be."

"All right."

"And these young women too. They're cadets, the future knights of this country. There are things they cannot say, things they cannot do. The liberation of each surface country is work for its people alone. It is out of our hands."

"Yes. I understand." As proud and haughty as Sistia could be, she complied with his orders to the fullest.

"I don't understand…! Why are you telling us this?!" Leone asked.

Liselotte was equally suspicious. "Indeed. This makes no sense. What are you after…?!"

"I have no ulterior motive. I'm simply sharing information. This serves your needs, doesn't it? The hieral menace in your care will be handed over in four days' time. A ship will arrive from Highland to attend the reception and the final signing of the agreement one day before then. Before the signing is complete, we will attack the Highland ship and strike down the signing ambassador—our only enemy is the Highlander who preys upon the surface," the black-masked man explained.

Leone and Liselotte gasped. This was a Steelblood Front plot to attack a Highlander. He had openly admitted it to them in advance too.

"You must have your own agenda, your own plans. If you're going to make any sort of move, you'll be moving with us. Make good use of this information."

"Why should we believe an enemy's words?!" Leone asked.

"Indeed!" Liselotte agreed.

"You're free to believe me or doubt me. Feel free to inform the head of the academy, or say nothing if you so choose. Hopefully, you'll pass this on and keep them from interfering with our plans."

Leone and Liselotte went silent. Neither could say what they'd likely do.

"And now that I've informed you of the situation, if you'll excuse me." The black-masked man turned on his heel, and Sistia followed immediately.

Only Leon called back to Leone and Liselotte. "I think you know this now...but if you choose to stop us here, your victory would just mean there'll be no one left to keep Ahlemin and Charot out of Highland's hands. So let's drop this for now, and pick it up again next time."

"Brother! Even still, I... No matter what reason you had...!"

"Yeah. Leone, you have your own thoughts, your own things you must do... Walk forward. Do what you must. Don't let anyone stop you. But hear me out on this... I know I wasn't there for you, but you've grown up well. I'm happy. Keep it up." Leon smiled faintly before following the black-masked man.

"Brother..." The kind smile on his face was just like the ones he gave her when she was little. Leone couldn't help missing her life with him when she saw it. That emotion was something she couldn't allow herself to feel, though. When the time came, it would dull her will. She shook her head forcefully, trying to clear away the sentimentality.

"Leone, what shall we do? Do we...?" Liselotte began to ask.

Chapter V: Inglis, Age 15—Orders to Defend the Hieral Menace (5)

"I think we should tell the principal. Let's go straight to her when we get back."

"Yes. We need to keep Ahlemin and Charot safe!"

When Leone and Liselotte returned to the academy, they relayed the night's events to Principal Miriela. Inglis was also there, so she got to hear the Steelblood Front's plans.

"Hmm… So we just need to capture the Steelbloods while defeating all the demihuman magicite beasts? Sounds like more fun than just taking on the magicite beasts alone." Inglis's eyes gleamed with glee.

◆ ◇ ◆

One night a few days later, the group sat in the knights' academy cafeteria.

Inglis and Rafinha, dressed in the attire of palace maids, placed plates in front of Leone and Liselotte. "And here you go, mistress!"

"A super-sized supreme blazin' hot pasta."

"A super-sized bone-in meaty cheese melt."

"A super-sized supreme Alfredo pasta."

"And for dessert, an entire cake assortment!"

Thud! Thud! Thud! Thud! The plates landed on the table intimidatingly.

"W-We didn't order this!" Leone protested.

"There's no way we can eat this much…" Liselotte groaned in dismay.

"Yeah, we know," Inglis and Rafinha said together. It had been a joke all along; the food was for themselves. "Let's eat!" They dug in ravenously.

"The cafeteria really does strike a great balance between flavor and portion size. And they have a menu just for us!" Rafinha exclaimed.

"And it's even free," Inglis added.

"But the principal is gonna stop paying for our meals soon. Our agreement is just about up."

"Yeah. But she promised that if tomorrow's operation goes well, she'll extend it."

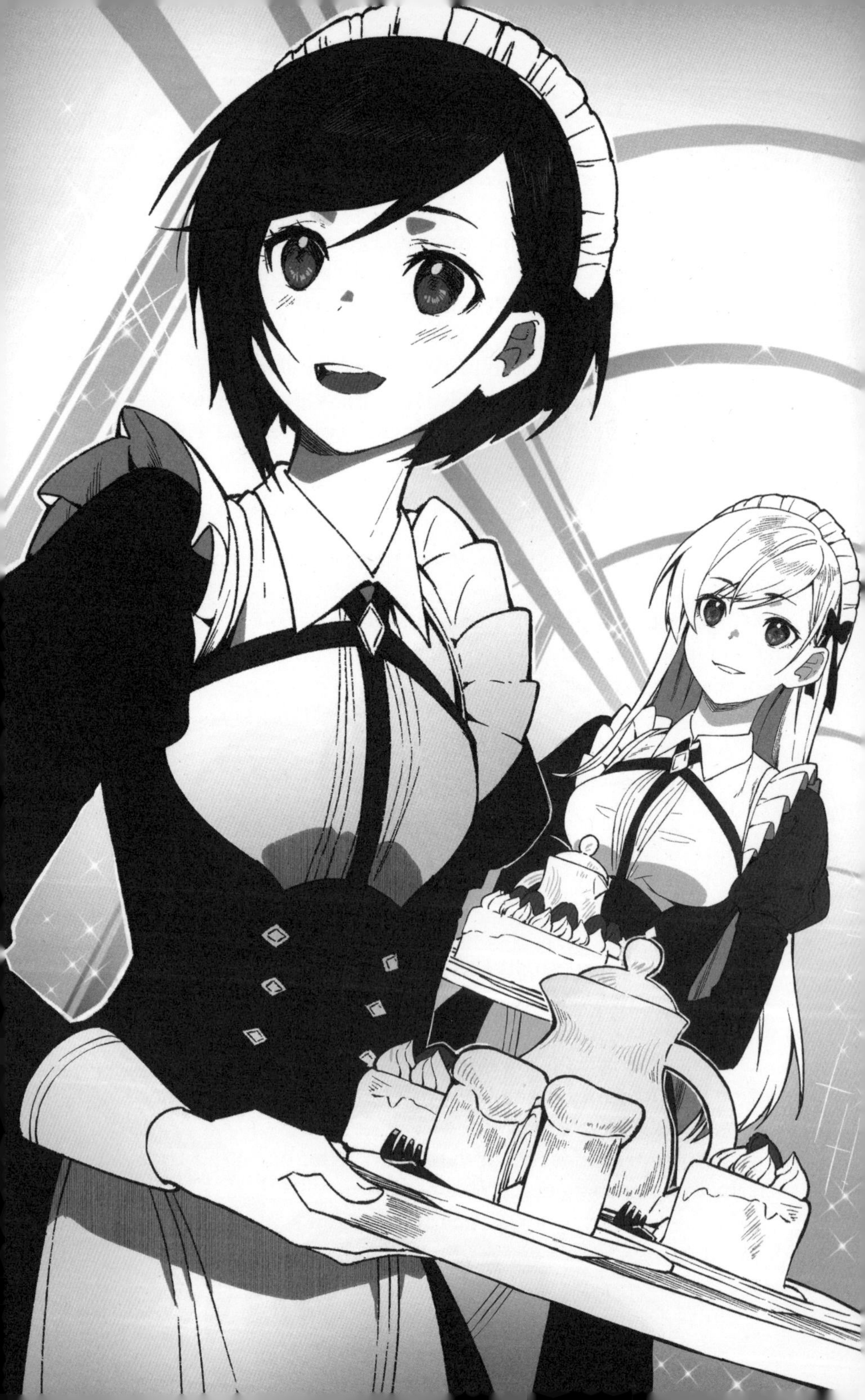

Chapter V: Inglis, Age 15—Orders to Defend the Hieral Menace (5)

"Really?! Nice, Chris! We absolutely can't mess it up, then!"

"We have to prepare ourselves for what's to come."

"Of course! All right, let's eat up!"

"That's exactly what I was thinking, Rani."

Nom, nom, nom, nom!

While the group talked, the mountains of food disappeared at an alarming rate.

Leone and Liselotte were so used to the speed at which the two ate that they didn't even comment on it—but one thing in particular caught their attention.

"So, why are you wearing those maid outfits?" Leone asked.

"Are you practicing for tomorrow?" Liselotte followed.

Tomorrow, Karelia and Highland would hold the official signing ceremony between the king's faction and the Altar faction. The maid outfits were necessary for Inglis and Rafinha's plans tomorrow.

"Yes, that's right," Inglis confirmed.

"We thought we'd practice blending in as maids. And besides, these are super cute, so isn't it great that we get to dress up Chris? We'll have bigger things to worry about tomorrow, so let's enjoy it tonight," Rafinha explained.

"It looks good on you, Inglis. You're really beautiful," Leone said.

"No matter what you wear, Inglis, you always look stunning," Liselotte commented.

"Thank you both," Inglis said with a laugh. *I think the same thing whenever I look in the mirror, so I'll just take the compliments in stride*, she thought.

"C'mon, Chris, spin for us! Spin around, say something like a maid would, and smile!"

"Sure, okay." Inglis swiftly but quietly stood. And as she spun around, the hem of her dress and her long platinum-blonde hair swayed softly. "Welcome home, mistress," she greeted with a grin.

Rafinha and the others struggled to hold back laughter. "Pfft—"

"...Heh heh."

"Aha ha..."

"Huh?" Inglis tilted her head in confusion.

Rafinha softly touched her cheek. "You have a crumb on your face. Going for the cute-but-clumsy look, huh?"

Leone laughed. "Ha ha ha, I was so worried about tomorrow, buuut..."

"Aha ha ha. You two are acting so normal. It really puts me at ease," Liselotte said.

They're laughing at me, but it's not so bad if that cuts the tension.

At that moment, Silva was passing by. He stared at them in surprise. "Why in the world are you playing around like this is dress-up?"

"Ah, Silva." Inglis said.

"Good evening. How does Chris look as a maid? Cute, isn't she?" Rafinha asked.

"I didn't acquire those for you to play around in them. Are you taking this seriously at all?"

Silva had used his connections to obtain temporary work for them as maids; the pair would be infiltrating the palace tomorrow. The Royal Guard was inseparably linked with the palace. Silva, brother of Captain Reddas and bearer of a special-class Rune, was a familiar face there.

"Silva, you seem a bit nervous." Inglis could see the tense grip of his hand on his dinner plate.

"Of course I am. So many things will be determined tomorrow—by our own hands, even. The country's future. Lady Ripple's fate. If things don't go well, Lady Ripple will blame herself and assume it's her fault. I don't want to let that happen. Your work will be crucial for our success. I won't be able to help on that end."

Inglis and Rafinha would be acting separately from the academy's main force tomorrow, and Silva would not be able to help them.

"So please. For Lady Ripple's sake," he added.

Silva had a deep concern for Ripple's situation. Actually, Ripple had mentioned that she had no problems with Silva and thought they'd make good partners. Maybe he treated her in a respectful, gentlemanly manner. Even when he'd been wounded severely, his first thought was for

Chapter V: Inglis, Age 15—Orders to Defend the Hieral Menace (5)

Ripple. Furthermore, Ripple's weapon as a hieral menace was a gun, while Silva also typically used a gun. Was there a link there?

"Silva, do you *like* Ripple?" Rafinha asked bluntly.

At times like these, it's good to have Rafinha around, Inglis thought. The kind of intrusive personal question that she'd want to ask but shied away from, Rafinha went straight for.

"Th-That's absurd! It's absolutely not that sleazy kind of thing!" Silva was flustered, his ears red—so it probably *was* that kind of thing.

Rafinha grinned while Leone and Liselotte watched with smiles. "Mm-hmm... Nothing wrong with that, right, Chris?"

"Agreed. There's nothing wrong with that."

"That would be inappropriate! I'd never think of something as rude as pursuing a hieral menace! I do have a great deal of respect for her, but..."

"Did something happen?" Inglis asked.

Silva's voice got quiet as he stared at the floor. "A long time ago... When I was a little boy, she saved me from a magicite beast. But before she arrived, the friends I was with were killed... They didn't have Runes, and yet they still protected me. My own weakness led to my friends' deaths."

Thinking back, Inglis remembered that Silva had been opposed to Inglis and Yua joining Ripple's guard because the two of them were Runeless. Inglis had thought he looked down on them, but then he'd taken blows meant for another squire, Lahti. He hadn't complained about that either. With all of this for context, Inglis now thought Silva actually wanted to keep the Runeless away from danger; he wanted to protect them at all costs. Inglis and Yua were exceptions to that rule, cases where such care was unnecessary—which caused some friction—but to the average Runeless, he was a reliable pillar of support.

"Ah, sorry to bring something like that up..." Rafinha said, her expression remorseful.

"No, it's fine. I simply want you all to know how important this is to me. Lady Ripple held me in her arms and comforted me as I sobbed. She told me to be strong for my friends who were gone, to be able to protect tens or hundreds in the place of each of them... I am who I am now because of her. Since then, I've been training with the intent to fight alongside her."

"By any chance, did you choose to use a gun Artifact to match her?" Inglis asked.

Pleased, Silva nodded. "Yes, I did. This Artifact makes it easiest to fight alongside Lady Ripple."

"Hieral menaces really are a divine presence, protecting the country and its people," Leone observed.

"Indeed. Lady Ripple is quite noble," Liselotte assented, nodding in heartfelt agreement.

"But please don't tell Lady Ripple I said that. I thanked her again recently—and she remembered, but for some reason she had a pained expression. I don't want to cause her any worry or distress."

"Okay, we won't. But why would she act that way?" Rafinha asked, tilting her head.

"Hmm. I don't know," Inglis said. "But I don't think we need to worry about it too much. If she stays in this country rather than returning to Highland, maybe someday she'll tell us of her own accord."

"Okay. Let's do our best tomorrow! Right, Chris?"

"Yeah. Leave it to us, Silva. On your end... Just give us as much time as you can. I want to go over there and fight when we're done."

"Just how much *do* you like to fight?" Silva asked.

"Well... If my appetite didn't get in the way, I'd like to never stop, I suppose," Inglis replied with a smirk.

Silva stared at her blankly. She'd rendered him speechless.

Once the sun rose, the day of Karelia and Highland's official signing ceremony would begin. Things were going to get busy.

Chapter VI: Inglis, Age 15—Orders to Defend the Hieral Menace (6)

"Hey, new girls! Can you get this one next?"

"Okay!" Inglis and Rafinha, dressed in maid outfits, cheerfully replied as they left the palace's kitchen pulling a wagon laden down with platters. Transporting food to the hall where the party would be held was a simple task. They were day laborers employed only for the busy event, so it was about all they were entrusted with. Even so, they were having a lot of fun.

"Wooow! It looks so good. It smells so good!" Rafinha said.

Inglis readily agreed. "The palace's food is in a class of its own!"

The vivid colors, the sophisticated aromas, the complex flavors—they were all thanks to the skills of the finest chefs using the finest ingredients. The food at the knights' academy wasn't bad, but it wasn't *this*.

"Ah, Rani, slow down. You're eating away at the mountain of shrimp."

"What about you, Chris? You're eating a lot of that sliced meat. That's no good."

The long hallway facing the courtyard afforded the pair many opportunities for snacking away from watchful eyes. They were quite aware that they weren't there to eat, but the party for welcoming the Highland ambassador would be cut short by the Steelblood Front's attack anyway. Surely, the food would be better off not going to waste.

* * *

Vrrrm... Vrrrm...

A low throb echoed from far away. It was coming from above—far, far above. A Highland flying battleship revealed itself in the skies, as if piercing through the sunset-tinged clouds.

"Wow, that's a big ship. As big as Theodore's, maybe even bigger," Rafinha remarked.

"I wonder who's in charge of such a large ship."

"Hopefully a nice person like Theodore or Cyrene," Rafinha said, nervous. "After all, we're supposed to protect them..."

Inglis and Rafinha were in the middle of an undercover mission to protect the king and the Highland ambassador from the Steelblood Front's attack. Neither the royal court nor the Royal Guard had been informed of the attack, a decision of Principal Miriela's that Inglis agreed with.

"But if it's someone like Rahl or Muenthe...then there's no real point in protecting them, hmm..." Rafinha said.

"Now that I think of it, we've never actually seen His Majesty, have we?"

"You're right. What if he's a mean person too? He doesn't get along well with Prince Wayne, but the prince is so nice..."

"Ha ha ha. I suppose." Inglis thought that was a bit of a naive observation. By Rafinha's reasoning, what made people incompatible was only if one was good and one was bad. But really, whether the people involved were good or bad, their conflicts would stem from their positions and thinking. What mattered was their chemistry, not whether they were good or bad.

"Well, I'm fine either way. There'll be plenty of other people to fight," Inglis said.

The fact that Leone and Liselotte had spotted the man in the black mask, Sistia, and Leon suggested that the trio would make an appearance. An aether user, a hieral menace, and a former holy knight...

Today Inglis would meet them on the same battlefield and take them all on at once. It was wonderful. Once she captured them, she planned to immediately return to the knights' academy, where she would rejoin

Chapter VI: Inglis, Age 15—Orders to Defend the Hieral Menace (6)

the squad led by Principal Miriela and Silva to wipe out the magicite beasts summoned by Ripple. Inglis would have the opportunity to fight tons of magicite beasts there, maybe even strong ones she'd never seen before.

She chuckled to herself. "I can't wait. It's my first chance in a long time to really let loose."

"You never change, Chris. Even I'm a little bit nervous about this one."

"Rani, you should learn to appreciate the simple pleasures of a good fight. There are strong enemies. Fight them. Enjoy the challenge. That's all you really need to think about."

"Uhhh... I think there's more to it than that... But oh well, I guess that's just how you are."

Preparations continued for the party as the day went on. Many people lined up in the hall: the party attendees, the musicians who would fill the hall with music, the knights to guard everyone, and even Inglis and Rafinha were there. They waited at the edge of the hall, ready to serve.

A middle-aged man in a luxurious gown made his leisurely entrance. He was tall and strong, with a scattering of white in his hair. The magnificent scepter held in his hand made his position clear. At his side was Reddas, captain of the Royal Guard.

"Ah, His Majesty makes his entrance!"

"King Carlias...!"

"Long live the king!"

Cheers echoed throughout the hall. From what Inglis and Rafinha could see, King Carlias seemed to have a dignified, well-liked presence. Inglis noticed something even more spectacular, though.

"Huh... His Majesty has a special-class Rune."

The gleam from the king's right hand was unmistakable.

"Yeah, so he must be strong. Protecting him should be a piece of cake!"

"That won't necessarily be the case. As a king, he probably doesn't have much free time to practice." Based on Inglis's experiences in her past life, that was definitely true if he took his role as king seriously. Some sacrifices were unavoidable when you were a king.

"Huh? This is unusual. You haven't said you want to fight him."

"I haven't said I don't want to fight him either."

Rafinha stared at her. "That's not a good idea, is it? If we get the chance to talk to him, please don't say anything weird."

King Carlias addressed the people around him. "It pleases me to receive an ambassador from Highland this evening. The ambassador has promised to send us a new hieral menace in response to the condition ours suffers. With this opportunity, the future of our nation will become yet more prosperous." His words, delivered with scepter raised, were met with applause.

"What about Ahlemin and Charot?!" Rafinha exclaimed, worried. "He didn't say anything at all about them—wait, is everything okay now, so they won't be handed over after all?"

"I don't think so. At times like these, it's normal to speak of accomplishments only, not what turned out poorly."

"Well, that's not nice."

Rafinha's disapproval was precious. Inglis smiled.

"Then, I direct your attention to the ambassador from Highland. Everyone, please join me in a warm welcome." King Carlias turned to the hall's entrance.

As everyone else followed, someone with the stigmata of a Highlander on his brow entered. His eyes were different colors—one red, one blue. His hair was a pale white, except for two tufts in the front that matched the colors of his eyes. He wore elaborately decorated armor—but within it was someone of small stature.

"Is he...a child?" Inglis said.

This young Highlander boy appears to be around ten years old, she thought.

"Wow, he's cute. His eyes and hair are beautiful," Rafinha said.

"Agreed." Inglis nodded. Rafinha was right; he was a beautiful boy.

"Let me introduce him," the king began. "This is the Highland ambassador, Lord Ivel. He's still young, but he is a great Highland general. This is the first time even I have met a Highlander of such great status."

"Wow, impressive."

Chapter VI: Inglis, Age 15—Orders to Defend the Hieral Menace (6)

"Then, this kid is even stronger than the usual ambassadors sent here?"

"So he's a big shot already..."

Ivel snorted at the crowd's buzz. "The ambassadors sent to the surface are mere diplomats. Don't compare them to an archlord such as I, entrusted with His Holiness the Pontifex's armies."

Rafinha pouted. "I take that back. He's not cute at all."

"Agreed." Inglis nodded again.

The other attendees were plenty pleased, though.

"How wonderful!"

"It's an honor to meet him!"

"I'll remember this for the rest of my life!"

Rafinha grimaced. "I don't like this. A kid's talking high and mighty, and everyone here's fawning over him..."

"Agreed." Inglis nodded yet again.

"C'mon, actually listen to me, Chris!"

"Huh? I was listening! Why are you angry?"

"You weren't! You were just nodding and ignoring me!"

"Well, what else was I going to say...?"

There wasn't anything else *for* her to say, was there? Inglis was sure it wasn't in response to looking at them, but Archlord Ivel began to laugh.

"Bwa ha ha ha ha! How ridiculous! Such shameful wretches you are. It's not as though you don't know that replacing your defective hieral menace comes at the cost of two cities. Are you truly so willing to sell the lives and properties of your own kin? Why do you smile? Why do you wag your tails and curry favor with I, your plunderer? Your psychology fascinates me." Ivel arched his shoulders, heartfelt amusement on his face.

"Well, that's annoying, but it's not off the mark."

"Agreed," Inglis repeated. This time, Rafinha didn't get mad.

"I suppose you don't care as long as the price doesn't fall upon you? Ha ha ha... How cruel, when tomorrow it will be your turn, fools. There's one word for you—ignorant," the ambassador ranted.

As could be expected, a chill fell over the hall, and all were silent. Still, Ivel continued.

"But that's quite well. The people of Highland are fools as well. They don't know, or want to know, of the dispossessed like you at their feet. They simply can't imagine life outside of their cozy little boxes. Six of one, half a dozen of the other. For me, it's much easier to work with the ignorant. As long as I can accomplish my mission for His Holiness, that's all that matters. I thank you for being such fools." He gave a polite bow; the gesture dripped with irony.

"Ha ha ha ha! No need to thank us, Lord Ivel. We truly are such fools! After all, that includes even I, the king. Thank you so much for your continued guidance and discipline." King Carlias smiled broadly while bowing to Ivel in an exaggerated manner. As he did, he prompted those surrounding him to do the same with his eyes.

"Th-Thank you so much!" Following the king's example, the others also bowed deeply.

"I don't want to watch this. It's humiliating," Rafinha said.

"Really? I find it kind of interesting."

Rafinha was right, though; the scene was hard to watch. But the normal human reaction would be to get angry, not cower in humiliation. Be too angry to speak, or raise one's voice to argue. King Carlias's reaction was not normal. To go along with the situation as if everything was fine meant he either lacked a human heart or had great faith that things would work out. Either motivation was a fascinating prospect.

"Bwa ha... And you, the king, are quite the amusing fool..." Ivel's lips curled into a smile.

Crshshsh!

The windows of the hall shattered as something huge flew in—a gigantic winged lizard. Its body shone with gemlike chunks of ore.

"A magicite beast?!"

As cries bound around the hall, magicite beasts in the form of a crow and a winged insect also appeared. From another entrance came dog and rat monsters. Screams rang out from all directions, not just from the hall.

"Here it is! The Steelblood Front's attack! Let's go, Chris!" Rafinha looked around. "Huh? Chris...?"

Chapter VI: Inglis, Age 15—Orders to Defend the Hieral Menace (6)

Although she had been right by Rafinha's side, Inglis was gone now.

Then shouts from the knights got Rafinha's attention. "Wait, that's dangerous! What are you going to do bare-handed?!"

"What are you doing?! Get back!"

"No! Stop her!"

"Stop that maid!"

Inglis had already rushed into the midst of the intruding magicite beasts. The winged lizard loomed over her, opening its mouth wide. It was about to chomp down.

"Haaaah!" Inglis nimbly leaped up, avoiding its fangs. Her jump carried her precisely up to the level of the beast's head. With a flowing somersault forward, she brought her heel down on the crown of its skull.

Bammmmmm!

The force of the blow was enough to cave its head in and bring it flat to the ground.

"What?!" the knights yelled in unison.

Such a lovely form had brought forth such loud blows, leaving the creature in a crumpled state; the power from her delicate frame was unimaginable to the knights. Their eyes went wide.

Inglis suddenly disappeared from their vision. From flat-footed, she leaped again, even higher, easily soaring above the winged insect magicite beast near the ceiling. She smashed it in another direction with a roundhouse kick and shot herself into melee range of the crow magicite beast. She moved with the strength of a powerful water rapid.

"Whoooa! She's so fast!"

"And her movements are so beautiful!"

"Is that girl really just a maid?!"

With the voices of the knights behind her, she gripped the crow magicite beast's beak in her hands.

"Mind lending a hand?" she called out.

She swung the magicite beast around while landing among the dogs and rats which had appeared at the entrance. "There!" Inglis flung the crow magicite beast toward the others, smashing them over the heads of the knights.

"H-How is she so strong?!"

"She doesn't have an Artifact! She's doing this bare-handed!"

"No, look! She doesn't even have a Rune!"

The magicite beasts piled on top of the lizard and insect magicite beasts she'd previously beaten on. She then threw the crow she was gripping, completing the pile. "As a maid, it's my responsibility to keep the hall clean and tidy." Inglis smiled and bowed to the knights.

"Her strength, her speed, her technique... Amazing..."

"And that's not all..."

"She's beautiful!" the knights yelled together.

The knights were distracted, but Inglis was already calling out to Rafinha. "Rani! Finish them off for me!"

Inglis's physical attacks were strong, but they couldn't finish off magicite beasts. This was precisely why people on the surface depended on Highland's Artifacts. Inglis had stunned the creatures, but they'd recover if left alone.

"Got it, Chris!" Rafinha pulled on the string of her Artifact bow.

Whoosh!

The thin arrows of light rained down on the heap of magicite beasts. Rafinha's single attack finished them all off.

"Thanks, Rani."

"You're welcome."

Inglis and Rafinha exchanged smiles, and Reddas, who was standing by the king's side, seemed to notice. "You... You're Inglis from the knights' academy?! And Sir Rafael's little sister—what are you doing here?"

"We had the day off, so we picked up a part-time job," Inglis answered.

"We love going out to eat, so we wanted some money to put toward that!" Rafinha said.

Chapter VI: Inglis, Age 15—Orders to Defend the Hieral Menace (6)

Inglis and Rafinha were, of course, not telling the whole truth. They both gave charming smiles to smooth things over further.

Luckily, Reddas had no particular suspicions. "Hmm, I see... Anyway, thank you for your assistance. I don't know how you two did it, but you have talent!" He laughed heartily.

"That's a grand compliment. Thank you, but please be careful. I don't think this is the end of them," Inglis warned.

The Steelblood Front's Prism Powder was likely responsible for all the magicite beasts. The Prism Flow wasn't falling, so this had to have been orchestrated. One of the Steelblood members had probably scattered Prism Powder throughout the castle. The black-masked man had even known the details of the negotiations between King Carlias and Archlord Ivel. Inglis didn't know who it was, but someone in this palace—someone in a very high position—was working with the Steelblood Front. These magicite beasts were just the first act. From where would the next blow strike?

"I know! Royal Guard! To arms! Surround His Majesty and the ambassador! Seal the doors! Prepare for attacks through the windows!" Reddas ordered.

"Yessir!" At Reddas's orders, the knights immediately sprang to action.

"Hmph. How dismal..." As Ivel chuckled scornfully, a knight who had moved to his side drew a glittering light-blue Artifact dagger.

"For justice!" The knight threw himself at Ivel from his blind spot. The Steelblood Front collaborator was already present!

"No! Stop him!" King Carlias called out.

"Understood." Inglis slipped between the knight and Ivel, catching the Artifact dagger with one hand.

"Ugh...! Let me go! The Highlanders who prey on the surface must be eliminated!"

"Sorry, but I have things I need to protect too." There was her promise to Principal Miriela, for one. If Inglis protected King Carlias and the ambassador, her days of free meals at the cafeteria would be extended— that was something she couldn't afford to lose.

"You there—this is none of your business. Did you really think a weakling like him had a chance?" Ivel spat.

"Ah, my apologies."

"Well, I suppose this is fine. Keep him restrained."

Ivel held his index and middle fingers together. From their tips, a strange dark light began to glow. He carefully raised his hand as if using his two fingers to draw through the assassin's body.

"Agh...?! Aggggghhh!" The assassin's body split in half, spraying blood as it fell to the floor.

Gasps arose from the surrounding knights, both in awe at the high-ranking Highlander who had cut a human in half bare-handed and in fear of how horrifically the assassin had died.

Because Inglis was standing so close, the assassin's blood fell on her face and hair.

"Chris! Are you okay?" Rafinha rushed to her and wiped Inglis's face with a handkerchief.

"Ah, yeah. Don't worry."

Ivel smirked. "Hmph. You've got a lot of guts to stand being sprayed with blood like that. Most of the men are terrified."

"You honor me, sir." Inglis bowed politely.

Never mind the blood—Ivel's power was fascinating. She'd felt something like mana, so it was probably some sort of magic, but it was so complex that she hadn't been able to grasp how it worked from witnessing it once. It seemed to be faster, stronger, and more refined than the flows that powered normal magic or Artifacts. However, not understanding it was a good sign; it showed that he was someone strong and formidable. Inglis didn't realize it, but a grin drifted to her face.

"What reason do you have to smile? Are you someone who smiles when they're angry?" Ivel asked.

"No. But as a maid, am I not supposed to greet a guest with a smile?" *A decent excuse, if I do say so myself.*

But even if Inglis wasn't angry, Rafinha was. "You did that on purpose, didn't you?! That's in bad taste!"

"Really? I'd say that inviting someone, only to try to kill them, is in bad taste," Ivel said. He shifted his attention to King Carlias. "And you,

Chapter VI: Inglis, Age 15—Orders to Defend the Hieral Menace (6)

King. Was that your reckless attempt at luring me into your territory to strike me down?"

"O-Of course not! This is not the will of my country!" King Carlias protested.

"I-Indeed! Recently, ruffians known as the Steelblood Front have run rampant over the surface! What just happened may have been one of their plots…" Reddas followed.

"It's as he says! It's shameful for a king to allow such a group to run wild, but…" King Carlias continued to plead.

"Hmph… I guess I can believe that. But that presents its own problem, doesn't it? You've endangered the precious ambassador from Highland through your own incompetence. How do you plan on atoning for that crime?" Ivel asked.

"I, Carlias, shall accept any punishment. By all means, I beg your pardon." He bowed deeply before Ivel, his head held low—nearly low enough to touch the floor.

"Y-Your Majesty!" Seeing their own king debase himself, the knights had indescribably conflicted expressions.

Rafinha was silent as well, but her eyes were full of sadness.

That wasn't enough to remove the cruel smile from Ivel's face. "Weak. That isn't enough, you so-called king. Accepting apologies is only for when both sides are equal, and you—you are not Highland's equal. You're nothing more than the leader of a herd of livestock. And those of us above livestock decide what to do with you, right? So…" Ivel quickly brushed across King Carlias's right shoulder, his fingertips swathed in a strange light—

"Gwahhhh!" The king's arm fell to the ground with a thud, spurting blood.

"One arm. I'll take that as an apology." Ivel's smile was as pleased as it was repugnant.

"Y-Your Majestyyy!"

"You bastaaard!"

"Even if you're a Highland ambassador…!"

"There are still some things you can't do!"

The knights surrounded Ivel in a frenzy. They had put up with his behavior before, but this had passed the limit of what they would endure.

"Oh? So you *were* trying to trick and assassinate me?" Ivel asked.

Reddas, in a rage, drew his sword and thrust it at Ivel. "Silence! I will not allow anyone to injure my king!"

"Stop! Silence, everyone! Anyone who does not stay their hand shall be put to death in my name!" King Carlias's voice echoed to the knights through the hall.

"Wh— Yes, my liege!" Reddas and the knights flinched as if his words were a splash of cold water.

"L-Lord Ivel... I thank you for your magnanimous treatment." Even missing an arm, King Carlias continued to bow his head to Ivel.

"Your Majesty..." Tears of pity or frustration welled up in the eyes of the knights.

"Ha ha ha... Very well. I forgive your failure. But you will be sure to protect me properly going forward, I presume." Ivel nodded, self-satisfied.

Rafinha and Inglis whispered to each other, in voices too quiet for anyone else to hear.

"Hey, Chris..."

"Yeah?"

"Is this really okay? Is this right? This kind of—"

"To each their own. If you think it's just, it's just."

Inglis, personally, could sense a certain kind of firm conviction from King Carlias, who was willing to cast away his status and pride as a king, even to the regretful tears of his knights. No matter how hard he was trampled on, he would maintain absolute obedience to Highland to keep his country and its people alive. She knew that much from watching him. He definitely wouldn't be able to reconcile this belief with those of Prince Wayne, who seemed intent on building power on the surface and reducing their dependence on Highland. What result would that contradiction bring? One, surely, that each of them should struggle for.

Nonetheless, it didn't involve Inglis. This new era had to be defined by its own people.

"More importantly, Rani, there's something you need to hurry to."

"Huh...? What?"

Chapter VI: Inglis, Age 15—Orders to Defend the Hieral Menace (6)

"This." Inglis brushed a finger over King Carlias's arm, lying on the floor. "Hurry, and you might still be able to stick this back on."

Rafinha's new Artifact had the power of healing. Rafinha nodded, her expression tense. "That's right! I'll do my best."

Inglis nonchalantly picked up King Carlias's arm. "Pardon me. Please hold still for a moment, Your Majesty." Inglis pressed it to the wound, and the king grimaced.

"Ugh... What are you doing?!"

"We're going to try to heal your wound. It may hurt, but please endure it."

"What...?"

"C-Can you do it, Inglis?!" Reddas asked.

"Yes. Rani can—"

Rafinha had already activated the Gift, and her hand glowed with a healing light. "Yes! I can!"

Her hand brushed over the gap of the wound. Her expression was tense and nervous, probably because the wound was so horrific. Inglis had already experienced various situations like this one in her past life, so she was fine with pressing a severed limb to its wound, but this was new to Rafinha. Even when she had healed Silva, though his wounds had been deep, he hadn't been dismembered.

However, her apprehension did not disturb her Gift. The two Gifts of her new Artifact each needed to be supplied with the proper wavelength of mana. In the case of Rafinha, when she used her Artifact without focusing, the Gift produced was the familiar rain of arrows of light. The new healing Gift was difficult to activate without significant concentration. But it shone, kindly yet strongly, unwaveringly. It seemed to reflect the strength inside Rafinha. Inglis was proud.

King Carlias's wound began to heal slowly, from the outside first. Reddas and the knights shouted in relief.

"Ah...!"

"His Majesty's wound...!"

"It's healing!"

"But..." King Carlias turned to look at Ivel.

Inglis knew what he wanted to say. And it would be cruel to make the wounded speak too long. So she spoke in King Carlias's place. "Lord Ivel, do you mind if we continue to heal him?"

"Well... Hmm. I don't really care."

"Thank you."

As Inglis bowed to Ivel, he stopped her. "Wait. I'd like something in exchange. Someone else's arm—I want to see the king wag his tail and beg, and sacrifice someone for me. It'll be so funny! Now, *King*, who will lose their arm for my amusement? Hurry up and tell me!"

"Ngh...! In that case, I need no healing! Not like this!" King Carlias protested.

"Such a shame. Your maids are working so hard for you. You can't let that go to waste," Ivel taunted.

"Please do not underestimate me! What's an arm, compared to king and country?"

Reddas stepped forward—but Inglis quickly stopped him. "Wait. I'm the one speaking with Lord Ivel." Leaving Reddas to support the king's arm, she stepped forward. "Then take my arm. Let me see you cut it off."

"Yours? You're decently swift, but still, you're just a Runeless. That would be worthless."

"Oh, really." Inglis smiled as she tilted her head. At the same time, she converted aether to mana and let it wash over herself. Surely a Highlander like Ivel would understand this—but his reaction was not what Inglis expected.

"Hmph. What are you grinning so proudly for? That's ridiculous. You do seem to be able to manipulate some rather powerful mana without a Rune—but that's quite amateurish, isn't it?"

Even Eris and the others had been astonished by it, but Ivel was unmoved, his mocking smirk unperturbed. This was proof of his confidence. Inglis suddenly had to revise her assessment of him; he was powerful, indeed.

"Ah, I see! Still, if you want to cut off someone's arm, take a swing at me!" Inglis's gleaming smile seemed to perturb Ivel.

"What are you so pleased about?! Very well, I'll cut off your arm.

Chapter VI: Inglis, Age 15—Orders to Defend the Hieral Menace (6)

Don't think I'll go easy on you just because you're a woman! I hate women like you who have bodies that stick out in places!"

"Excellent, then!" Inglis could tell he wouldn't hold back against her.

"Chris!" Rafinha called out, worried.

"Don't worry, Rani. Keep healing His Majesty." Inglis smiled at her reassuringly.

"Okay...!"

Ivel's fingertips began to glow. "Bwa ha ha! I can't wait to hear how you scream when your arm comes off!"

Inglis focused on the power swirling around Ivel's fingers. "I knew it. That isn't a simple flow of mana. Are those different wavelengths overlapping to create a new flow?" She could sense that the light was composed of a complex control of power. So this was why Ivel was so confident in declaring her mana amateurish.

"Don't talk like you know anything! Now, scream for me as your arm comes off!" Ivel's fingertips brushed over Inglis's upper arm. It was the same fearsome attack that he had used on the assassin and King Carlias.

It made a small tear in her maid uniform.

"What?!" Ivel's eyes widened in shock.

"Hey... That's what he did before, wasn't it?!"

"Yeah, it definitely was! But that maid girl—"

"She's untouched!"

A buzz arose from the knights.

"Ahhh! Amazing! Incredible!"

However, Inglis's eyes opened in shock. The power behind Ivel's attack was higher than she'd expected. If he'd announced he was going to take her arm and had slowly used his technique, she could have easily defended against it.

In that moment, Inglis had consciously activated the aether in her body in response to Ivel's movement and blocked it. She had held back her power while activating Aether Shell. By using less than half of what she usually did for the technique, she could increase her defense without the flashy glittering. It was a simple thing, but that level of control was thanks to her steady practice.

Previously, she had to use Aether Shell at its maximum strength. But right here, she'd had no intention of taking any damage to her clothes, never mind herself. She liked that maid uniform. She'd wanted to keep it in one piece. Yet, above her expectations, he had torn it. A high-ranking Highlander like this was not to be trifled with. It was almost praiseworthy.

However, Ivel seemed displeased. "What... What the hell?!" This time, the light covered not just his fingertips, but the entire edge of his hand. He swung his arm forcefully. It would probably be more powerful than the previous time. Then—

"Haaah!" With a short breath, Inglis fully activated Aether Shell. Her body was covered with glowing pale blue aether.

This time, his blow cut neither skin nor cloth.

"Grahhhhh!" Next, both his hands lit up.

So he can channel the complex wavelengths in two places at once. He's talented, Inglis thought.

Ivel's glowing hands struck Inglis over and over from all sides. Nonetheless, Inglis stood motionless and unharmed while wrapped in Aether Shell. The knights, only barely following their motions, were taken aback.

"What?! It's not actually that powerful?"

"But we saw it cut a man in two. It even took His Majesty's arm."

"Maybe he can only keep up its strength for so long?"

A new wave of magicite beasts suddenly made their presence known in the hall. Around ten four-legged creatures appeared. That was a rather large group to handle together.

"So bothersome! Silence!" Ivel, irritated, swung a chop in their direction. Light flashed over the gap between them, and the magicite beasts were collectively cut in half in a single blow. The knights were transfixed by the sight.

"Wh—?!"

"No, it's—!"

"Is it because that maid girl is just that amazing?!"

Having seen and taken Ivel's attacks repeatedly, Inglis realized something. "Now I understand. You don't just use mana, you use something like it but more powerful... Fascinating."

Chapter VI: Inglis, Age 15—Orders to Defend the Hieral Menace (6)

From the perspective of someone who could use divine aether, mana was wasteful. In Ivel's case, he was controlling something like mana, but it was much more efficient. She could consider it a sort of refined, higher-level mana. As a source of power, it lay between aether and mana. The basic idea of enhancing magic was to simply pump more mana into it. But in Ivel's case, he could improve the mana, the source of magic, itself.

Inglis hadn't seen a technique like this in her past life. If it continued to be advanced, it could even catch up with aether. *I don't know how much time has passed, but humanity has advanced.*

It was wonderful. It was enthralling to witness.

"The technique is called Mana Refine! By forcing the mana wrapping around me to crash into itself before I then shave off its waste, I can increase the power's purity and efficiency!"

"I see, so such a thing is possible... Amazing!"

Ivel, breathless, attacked furiously, but to no avail. "I don't understand your power! I can tell you're strong, but I don't know why! Just what *are* you?!"

"I'm simply a maid."

"What the hell... Don't make fun of meee!"

Ivel put everything he had into one all-out attack. It struck Inglis's chest, but her Aether Shell blocked it.

"Ughhh... Why won't it work?"

"Pardon me. Even if you're a child, it isn't proper to keep your hand on a woman's chest."

Ivel had, unthinkingly, left his hand on Inglis's breast. Inglis smiled and grabbed him by the wrist, twisting it away.

"Gwah...?!" Ivel's face contorted in agony. Even from his perspective, Inglis's power was overwhelming. He had no way to resist it.

"Ah, I'm sorry."

Inglis released him. Even at this point, she wasn't here to fight Ivel. She was here to receive the punishment of having her arm cut off. "Now, go ahead. Please remove my arm."

"Wh—!"

* * *

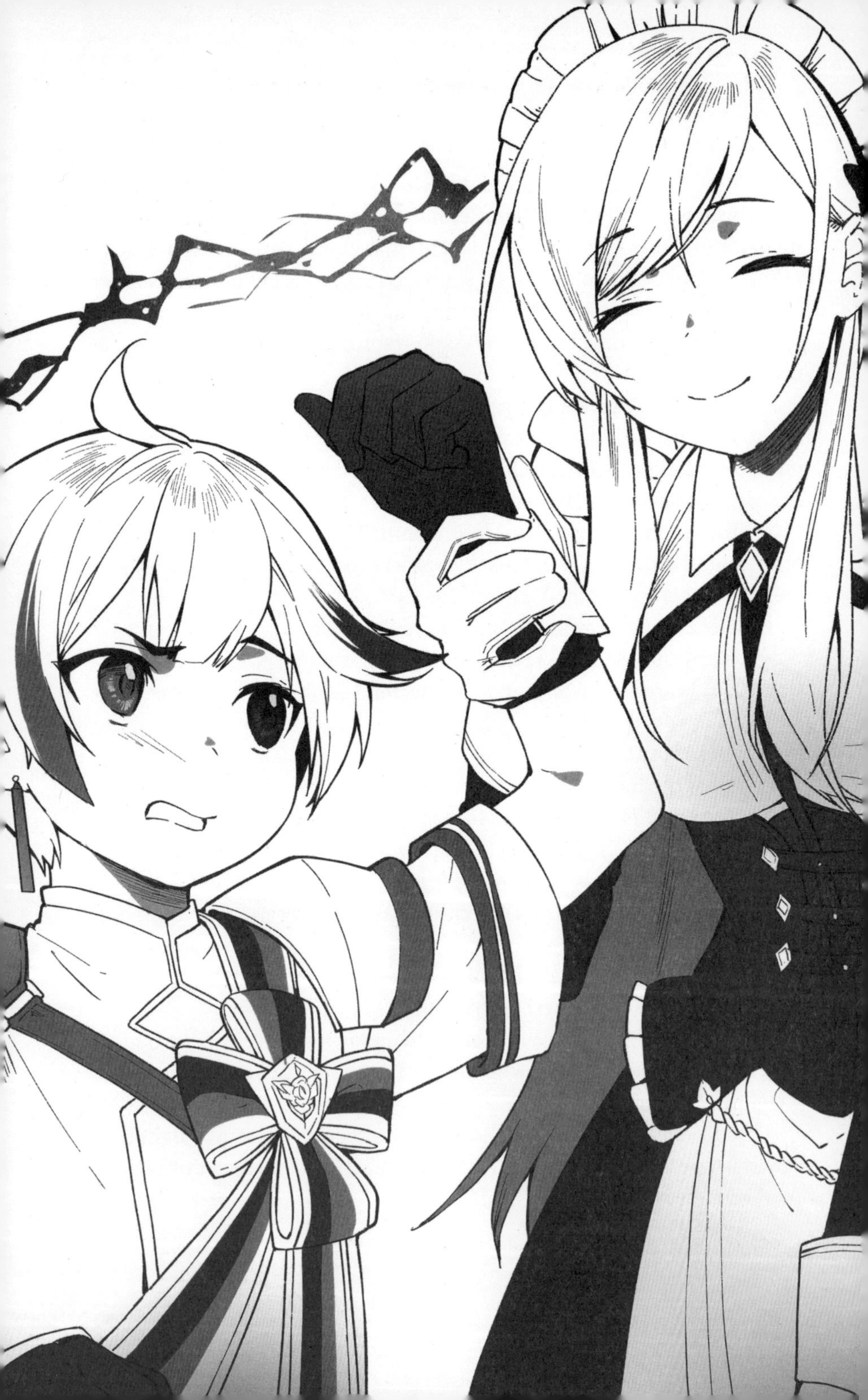

Chapter VI: Inglis, Age 15—Orders to Defend the Hieral Menace (6)

To Ivel, this servant's ladylike smile was terrifying. He couldn't figure out what she was. She looked like a beautiful flower, but she was an extraordinary monster.

"Your name's Inglis...? You don't seem like a normal maid!"

There's no way a monster who can withstand an archlord is a servant girl in some rock-pile on the surface! She must have some kind of background, some kind of purpose, Ivel thought, his mind racing. He assumed she was some new force prepared by the Triumvirate faction of Highland.

Technology improved constantly. It was possible that they'd created a weapon to surpass hieral menaces without him knowing. The Throne faction—unlike the Papal League, which valued doctrine and tradition—was exceptionally willing to innovate. In other words, they were nuisances whose intellectual curiosity outweighed considerations of safety and stability. The reason they were willing to drop the ban on granting arms like the Flygear to the surface so lightly came from a misplaced self-assurance that they'd be able to create yet higher performing weaponry and maintain the balance of power.

Ivel agreed, in a way—even if the world were turned upside down, humans from the surface would never be able to threaten Highland. But his master, the Pontifex, was more concerned. And to him, the Pontifex's orders were absolute.

Plus, while the rubbish on the surface could not threaten them, their fellow Highlanders of the Throne faction could. In particular, Theodore, now the ambassador to this country, was a young engineer of much renown. He couldn't reject the possibility that Inglis was a trap laid by Theodore and the Throne faction.

Is Theodore trying to twist our own plan around to test the power of a new weapon he's been keeping a secret? Then I'm glad I came here myself. I need to know exactly what this Inglis can do. If I don't, this could become a disaster for the Papal League. This woman is as beautiful as she is dangerous.

"Speak! What plan brought you here?!" Ivel demanded.

"Honestly, to earn a few coins and eat out more... Most of the time, I'm a student in the squire program at the knights' academy."

Inglis had repeated the same explanation Rafinha had given before, but she could see that didn't satisfy Ivel.

"Hmph. So you're not going to give me a straight answer..."

"I'm telling the truth," she insisted.

"No matter. Say whatever you want—I'm more interested in your power! Show it to me!" Ivel beckoned Inglis to attack.

"You say that—but I'd just be asking to be punished."

If she could do so without repercussions, she'd welcome an all-out fight, but it would obviously be ill received. King Carlias would never approve of her attacking a Highland ambassador. He'd said earlier than anyone who did so would be executed. Going against that would cause big problems.

"I don't care about that! In fact, if you defeat me, I'll let you off the hook! So come! Strike me!"

"If you say so, but..." Inglis looked toward King Carlias questioningly. If she could fight him, she'd like to, but—

"Stop! Laying a hand on a Highland ambassador can only end in ruin! We will keep this civil!" King Carlias gave the response she'd expected.

"Thus, sadly, I'll have to decline." Inglis bowed. Her expression was calm, but she really was disappointed. *Life doesn't always go how you plan.* She felt like she was about to cry.

"Hah! A foolish dog of a king! Your obeisance means nothing! Listen, I didn't come here to negotiate with you! That's for mere diplomats! The hieral menace exchange is called off. You can consider your relationship with the Papal League soured! His Holiness the Pontifex is angered, and someday this country will be wiped from the earth!"

"What...?! Then why are you here?!" King Carlias's eyes widened. He seemed quite shocked, which was understandable. The negotiations he'd worked so hard to put together had been a farce all along.

"There's been talk of an anti-Highlander organization, the Steelblood Front, running amok—we knew they wouldn't be able to resist sabotage if they heard of negotiations to sell land, so we laid a trap! Once they show up, I'll wipe them out with my power! That's why I, an

Chapter VI: Inglis, Age 15—Orders to Defend the Hieral Menace (6)

archlord, am here! Your country has never meant anything to me! Ha ha ha ha!"

Ivel's mocking laughter was enough to rouse the anger of the knights.

"What?!"

"You were just using us?!"

"Then for what reason did His Majesty submit himself to such humiliation?!"

Ivel provoked their anger further. "For nothing! It was worthless! At least, it was for you worms squirming on the ground!"

"You bastaaard!"

The knights' screams of rage brought a smile to Inglis's face. It was completely out of place, but as adorable as a blossoming flower.

"Wonderful," she said. "In conclusion, you're the villain who betrayed our king and even cut off his arm. Am I getting that right? Is that what you're asserting here?"

If he wanted to be a villain, then she'd get what she wanted. She could fight. She could have fun! She didn't know what Ivel's reasons were for revealing his plans, but it didn't matter at this point.

"Yes, that's it! That's exactly right!" Ivel shouted.

Inglis never dropped her grin. "Your Majesty, if you command me to strike this criminal down, I will do your will. What shall be done?"

Nearby, Rafinha, Reddas, and the other knights all nodded forcefully.

After a pause, the king answered, "We cannot kill him. Take him alive!"

"Yes. As you wish." Inglis bowed deeply and accepted the order. She was practically jumping for joy on the inside.

Vrrrm... Vrrrm... Vrrrm...

The sound of a flying battleship overhead interrupted her internal reverie. It was a new noise, different from that of the ship which had anchored above the palace.

* * *

Boom! Boom! Boom!

A series of explosions echoed from the sky; it was a volley of cannon fire. The palace shook like an earthquake as the explosions echoed throughout. Through a broken window, Inglis saw that new battleship firing its cannons.

"That's the Steelblood Front's battleship!" she said. Finally, her *real* hope for the day had arrived: the masked man and his followers.

Looks like things are getting busy.

Ivel also glanced outside, fully aware of the situation. "Hmph. As expected, the rats enter the trap."

A swarm of Flygears was already emerging from the attacking battleship. From what Inglis could see, its armaments were on par with the combined force of Ambassador Theodore's ship and its complement from the Paladins. The Steelblood Front was something far beyond simple guerillas—it rivaled the strength of an entire country's knights. And it had deployed quickly, meaning the crew had a lot of experience operating flying battleships.

The scene in the sky became hectic in no time. The flying battleship that had carried Ivel and the Royal Guard squadrons assigned to the area scrambled its Flygears to intercept their foes.

"Um... Is the bout canceled because of their appearance?" Inglis asked Ivel.

"Of course not! I don't want rats scurrying about, but you are of far greater interest! Unfortunately, I have a great many things left to do, so let's get to business—show me everything you've got!"

"Thank you very much! Then, as you request..."

Inglis again activated Aether Shell. Then she lowered herself slightly, ready to pounce, her gaze fixed squarely on Ivel.

Straight-on. Thrust directly forward and attack. That's fine. No clever tricks or twists, just all I can give it. How will Ivel take it? I'm looking forward to finding out.

"Here I come!"

Crrssshhh!

Chapter VI: Inglis, Age 15—Orders to Defend the Hieral Menace (6)

* * *

As Inglis sprung forward, the flagstone beneath her feet shattered as if it had been hit by an explosion. Fragments of rock went flying.

Ivel had clearly seen her jump. He knew he had. But he'd lost sight of her and couldn't find her.

"She disappeared?! No!"

He could feel the air shift against his skin as a shadow danced at the edge of his vision. His instinct—a warrior's intuition—warned him of danger. Just as he threw himself back, Inglis's kick passed before his face.

"Wow, you dodged? Amazing!" she exclaimed, her eyes gleaming.

She obviously saw him as a worthy challenge. Even Sistia, a hieral menace, hadn't been able to react in time to Inglis's all-out attack with Aether Shell, yet Ivel had. Furthermore, Inglis wasn't the same fighter she'd been then. Since then, she'd grown through her training at the knights' academy. Nonetheless, Ivel had successfully dodged her kick. That was the skill a high-ranking Highland warrior possessed.

"Guh—?! Impossible!" Ivel grunted. While it was true he had evaded her first attack, he'd only guessed where to move. He just happened to be right. He had an idea of how to counter, but he hadn't been able to attempt it. At Inglis's speed, he couldn't respond in time.

It didn't matter that her smile was beautiful or that her leg was captivating as it swept through the air. She was a serious threat. An unfathomable one.

"In that case—!" Ivel took a forceful leap backward, concentrating as he activated his magic. The same light which had covered his fingertips, then the side of his hand, formed a sphere that covered him. It was hard to control his stance as he flew backward.

He assumed that Inglis could probably easily follow his trajectory and counter him, but he didn't care. That was why he had covered himself with this wall of light.

Ivel's specialty in magic was Annihilation, which destroyed all things. It couldn't be invoked with normal mana, but it was possible through his use of Mana Refine. Just a light brush with such power would cut through the human body easily. To be precise, the magic annihilated what it touched in such a thorough manner that it seemed to have been severed.

This wall of light can annihilate any sort of attack! Ivel thought. *If you try to cut it with a sword, the blade will be annihilated. If you try to punch through it, your fist itself will be annihilated!*

That was, at least, if the opponent was within Ivel's expected range, but Inglis defied expectations. He had no idea what the pale blue light covering her body was, and he couldn't sense any power from it.

But this is the kind of opponent I need to put all my effort into fighting!

At first, he'd planned to concentrate his power in his palms, blocking Inglis's attack and annihilating her arm or leg. However, she had moved too fast for him to react in time to block. Extending his power from his hands to a wall would make any given point weaker, but sacrifices had to be made. Covering his whole body was the safest viable option. *Now, come!* Ivel willed within his heart.

But Inglis stood still. She silently stared at Ivel, missing a perfect opportunity to attack.

"What are you doing? Are you making fun of me?! I was just wide open!" he yelled.

"You're likely using the power of Annihilation, which destroys anything it touches. If I were to punch you directly, my fist would be gone."

Ivel shuddered in shock. *How does she know that?! I didn't tell her, of course. Did she figure out my magic just from looking at it for a few seconds?! Does she have the power to read my mind or something?!*

Despite what Ivel was thinking, he challenged her. "So you're afraid to attack? You're more of a wimp than I expected!"

"Why, of course not." Inglis shook her head. "From the looks of it, since you've covered your whole body, your power is spread out. If you focus it on one point, the effect should be stronger."

He raised his voice, his heart trembling. "What does that matter?!"

Inglis was absolutely correct. She'd seen through him so easily.

"I don't want to defeat an opponent who can only give me incomplete power. Brace yourself, focus all your power on one point—I'll attack there."

Chapter VI: Inglis, Age 15—Orders to Defend the Hieral Menace (6)

"Ha ha ha ha! What are you, an idiot? If I'm stupid enough to do that, you'll just attack somewhere else!"

"If I intended to do that, I would have already done so."

Ivel stood in chilled silence.

"Will you believe me?" Inglis continued. "Or, to turn your words around—are you more of a wimp than I'd expect from an archlord of Highland?"

"Hmph! Very well—you can face me at my full power!"

For Ivel, this was a chance to assess Inglis's character. Was she willing to deceive people? The answer to that would be vital information.

"Rrraaahhh!" Planting his feet firmly, Ivel overlapped his hands in front of his chest and prepared for the attack. A wall the size of a hand mirror appeared in front of his palms. It was small, but it glowed intensely. It was a dense concentration of magic.

"That's good! The sublimated mana is very strong when it's focused!" Inglis said.

"Now come! I hope you're not a coward!"

"Of course! Get ready!"

It took only a second for Inglis to explode off the ground again. She disappeared from Ivel's vision.

Inglis once again rushed toward Ivel at full speed, twisting her body into a kick aimed directly at the wall of light. "Haaaah!" she cried.

Touching Ivel's wall is terrifying, but if I strike it with an attack sheathed in aether and break through the structure of the magic itself, then maybe...

Crrraaaccckkk!

Ivel's wall distorted, bent, and shattered. "What?!" His face twisted in shock. The force of Inglis's kick struck his arm.

Bammmmmm!

The attack blew him away with the force of a bullet.

"Gwahhhhhh?!"

His body crashed into and broke through the stone wall, leaving a great hole as he soared far, far away.

I wonder where he'll land, Inglis thought. He was already so far away that she couldn't track him with her eyes.

"Oh no. I tried to capture him, but he seems to have disappeared somewhere."

Maybe I went too far because he was egging me on?

King Carlias, Reddas, and the other knights were left in speechless awe.

Chapter VII: Inglis, Age 15—Orders to Defend the Hieral Menace (7)

Breaking the hall's stunned silence, the Steelblood Front's cannonade fired through the hole in the wall—the same hole Ivel had left after Inglis had launched him.

Baaam!

A cannonball landed near King Carlias, smashing a hole in the floor next to him. He was the first to recover from the sound of the impact, and he raised his voice.

"Harrumph...! All of you, this is no time to hesitate! They've made their intentions clear, so we will destroy the Steelblood Front here and now! Accomplish such a feat and Highland will look fondly on us! Reddas, your duty here is done. Take command of the counterattack!"

"Yes, Your Majesty! Then, you must take shelter! We'll leave a force to keep you safe—all others, sally forth! Attack!"

"Haaa!" A spirited roar of acclamation arose from the knights, whose expressions showed that they preferred a fight with the Steelbloods to enduring Ivel's behavior.

Reddas added, "And Rafinha! Please, continue healing His Majesty's wounds!"

"Yes…!" Still focused on healing King Carlias's wounds, Rafinha was sweating heavily from the strain of her Gift. However, thanks to her effort, the king's arm was returning to normal.

"No, wait. Rafinha's coming with me," Inglis announced.

Reddas paused, taken aback before he said, "Huh?"

He probably didn't expect anyone to object, Inglis thought. *But this is a battlefield. I'd be worried leaving Rafinha anywhere out of my sight. She'll be safest somewhere I can keep an eye on her.*

The healing of King Carlias's wounds, Rafinha's safety—if Inglis were asked which was more important, she'd have no hesitation in choosing the latter. In this life, she'd chosen to pursue what was important to her, and she knew what she valued more.

Reddas weakly protested, "But His Majesty's wounds…"

"Yes. We'll be done with that in a moment." That didn't mean that she was going to leave anything undone. Inglis approached Rafinha close enough to hug her and gently touched her shoulder. Then, synchronizing her own mana with Rafinha's, she let it amplify Rafinha's mana wavelength. It was the same technique she'd used when healing Silva's wounds. "Good work, Rani. Let me help."

"Thanks, Chris…!" The healing light emanating from Rafinha's Artifact shone even more brightly. King Carlias's arm, which had been connected but still had a bloodless pallor, regained its healthy color as everyone watched.

His fingers twitched. "Ah! It moves!" the king exclaimed. He clasped his hand. He opened it. He bent his arm, stretched it. He repeated the motions over and over. He seemed to be fine now.

Reddas and the knights cheered.

"H-His Majesty's arm…!"

"It's healed! That's amazing!"

"Thank you both! Thank you so much!"

"I'm sorry, both of you… That must have taken much effort. But as you can see, I'm fine now." King Carlias bowed his head.

"Ah, no…! We—" Rafinha began to speak.

"We only did what needed to be done," Inglis finished. *Rather, I did what needed to be done to take Rafinha along with me without making*

Chapter VII: Inglis, Age 15—Orders to Defend the Hieral Menace (7)

waves. "Then, if you'll excuse us, we'll turn our attention to defending everyone from the Steelblood Front." She bowed politely.

"Us…? Chris, I'm tired. I could use a quick break…"

"That's a bad idea. Being anywhere but by my side is dangerous. Let's go. If you need to rest, you can rest near me."

"Won't that mean I'll be in the midst of the fiercest fighting…?!"

"It'll be fine! C'mon, c'mon, let's go!" Inglis said excitedly. The black-masked man of the Steelblood Front was waiting for her aboard that battleship floating in the sky.

Inglis gripped Rafinha's hand tightly and pulled her along. *Finally, a rematch with the man in the black mask! This is the perfect chance to see how much I've progressed!*

"Okay, okay…! Then, pardon me! I'll be going!" Rafinha said.

"All right, then! We're off!"

"Eeek! Chris, stop pulling me so hard!"

In the blink of an eye, Inglis, with Rafinha being pulled by the hand, flew through the hole in the wall. Many Flygears flitted through the sky like flying insects in a chaotic dogfight.

"Over there! Let's go!" Inglis pointed at the Steelblood Front battleship, which was closing in on the Highland battleship.

"There are Flygears! We need to find an open spot somewhere…!"

"Well… We don't have time for that! Let's go, Rani!" Inglis held onto Rafinha's hand tightly and leaped high. Her destination was the closest low-flying Royal Guard Flygear.

Thud!

She landed precisely on the edge of its hull, just as she'd planned.

"Whoa?! Wh-What…?!" a person inside yelled.

"Sorry to drop in. We'll be gone in a moment," Inglis said.

"Sorryyy!" Rafinha added apologetically as Inglis pulled her upward to another Flygear higher up.

Thud!

* * *

"Whoooooa?! Wh-Where did you come from?!"
"From below. Pardon us."
"Hello! Goodbye!"

Thud! Thud! Thud! Thud! Thud!

They leaped higher and higher, using Flygears as stepping-stones.
"Wh-What's that?!"
"It's a maid! A maid is flying!"
"She's fast! How's she moving like that?!"
Gasps of surprise arose from the fighting knights each time the pair jumped from ship to ship, until finally Inglis and Rafinha reached the deck of the Highland battleship.
"Mm. That was a good workout."
Rafinha gasped for breath. "I knew it! You're not going to let me rest—"
"C'mon, Rani. The Steelblood battleship is right there."
"I knew it! We're on the front lines…"
"Indeed. Isn't it fun?"
"Ugh, Chris…! You really need to chill!" Rafinha objected as loudly as she could.
"We won't get many chances like this, so why not enjoy it?"
Just then, the Highland ship began returning fire, and the battlefield got more and more chaotic. *This tumult, this ambiance—this is a battlefield. I can feel my blood boiling.*
"I wouldn't call this fun, but…!" Rafinha pointed down at the city surrounding the palace. Stray shots from both the Steelblood Front and Highlander battleships crashed down. The cannon fire would obliterate a house without a trace.
"We need to do something about that! If we don't stop it quickly, more and more innocent people will be caught up in it! So let's do this, Chris!" Rafinha's gaze tightened.
This is Rafinha's sense of justice. She can't ignore powerless average civilians being caught up in this. "Oh. Looks like you've got your enthusiasm back, Rani."

Chapter VII: Inglis, Age 15—Orders to Defend the Hieral Menace (7)

"After seeing that, of course! I'm going to try to stop that cannon fire!"

"How?"

"Like this!" Rafinha forcefully drew her white Artifact bow. An arrow of light condensed in her hand. "Fly!" When the light reached its brightest, Rafinha let loose the arrow into the sky. "Burst! And swallow that ship!" The huge arrow of light split into countless smaller arrows, each leaving a trail, not striking the ships but instead swarming around their turrets.

"I see... You're blinding them."

She's using a swarm of arrows of light as an ersatz smoke screen. As long as she doesn't let them impact, she'll be able to keep them on station for a long time, continuing to interfere.

"Yep! This way, they'll probably have to stop firing."

"But you're also keeping the arrows from impacting. That's pretty impressive." Inglis noticed the rate of fire from the battleships had slowed in confusion at the light whipping around them.

"Ha ha ha. See, I'm getting better too! Anyway, I'm gonna keep shooting these off to keep them from firing. Chris, you stop the Steelblood Front battleship!"

"Yeah. Got it!" Inglis moved further forward, and stood on the tip of the prow. Then, she thrust her palm toward the Steelblood Front ship. In her palm, the pale blue light of aether swirled, condensing. The light swelled and swelled, quickly forming into a gigantic bullet of light. "Aether Strike!"

Blammmmmm!

It would strike the bow of the Steelblood battleship and then tear through from front to back before blasting out the stern—but that's not what happened. As it pierced the bow, it was met with another pale blue light.

Fwoosh!

* * *

Inglis gasped. As a result of the two forces struggling, the Aether Strike deflected upwards from its path through the Steelblood ship, scraping off the ship's cladding as it disappeared into the sky. "I can't believe you deflected that..."

There was only one person who could achieve such a thing. Inglis stared at the newly exposed lower decks of the ship. There, on what must have been the bridge of the ship, stood a man with a black iron mask and a black outfit, including a matching cloak.

"I knew it...!"

Their leader, the black-masked man! Sistia and Leon don't seem to be nearby, though...

He was surrounded by men who seemed to be his subordinates, all pointing at her.

"That girl did that?!"

"A maid from the palace?!"

"How is a maid that powerful?! What's going on?!"

Inglis decided she was in the mood to play along. "Welcome! It's my duty to provide you hospitality, isn't it? That was just in place of a greeting." Inglis smiled and curtsied to the men.

"H-Hospitality?!"

"That was in place of a greeting?! What kind of maid are you?!"

"No way! That could've taken the ship down!"

The black-masked man held back the panic of his crew. "Be careful, everyone. The prettier the rose, the sharper its thorns. And look, isn't she beautiful?"

"Y-Yes..."

"She is..."

"To be honest, she's cute..."

"Precisely," their leader said. "Be careful, or she'll eat you alive."

They fell silent.

"I'm the only one who can stop her. Stick to the plan. I'll hold her back."

"Yes!"

Upon hearing his men's response, the black-masked man leaped

Chapter VII: Inglis, Age 15—Orders to Defend the Hieral Menace (7)

forth, landing on the Highland battleship near Inglis. "Well, well. I thought I'd leaked that information to you so you *wouldn't* interfere. Is your plan to save the hieral menace going well?"

After a short pause, Inglis answered, "The principal and the other students are doing their best."

"Too bad for you! I'm not gonna let some guerillas' plot go off!" Rafinha shouted from the other side of him.

"If we let the attack go off without doing anything, it would look like an inside job. So Rani and I are here to protect His Majesty and the Highland ambassador."

"Hmm. Here I'd thought the knights' academy would stay out of things due to its relationship with the prince," the black-masked man mused.

In fact, Principal Miriela had considered that. However, factional politics had never been a priority; she only hoped that her split forces would succeed.

"Surely, by splitting your forces, there's a danger that both operations will fail," he continued.

"I don't think so." Inglis quietly shook her head. "If I clean things up here before they finish, I'll be able to be in both fights. Best of both worlds."

"Well, well. Brave words. While you're at it, would you mind telling me where the Highland ambassador went? If you're so sure you'll win, it shouldn't bother you at all."

"My apologies. I don't know." That wasn't a lie. After all, she'd kicked him too far away to see where he had landed.

"I see. That's a shame."

"That doesn't even matter! He wasn't here to—" Rafinha began to protest.

"Wh—?! No, Rani!" Inglis activated Aether Shell and circled as fast as she could behind Rafinha before covering her mouth.

"Mmph?!"

Inglis knew what Rafinha wanted to say. Ivel had had no intention of negotiating to begin with, so attacking to prevent the ceding of land to Highland was pointless. The black-masked man's initial read on the situation had been wrong. They could point out that his plan had been a swing and a miss. They could, but—

"No! You can't say that!" Inglis insisted.

If the masked man knew the truth, he might lose his will to continue his mission and leave. That couldn't happen—not until she had fought him.

"You're fast. I see you've gotten even stronger since we last met."

"I don't know to what extent I have, but I know how to find out. You're just the man for the job."

"So would you take me as your measure?"

Inglis grinned. "Putting it that way makes it sound a bit rude, but if you don't mind."

"If I must." The pale blue light of aether enveloped his body too.

◆ ◇ ◆

Before Inglis began her battle with the black-masked man, the Royal Guard knights deployed to the knights' academy noticed the commotion at the palace when the Steelblood Front used magicite beasts to attack.

"H-Hey! Something's going on at the palace! It's on fire!" a knight yelled.

"Wh-What?!" another cried, pausing to ascertain the situation. "Oh no! It really is!"

Assigned to work with them, Silva urged on the knights. He had been helping prepare for the transfer of Ripple to the Royal Guards at the palace, planned for later that night.

"I don't know what's going on, but it looks serious!" he said. "We'll be fine here, so your forces should probably return to the palace. I'll keep myself stationed here!"

Silva was the younger brother of their commander, Captain Reddas. They couldn't ignore his words—and he was right, in any case.

"You raise a good point. Understood, Silva!"

"Yes! We can't take Lady Ripple there without being sure it's safe!"

"If you'll excuse us, then! Please take care of the rest!"

The knights boarded their Flygear and flew toward the castle.

As he watched the aircraft disappear into the distance, Silva felt a nagging guilty conscience. *I tricked them. I didn't tell them what's actually happening, and I've prolonged this as long as possible so they wouldn't take Ripple back to the palace until today. I'm sorry. I'm so sorry—but it's for Ripple's sake. I had to do this.*

"All right! I need to hurry!" he said, shaking off his worries.

He soon met up with Principal Miriela, Ripple, and the other students assigned as guards. They had gathered in a large lecture hall in the school building; it was the room where Principal Miriela had first gathered her best students, those assigned to protect Ripple. Other than Inglis and Rafinha, who had been sent to guard the castle, all of their available forces were present.

Leone and Liselotte were among them, seated with tense looks on their faces. Nearby, Yua cradled her cheeks, rocking back and forth as if she were about to fall asleep.

"Principal Miriela and Lady Ripple, I apologize for having kept you waiting! Let's get started! There's no time!" Silva said as he entered the room.

Principal Miriela nodded with a serious expression. "Yes, let's begin. Everyone, I don't know what will happen during this operation, so I'll say this again—you may sit this out if you so choose. Please don't push yourselves too hard."

Miriela expected no one would actually take her up on her offer. She proceeded on to the next part—wait, but one person *had* stood up.

"Ah... Then I'll leave, I guess," Yua announced, bleary, beginning to make her way to the door.

"Whoa! Wait! Wait, please, Yua! We need you here!" Miriela protested.

"Huh? Principal, didn't you just say we could choose to sit this out?"

"I know I said that, but I didn't actually mean it! It's just a cliché!"

"A cliché?"

"When an authority figure says people can stay back to protect themselves, no one's supposed to go along with it! You're just supposed to feel grateful! It's for getting you fired up, ready to take on what's ahead! Right? Am I wrong here?"

"I dunno…" Yua crooked her neck, expressionless. No one could guess what was going on in her head.

"The principal may have said that, but as far as you're concerned, participation is mandatory," Silva said. He bowed to Yua. "We need your help. Please, lend us your strength."

This is all for Ripple. Submitting myself before her *does not bother me—not when it's for Ripple.*

Yua, unaware of what he was so concerned about, could only find Silva's behavior extremely unusual though. "Four-Eyes, do you have a fever?"

"No! I feel perfectly fine!"

"Ah, yep. You're still prickly like usual."

"That depends on who I'm talking to!"

It was Ripple, not Principal Miriela, who interceded. "Now, now, calm down. Yua, I'd also appreciate it if you helped in this operation." She bowed alongside Silva.

"Lady Ripple?" Silva thought that was unusual; Ripple's attitude was different. She always put on a cheerful face during normal situations, but in the current situation with the magicite beasts, she tended to keep her head down and listen quietly.

"Ripple…is something wrong?" Principal Miriela asked. She had also noticed the change in Ripple's demeanor.

"Yeah… Up until now, I thought I had to just accept everything going on about me. After all, a hieral menace who can't protect others isn't worthy of being a hieral menace, but…everyone's trying so hard to help me, right? Well, except for one kid who's just here to enjoy the ride…"

"Ha ha ha, yeah, there is that one—of course, we won't say who it is." Principal Miriela chuckled wryly.

"I'm sure the hairs on the back of her neck are standing up right now."

"Yes. I'm sure of it."

Chapter VII: Inglis, Age 15—Orders to Defend the Hieral Menace (7)

Leone and Liselotte nodded to each other. There was no need to name her. After all, everyone could tell.

"But with all that in mind, looking at everyone—my homeland where I was born is pretty much wiped out, but this country is now my…" Ripple paused briskly before smiling brightly. "I'm really moved. I understand how I feel now, so… I don't know if a hieral menace is supposed to think this, I know it's going to cause you trouble…but I still want to stay with this country's people. Knowing that, it's only natural for me to ask for your help, right?"

"Lady Ripple…" For some reason, Silva felt oddly at ease. For the first time, it felt as if Ripple was relying on him fully.

Not just on him—on everyone, really. But it still felt good.

"So, Yua…" Ripple began.

"Please, for Ripple's sake…" Silva followed.

"Yua, if Ripple's going this far…" Principal Miriela was the last to appeal to her.

Everyone's gaze turned to Yua, whose breathing was the steady, comfortable sort of someone sleeping.

"What's wrong with you?!" Unable to stand by and watch, Silva slammed his red long gun down toward Yua's head—and her hand shot out to grab it.

Her reflexes were impressive. "Violence is wrong."

"That depends on the person's attitude! And yours deserves it!"

Yua scurried behind Ripple and hid herself. "Scary. Save me, Lady Dog-Ears."

"Now, now… Yua, will you help us defeat magicite beasts?" Ripple asked.

"I do that all the time."

"There'll be a lot of them this time, and I think they'll be strong. Can we still count on you? If it goes well, I'll treat you to something, okay?" Principal Miriela offered.

"Rather than food, I'd like you to introduce me to someone," Yua countered.

"Huh? Well… What kind of person?"

"Someone cool like Four-Eyes—"

"Wh-What?! Flattery at this point..." Silva couldn't help but feel a bit flustered.

"But I could go without his temper."

Turns out Silva had been imagining things. Yua was incapable of flattery.

"Someone not as weak as Four-Eyes either."

"Why you—! You're just making fun of me!" *I really don't get along with Yua. We're never in sync*, he thought.

Principal Miriela raised her voice. "Argh! Let's get started before this turns into any more of a mess! Leone, please split us off into the sub-dimension!"

"Y-Yes, ma'am! Here I go!" Though she was taken aback by the sudden turns the conversation had taken, Leone immediately focused. Her new dark greatsword Artifact had a Gift that would transport everyone to a dark dimension.

"That's it!" the principal encouraged. "This is much smoother than before! You've gotten good at this in no time at all, Leone. That's wonderful!"

"Thank you." The praise took Leone by surprise, but it was true that she'd gotten used to the Gift; the speed of its activation, the strength of the dimension, and its size had all stabilized.

"Let's begin! For Ripple's sake...let's work together! Not only for her, but surely for the sake of this country and its people too!" Principal Miriela announced.

The students answered in unison. "Yes!"

Silva explained the plan. "The principal and I will let Lady Ripple drain our power to summon magicite beasts! Everyone, we're relying on you to handle them! Now, Ripple, go ahead!"

Silva extended the barrel of his charged Artifact gun to Ripple. At the same time, Principal Miriela also held forth her Artifact staff.

"Ripple, leave this to us! My students are talented, it'll be fine!" Principal Miriela assured.

"Yeah... Thanks, everyone. Good luck!" Ripple nodded before

Chapter VII: Inglis, Age 15—Orders to Defend the Hieral Menace (7)

placing her hands on the offered Artifacts. As proof that she was absorbing the mana of each, the glow surrounding them disappeared.

Vwoom!

The usual dark sphere surrounded Ripple's body, signaling that the magicite beasts would arrive soon. While supporting the now-unconscious Ripple as he laid her down, Silva gave orders to the other students. "Everyone, form a circle around Lady Ripple! We don't know how many enemies there will be! Support each other as you fight!"

"Leone and others with dimension-slipping Artifacts, to the center of the circle! Step back and let the others take the lead!" Miriela instructed.

"Yes!" The elite students reacted quickly, moving at once.

As they did, a number of vortex-like distortions appeared around the circle. From them, demihuman magicite beasts appeared. They were powerful magicite beasts, comparable to the transformed Rahl or Cyrene. The students had to be wary of these foes, which could severely wound even Silva if a blow struck true. Five of them had appeared, spreading out to surround the students circled around Ripple.

Leone gasped. "Five of them?! They're starting out strong!"

"But we've got to do this! If we pull this off, we can help protect Ahlemin and Charot!" Liselotte reminded her.

"Yes! Let's go!" They nodded to each other intently.

"Um... Ah, enemies. But, uh, we all do this together?" While everyone else was wrapped up in a sense of urgency, only Yua was left behind, unsteady.

As the leader of the second-year students, Morris yelled, "Yua! You don't worry about anyone else, just beat the enemy in front of you!"

Yua was talented, but she wasn't the kind of person suited to coordinating things. Someone else was required for that role, and Morris was well suited for it. He was open-minded, and his relationship with Yua wasn't bad.

"Beanpole..."

"My name is Morris! But whatever, go wild!"

"Okay, but if they get mad it's your fault, Beanpole," Yua mumbled as she lightly rushed to the nearest magicite beast.

However, those light footsteps weren't lazy at all. In fact, from the others' viewpoints, Yua's footwork was exceptionally swift and sharp.

"Gotcha." It was a palm strike that seemed gentle enough to be a caress.

Bash!

Nonetheless, the magicite beast flew away and twisted unnaturally.

The students involuntarily gasped in astonishment. Even the magicite beasts seemed to freeze for a moment. Were they shocked by the overkill?

"Better to just leave her to that, right?" Morris asked, turning to Principal Miriela and Silva.

Silva nodded. "Indeed. I don't mind!"

Yua was not the cooperative type. Better to set her loose than try to coordinate and fail.

After sending one enemy flying, Yua turned to face another. But the group of them was spread out.

"Rrroooaaarrr!"

On the other side of the circle from Yua, a beast roared. Specks of light began to converge around the creature—it was going to let loose a scattered heat ray! When the students were assembled in a tight formation like this, it was hard to deal with large-scale attacks from a distance.

"Not on my watch!" Liselotte, with her Gift of white wings, flew through the air at full speed toward it in the nick of time. Her halberd's thrust combined with her own momentum deeply pierced the magicite beast's neck; the heat rays it had been condensing dissipated.

Liselotte removed her halberd from the enemy. "I shall go forth and leave the enemy in disarray! If I may?"

Miriela nodded. "Don't push yourself too hard! Just disperse the enemy's attacks!"

Chapter VII: Inglis, Age 15—Orders to Defend the Hieral Menace (7)

Liselotte's Gift of free mobility would be far more effective when used to move around and leave the enemy in disarray than if it were bluntly incorporated into a formation. Since Yua alone wasn't enough to play the decoy, having Liselotte do so as well was best.

Liselotte kicked the magicite beast's body down as she took to the air again, charging toward another foe farther away, which was also charging a heat ray. "You too! I won't allow it!" The ax-head of her halberd slammed into the magicite beast, with all of her momentum behind it. The concentrated power faded. When the creature went to strike, she used her white wings to fly to safety.

She danced through the air to and fro, interfering with the enemies' big attacks. She thrust forward once more, and then her foe tensed its muscles, trying to keep her from pulling out the tip of her halberd.

"Ugh…! Too clever by far!"

Another beast approached her from behind. Magicite beasts were unintelligent, but in battle, they coordinated surprisingly well. Liselotte wondered whether she should drop her halberd for a moment or twist around and respond with a kick, and as she hesitated, a dark iron blade stretched out from the edge of her vision.

"Liselotte, I'm here!"

Leone's sword was there in a flash. She used an attack that combined a fierce thrust and the Gift of extending the blade, gaining speed from both. It had worked even on Leon. From far away, she stabbed the magicite beast in the back as it tried to close in on Liselotte. Skewered, it stopped in its tracks.

In the meantime, Liselotte had freed her Artifact and managed to escape. "Thank you, Leone! I see you can use both Gifts at once now!"

"Yeah, I've been practicing!" Leone smiled.

"Amazing… That's great, Leone!" Principal Miriela couldn't hide her surprise as she watched.

Leone had just used a Gift while already controlling another. Miriela had hoped Leone would eventually be able to use multiple abilities simultaneously, but for it to be so soon… She was amazed. She had expected Leone would have to focus exclusively on maintaining this dimension, so this was a pleasing development.

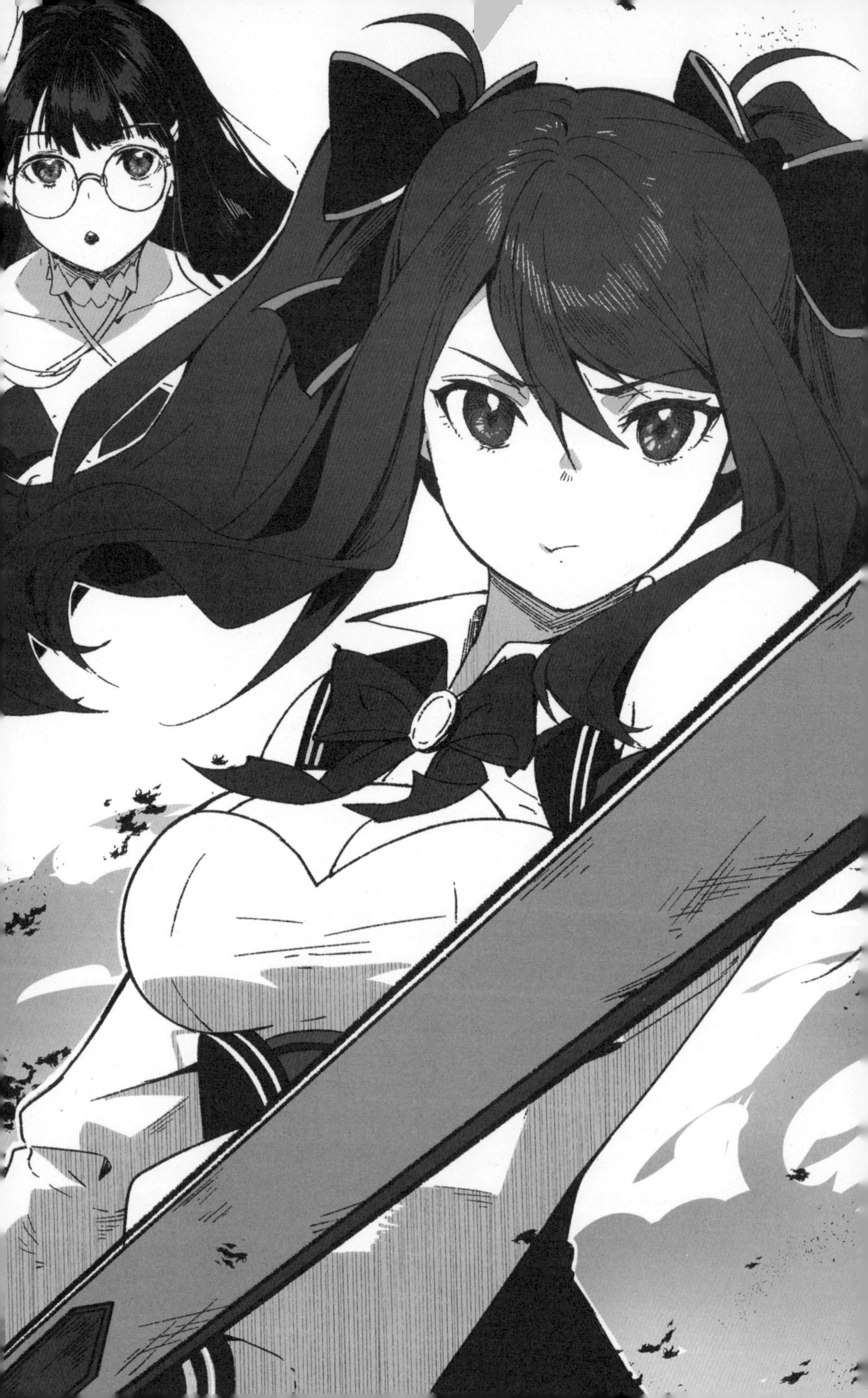

Chapter VII: Inglis, Age 15—Orders to Defend the Hieral Menace (7)

"All right, let's keep it up and wipe out these magicite beasts!" Miriela said.

Ripple, enveloped in the dark sphere, continued to absorb mana from Miriela and Silva. More and more enemies would be summoned.

◆ ◇ ◆

Sounds rang out atop the flying battleship, high above the palace.

Bammmmmm! Clannnnnngggg! Rrrummmble!

Ear-splitting clashes echoed all around Rafinha from the fight between Inglis and the black-masked man. They were in a fierce close-quarters battle, moving so fast that Rafinha could only occasionally make out their forms, and both wrapped in a pale blue light as they flickered in and out. When she couldn't recognize who was whom, she had no way of knowing which attacks might hit her like stray gunfire.

Normally, a person in that situation would be terrified and want to escape, but Rafinha stood unflinching, continuing to impede the two battleships with the arrows from her Artifact. *I need to do this. If I stop, things will get even worse in the city. I have to stay. And besides, I believe in Inglis. She'll protect me, no matter what.*

Rafinha caught the occasional peek of Inglis, who had a completely out-of-place smile on her face. Inglis was truly enjoying this battle. No smirking, just a broad grin with a hint of danger behind it.

But that was normal for Inglis. *And if things are still normal for Inglis, I can definitely count on her to keep me safe*, Rafinha reminded herself. That had been true of Inglis for their whole lives.

Suddenly, Inglis flitted into her vision again, delivering a backhand blow so forceful that her opponent's arm raised in defense was swatted away.

Clang!

* * *

Rafinha heard the sound a moment after she saw Inglis's attack. Another moment later, Inglis disappeared from her vision again.

"There!" came Inglis's shout.

Ker-thonk!

"Gwuh?!"

Rafinha hadn't seen what happened—had only heard their voices—but Inglis reappeared in a flash a second later.

Inglis appeared again, crouched as if she'd just rammed into him with her shoulder. The masked man flew like a bullet toward the other ship.

"And there's more!" Inglis leaped forth for a continued attack. But suddenly, the pale blue light around her body disappeared as she spun toward Rafinha, that same light converging on her raised index fingers.

Rafinha gasped. "Chris?!"

"Don't move!"

Whoosh! Whoosh!

Twin beams of light shot past Rafinha on either side.

"There she is! She's the one getting in the way of— Gahhh?!"

"Get rid of her! Otherwise we can't return— Ughhh!"

They were soldiers from the Highland battleship. Realizing Rafinha's barrage of light was acting as a smokescreen, they'd come to get rid of her.

"Watch yourselves," Inglis warned. "If you hurt Rani, I'll show no mercy."

"I don't think they're listening, if they can even hear you," Rafinha said.

Inglis's shots had precisely pierced between their eyes. They silently slumped from the deck of their Flygear, slid off the battleship, and fell to earth. All that was left was a pilotless, hovering Flygear.

"Rani, you may as well take that Flygear. It's safer there."

"Y-yeah... I will."

Chapter VII: Inglis, Age 15—Orders to Defend the Hieral Menace (7)

Inglis is right. It feels a bit creepy to be taking it from the recently deceased, though...

Breaking away from her thoughts, Rafinha added, "You should get on too, Chris!"

"Well, I'm still not quite done here."

Inglis turned her focus back to her target.

The black-masked man who'd been blown away regained his balance midair and rocketed back toward Inglis by kicking off the hull of his own ship. "Sorry, but I'm not done yet!" Thrusting his upper arm forth, he prepared to respond in kind.

"No, no! You're welcome anytime!" Inglis replied.

It's rare to find such a worthwhile foe. I've always wanted the chance to fight him, Inglis thought.

Inglis again activated Aether Shell and swung her leg up, trying to kick her foe away. But before that, she realized something: *He's bringing his shoulder forward to hide his body. And I feel another flow of aether, different from the one wrapped around him. Are his movements hiding another aether technique?*

"Haa!" Inglis immediately leaped up, somersaulting backward with all the force she'd been putting into her kick.

Vvvoom!

Too quickly for Rafinha to see, a light-blue sword, glowing brightly, swung through the space where Inglis had been.

"An aether sword?!" Inglis gasped.

The black-masked man's shoulder rush was hiding an aether sword from my vision. That's certainly a fascinating technique, even if I did figure it out in time!

He had condensed aether and manipulated it to take a physical form. Inglis did the same to turn ice into blades, but his skill was on a completely different level.

Controlling aether was far more difficult than controlling mana. Even so, the man in the mask had manipulated aether while keeping up his own Aether Shell-like technique—that made two major aether techniques he had used simultaneously.

When they'd met before, he'd said that Inglis was the superior in raw power but he had the upper hand in technique; Inglis supposed he was right. A combination like that was still impossible for her.

"So you see how things are now… Sorry, but I'll be finishing this!" Before Inglis could land, the black-masked man readied a follow-up slash.

He's caught me flat-footed. And even with Aether Shell up, a sword like that will do some serious damage. I can't let it hit an arm or a leg. No matter!

Inglis let out an assertive cry. "I don't think so!"

Clink!

Inglis formed a blade of ice in her hand. With Aether Shell active, these ice blades would shatter in a single blow. They couldn't handle the strain that aether put on them.

But in this situation, a single blow is enough!

Shoom!

As Inglis twisted in midair, her weapon struck against the masked man's own.

"Ugh…" Inglis's blade took the brunt of the blow. While it parried his slash, it also shattered to pieces in the process. But that had given Inglis time to land and recover her footing. That was enough.

"A weak blade like that is nothing next to mine!" He followed up with another fierce slash.

"Indeed. That's fine, though."

As long as it got me through the moment where I was vulnerable—I just need to keep up my footwork, dodge his sword, and strike with my fists!

The black-masked man grunted. "Is this—?!"

Every time he swung his sword, it missed, and every time it missed, Inglis came closer and closer. He couldn't land his blows. She advanced with small, precise movements through the rain of slashes, as if each

Chapter VII: Inglis, Age 15—Orders to Defend the Hieral Menace (7)

and every one of his moves were at her will. Even though he was the one on the attack, he was being forced back in order to keep his distance.

Anxious thoughts raced through the black-masked man's head: *I know she's faster than me. I know she's stronger with aether, but that's why I'm using two aether techniques at once. So why is this happening? This isn't just a matter of aether control. I can feel an overwhelming sharpness from her predictions. She possesses vast knowledge of combat, as if she has a lifetime of experience.*

Just what is this girl?

"Haaah!" Inglis had made her way completely inside the black-masked man's defenses; she delivered a palm strike to his gut.

"Guhhhh?!" The blow flung him backward. He fell to his knees but somehow didn't completely collapse. "Ha... Ha ha ha... It seems like things are getting completely out of hand. I don't remember you being this strong last time."

"You seem to have been quite busy, but I've been focusing on my training."

"I like to think I've been working hard for the greater good. Though I'm not childish enough to insist that 'justice will always prevail' or anything."

"Justice, injustice—power doesn't care. Strength is talent, training, experience. Isn't it unfair to tie ideology to strength?" she challenged.

Whether for good or ill, power used for a cause becomes the means to an end. Even if you realize those ideals, your power becomes meaningless to you in the end. That sort of mindset doesn't respect power itself. If you desire true mastery, you need to be more sincere. Let go of ideas, let go of reasoning, and reach for power without needing a cause to guide you.

"Ha ha ha ha! Beneath that dainty appearance rests a true warrior!"

"It's the only way I can live my life. Now, you must be hiding something else. Show me."

He repelled the Aether Strike I fired at his battleship. I'm sure of that— but that's impossible with what I've seen from him. His aether shouldn't be powerful enough for that. There has to be something else going on... And if I've got the chance, I'd like to find out.

The black-masked man feigned ignorance. "Hiding something? Like what?"

"My attack on your ship. You must have been the one who repelled it. I'd like you to show me how."

"Hmph. You're sharp, aren't you…? But I don't think the answer will particularly interest you."

"I won't know for sure until I see it, now will I?"

"How persistent. Very well. Allow me."

The color of the aether around him changed from a pale blue like Inglis's to a golden tinge.

Inglis gasped. *It's aether. I can tell that much. But I've never seen golden aether. Not even in my past life.*

Even the goddess Alistia, who had made Inglis a divine knight and demigod, had been wreathed in aether of the same pale blue. Even the other gods of that pantheon had.

"Is that the spirit of a demon?!" Inglis shouted.

Demons were the enemies of the gods. They had existed in her past life, but she had defeated them, thus becoming recognized by gods and mortals alike as a hero, leading to her kingship. Demons' spirits were characterized by a golden hue.

"But that can't be it…" she murmured.

The power wrapped around him was definitely aether; it wasn't ominous like a demon's. All aether was the same at the end of the day, but it flowed with very different wavelengths.

He seems to be able to control the nature of the aether itself, Inglis thought. *Astonishing control over it, really. I never would have thought this was possible. But is this color just coincidence?*

Now that I think about it, what even were "demons"? Inglis began to have belated doubts.

But more importantly— This is so exciting! A power I don't know, and techniques I don't know!

"So you did have something hidden." Inglis chuckled. "This is a lot of fun." She beamed at the black-masked man, her smile as beautiful as it *seemed* innocent.

Chapter VII: Inglis, Age 15—Orders to Defend the Hieral Menace (7)

"I wonder why... Such words from a young lady, yet I feel no joy," he mused aloud.

"I wouldn't mind if you enjoyed yourself."

"That I cannot do. I'm different from you—I'm just a misguided fool dedicated to my cause. I don't have time to fight all the time. So, come!"

"Very well, then!" Inglis rushed forth at full speed, her fists at the ready. *First, see what happens. Head straight in and strike. No twists, no tricks, but no mercy. A punch with all my might.* Her arm surged toward her opponent and the golden aether covering him.

Voom!

She felt a strange sensation as her fist swung off-target. "Wha...?!"

She tried again, then again. But a strange power kept her from touching the black-masked man. "Then—!" She raised her leg high for a kick.

Vo-voom!

Even that failed to connect. It practically slid away from him.

What is this? The closer I get to him, the harder it pushes back—I can't touch him! I'm being repelled as if we're two of the same magnetic poles approaching each other.

"What is this?! Is this how you repelled my Aether Strike?!"

"It is, indeed. By transforming the nature of my aether, I can make the forces repel each other. Thus, they will never meet, and I cannot be hurt. It's a matter of quality, not quantity."

"So it functions both as an absolute defense and the complete nullification of any offense from either of us?"

"That's right. There can be no more conflict between us, only peace."

Inglis took a moment to pout in frustration. "That's boring." *That means I can't fight him!*

"I told you it wouldn't be of interest to you."

"I suppose that limits my options here." Inglis sighed.

"I'm glad you understand."

"Yes, I understand completely—understand that this is my only option!"

Clink!

The Aether Shell surrounding Inglis faded as an ice blade appeared in her hand. *Aether techniques can't touch him, so I have to turn my aether into mana and fight him that way. His aether won't be able to push away mana.*

Incredulous, the masked man said, "And yet you still want to fight? Even though dropping your power places you at such a disadvantage?"

"That's the thing—creativity is also a part of fighting."

"I don't understand. Why would you go so far?"

"Because life is short. I can't afford to waste a single moment."

He sighed. "My, my. So young, yet in such a hurry. Then I suppose I must continue to take you on…" He got into position.

Rafinha's voice interrupted the atmosphere of their duel. She called out from the Flygear, "Chris! Something's coming! Be careful!"

Something wrapped in light was flying toward Inglis and the black-masked man.

Booooom!

Something had landed by them with an explosive noise.

"Wh—! You're—"

"Ha ha ha! Did you think that would be enough to kill an archlord like me? Too bad!" Ambassador Ivel had returned from Inglis's kick that had sent him far away.

"Lord Ivel! I'm so glad you're safe!" Inglis's face gleamed in joy at his survival.

"That's an obvious lie! You're the one who kicked me!"

"It isn't a lie. I really am glad you're safe." Inglis was being genuine; after all, the more fights with strong foes, the better. With Ivel safe, she could fight him again.

"An archlord…" the masked man said. "That would mean you're

Chapter VII: Inglis, Age 15—Orders to Defend the Hieral Menace (7)

high among the Highland generals. If you're here, that means you were in charge of the negotiations, right?"

"Hmph. So, what, you're the leader of the Steelblood Front? I'd heard you were a man in all black, but this is truly a terrible way to disguise yourself. Let me guess, you're self-conscious about your ugly face?"

The black-masked man sighed in exasperation. "Well, it's true that I'd feel uncomfortable in anything else. Nonetheless, taking down the Highland ambassador is our goal—I don't take pride in harming a child, but I'll complete our objective."

The tension between Ivel and the masked man heightened. Inglis cut through it, stepping between them. "Fall back, Lord Ivel. He aims to take your life." Then, she turned to the black-masked man. "Lord Ivel never had any intent of working with our country. You don't need to worry about the king and the ambassador negotiating over Ahlemin and Charot."

Inglis's mind was moving fast. *I don't want the two of them to face off. If they hurt each other in a fight, that will result in fewer people for me to duel. That would be a waste. If they do choose to engage, I'll have to protect Ivel. At the moment, he's far weaker.*

"Hmph! Things are going exactly to plan! Now that the Steelblood Front has stuck its neck out, we can swat you down like a pesky fly! I'll crush its leader here!"

"Dealing with your thorns now is better than letting you take root later!" the black-masked man said. "Taking the head of an archlord has its own value!"

Inglis interjected, "Wait, you can't fight! Sheath your weapons! Peace is vital!"

"What nonsense is coming out of your mouth?!" Ivel and the black-masked man replied in unison.

"I do not wish for anyone but me to be involved. If either of you wants to fight me, you're welcome to."

"That's absurd!" Ivel snarled. "It would be pointless!"

The black-masked man concurred. "Unlike you, we don't fight for fun."

"Then you leave me no choice." Inglis faced the black-masked man and activated Aether Shell once more. First, she needed to protect Ivel.

Just as Inglis made her decision, a single Flygear darted out from the Highland ship and flew toward them. Aboard was a familiar face. She was a hieral menace with long, lustrous red hair—Sistia. "Sorry to keep you waiting! We've taken the bridge!" she called.

"Well done. Get the captured ship out of here!" the masked man replied.

"Yes! I've already given the orders!" Just as she'd said, the Highland ship began to drift away.

"You bastard! You're trying to steal my ship? You thief!" Ivel yelled.

"In future battles, we will make the most of what we have gained today. We increase our strength whenever the opportunity arises."

Was this perhaps their objective all along? Inglis wondered. *If not, why would Sistia try to take the bridge? No, they were trying to fly to the palace to encounter Ivel. That must have been the main objective.*

The Steelblood Front had discovered Ivel was no longer at the palace, probably from a Steelblood sympathizer who reported back. As a result, they switched their main objective to taking the Highland ship.

A clever, resourceful move.

Ivel sneered. "Well, no matter. I can kill you here and take it back!"

"How insolent! Who do you think you are?!" Sistia demanded.

"That's the Highland ambassador, Sistia," the black-masked man filled in.

"Eh?! Then we should take him down before we get out of here! It's an excellent chance!"

"Yes, that was my plan."

"I won't let that happen," Inglis declared. "I can't have you all hurting each other. That would be a shame." *Especially for myself*, Inglis thought.

The masked man laughed. "We seem to have gotten ourselves into quite the mess, Sistia."

"Yes, you're right. Not to mention Leon's—"

"Indeed. At times like these, it comes down to power. Alone, I can protect myself but not overwhelm her. So I'm forced to borrow yours."

Chapter VII: Inglis, Age 15—Orders to Defend the Hieral Menace (7)

Sistia gasped. "Yes, then I'll—" She nimbly leaped from the Flygear and lined up next to the black-masked man. Her body glowed from within. "My existence, my power... Use it as you will. I offer it all to you."

Wait, is this—?! Inglis thought. *"A hieral menace's transformation into a weapon?!" I really want to see this!*

Sistia, enveloped in bright light, reached out her hand to the masked man. He took it, and she began to glow even brighter.

"So bright!" So close to the light, Inglis struggled to keep her eyes open. All she could see was a shadow that transformed into a long, thin weapon—a spear. It was hard to know that for sure from her vision, but she could sense its power. Inglis focused as hard as she could. She understood what was happening.

This is—

"Amazing..." was the only word that came from her lips.

She could sense Sistia in her weapon form taking his aether in and amplifying it. It wasn't mana—it was definitely aether. That came as a shock. Even an upper-class Artifact would shatter when infused with aether, like when Inglis had broken Leone's upper-class Artifact.

But a hieral menace does more than handle aether safely; they can take that aether and amplify it incredibly. Five, no, maybe ten times, Inglis observed. *Even an Aether Shell with all my might couldn't possibly stand up to an attack like this. Hieral menaces really live up to their reputation as the ultimate Artifacts.*

Inglis could understand a hieral menace handling mana, but aether as well...

This is on the level of the holy sword, a weapon of the gods, from my past life. Yet now, it's born from human hands, even if they are from Highland. Inglis had to admit to herself that she was dumbfounded. *The world has moved on so much from my past life. It's wonderful. Absolutely wonderful. Everything I'd want from a foe.*

"Ugh...! Is this the same power as that maid's?! But the hieral menace is responding to it!" Ivel said.

"Please, escape, Lord Ivel. It's too dangerous," Inglis said. *With Ivel out of here, I can experience that power to the fullest.*

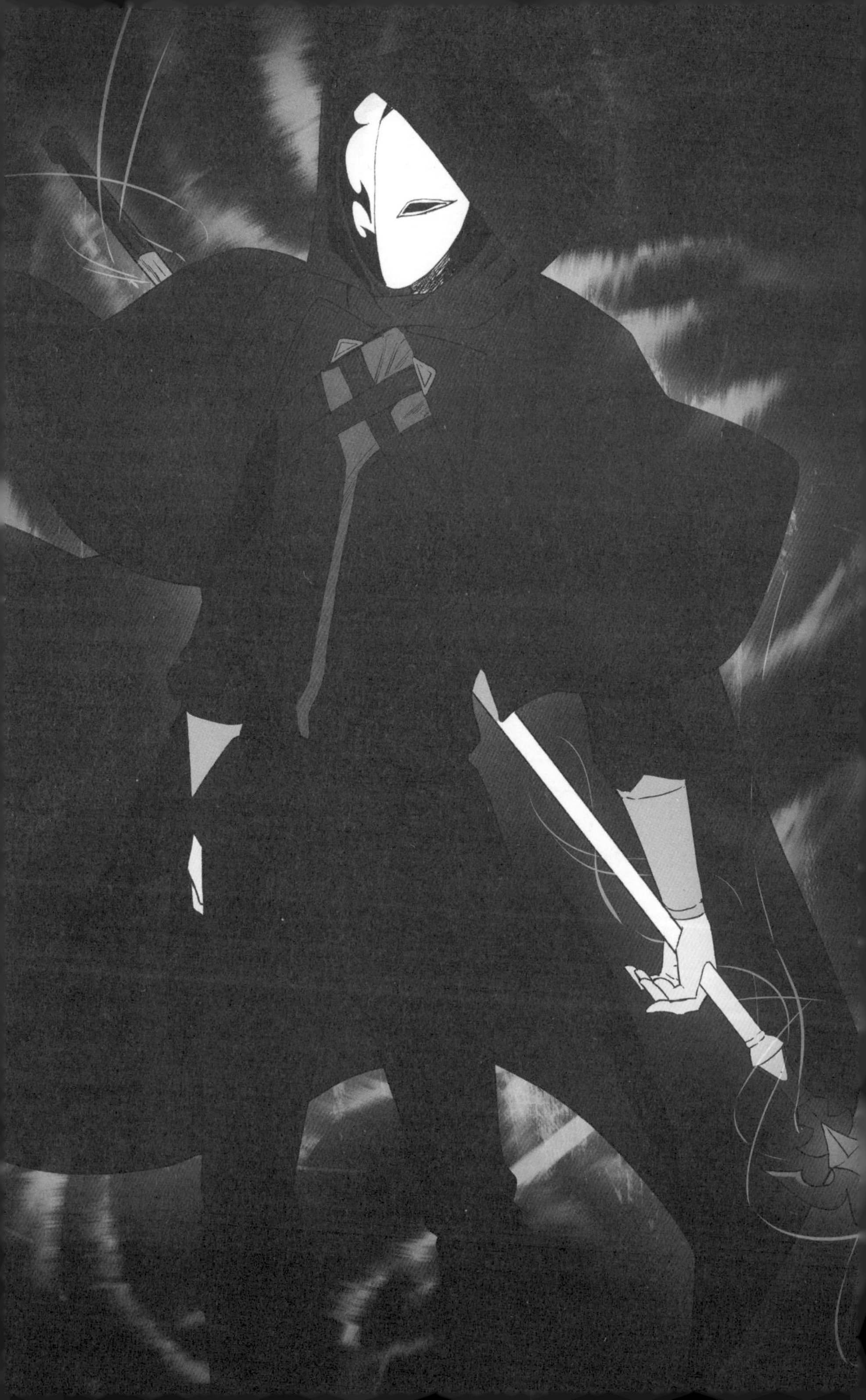

Chapter VII: Inglis, Age 15—Orders to Defend the Hieral Menace (7)

However, Ivel rushed the black-masked man himself. "I don't take orders from you! I know, I'll take it out while it's still transforming!"

"No! That's rude!"

Attacking a foe rather than waiting for them to reach full strength showed a lack of respect. Inglis leaped after Ivel, but she had no time.

Sistia had completed her transformation into a weapon, and a golden spear appeared in the masked man's hand. It looked like a longer and more impressive version of the golden spear Sistia had used. He thrust the spear forward with one hand. Even to Inglis, who had activated Aether Shell, the tip of that thrust was just a flash of light.

The spear pierced Ivel's shoulder—and his shoulder and upper arm disappeared without a sound.

Inglis gasped.

The flurry of thrusts flashed aggressively. As each blow landed, Ivel's torso, hips, legs, and head each disappeared. In the end, there was nothing left. It was all over in the blink of an eye.

"What?!"

Skreee-skreee-skreee! Vwoom!

Inglis heard the spear pierce the air multiple times, resonating with the masked man's aether.

Then another series of sounds followed.

Bssh-bssh-bssh-bssssshhhh!

Ivel's body burst apart, each body part exploding. It had all happened so fast that Inglis hadn't heard the sounds of the masked man's assault until after it was over.

But now there was something else headed her away.

Whoosh!

The fierce aftershock of the spear's thrusts fell upon Inglis. "Ugh?! It's too strong!"

Unable to stand against it, she found herself blown away—and where she was flying to, there was no floor. The blast had thrown her from the ship into the air.

"Oh, I'm falling," came her realization.

Well, then, how do I get back? was not a question she had to think about.

Rafinha brought her Flygear below Inglis. "Chris, grab on!"

"Thanks, Rani!" Inglis twisted to adjust her trajectory and landed aboard the Flygear. "All right, now back up over the ship! I'm ready for a big fight!"

"A-Are you sure that's a good idea?" Rafinha was understandably uneasy now, having seen the power of a transformed hieral menace.

"I don't know. But that's what makes it so exhilarating, you know?"

"Th-Then isn't it okay if we leave now? I'm worried about Ripple, Leone, and the others too..."

As if he'd overheard, the Steelblood Front leader said, "The Highland ambassador has fallen. Their battleship is ours. Those are sufficient results for us. If you wouldn't mind, we'd prefer to leave."

"I cannot allow—" Inglis began to shout.

Boooooom!

The huge sound did not come from the center of the capital, where this battlefield was. A pillar of light rose high into the sky. The pair of students recognized that location.

"Chris, that's—"

"Yeah. That's from the knights' academy."

The pillar of light faded, and a gigantic humanoid form appeared in its place. It was a demihuman magicite beast, far larger than any Inglis had seen before. It seemed as tall as the palace. Gems were shining on its body in all the colors of the rainbow, meaning...

"It's a Prismer!" Inglis and Rafinha exclaimed together.

"Wow, it's amazing... Hey, Rani, you see that, right? It really is a Prismer."

"Y-Yeah, it is..."

Chapter VII: Inglis, Age 15—Orders to Defend the Hieral Menace (7)

It was different from the frozen, birdlike one they had seen in Ahlemin, but still, Inglis had longed to fight one of these powerful creatures for a long time. A Prismer was the ultimate magicite beast, said to be strong enough to destroy an entire country. Only a holy knight wielding a transformed hieral menace could supposedly be its match in a fight.

Ever since Inglis had heard of them when she was little, she had trained with the pursuit of defeating one.

At last, I've found one that's still moving! Now I can fulfill the goal I set for myself back then! How could I not tremble in excitement?

"To be precise, it's still not complete," the black-masked man interjected. "Only half of its body is covered in those rainbow stones. But if left alone, it will become a full Prismer sooner or later."

He was right. Half of the demihuman Prismer's body was speckled with colors rather than with the full rainbow sheen. It reminded Inglis of a larva, but she could sense an enormous amount of power within it.

"Ahh... I can't decide, which one do I wanna fight..." Inglis's eyes glittered as she looked back and forth between the black-masked man and the growing Prismer. *Fighting the black-masked man means fighting him* and *a transformed hieral menace, so he'd be a great enemy too. So many choices! This is a grand battlefield; there are so many powerful foes!*

"Get a hold of yourself, Chris!"

Rafinha's fingers tugged on Inglis's cheeks sharply. "What are you thinking?! That doesn't matter! We need to get back to the knights' academy! Leone, Liselotte, Ripple—everyone needs us there!"

"Vuh! R-Rahi, vuh..."

"What?" Rafinha let go of Inglis's cheek, unable to understand.

"Everyone's there, so that means they should be fine for a while. See?"

A large ward appeared to isolate the larval Prismer, likely the work of Principal Miriela; the ward was powerful enough for them to see even from far away. There were other impressive people there too. Principal Miriela wasn't a holy knight but had a special-class Rune regardless, and there was Silva with his own special-class Rune. Leone and Liselotte were there, and most importantly, Yua was probably helping too, although

Inglis and Rafinha had no way of knowing how seriously she was acting. The depth of Yua's strength was unfathomable.

They won't be taken down that easily, Inglis thought.

"A ward...?! Ah! But still, it's dangerous!" Rafinha said.

Spots of light appeared all over the larval Prismer's body, scattering rays in all directions.

"It's okay!" Inglis insisted. The ward held the rays back, preventing them from leaking out. The city surrounding the knights' academy was untouched, and the ward was holding up.

Rafinha sighed in relief. "Good. The city's safe..."

"See? I told you they'd be okay. You need to believe in your friends."

"Or maybe you just want time to fight the guy in the mask first? Knowing you, you want to fight them both at the same time—"

"Why, of course not. I'm just thinking of the circumstances. If we let him go, who knows what he'll do after we leave? Worst case, he might even go after His Majesty." Inglis inwardly cringed, but kept her face as if nothing had happened.

"But he said he just wanted to leave?"

"What are you saying? He's a bad guy. A guerrilla. We shouldn't trust him. After all, we're supposed to be on the side of justice."

"Well... I think you're about as trustworthy as he is..."

"Huh?! Why?!"

"You, talking about justice? Sounds fishy to me. I know you're up to something!"

"But don't you like justice, Rani?"

"It's fine when *I* talk about justice! My pure heart is honest about it!"

A disdainful voice interrupted their squabble. "My goodness, what a troublesome pair. Get out of here. We don't have time to play with you," Sistia said. She was back in her hieral menace form.

"Wait, don't change back! I still want to fight you!" Inglis said.

"Silence! I'm neither a circus act nor your plaything!"

"Sorry, but she's right," the masked man followed. "I'm also worried about the strain on her. Example is better than precept. We'll be taking our leave. Let's go, Sistia."

"Yes!"

Chapter VII: Inglis, Age 15—Orders to Defend the Hieral Menace (7)

"I won't—" Inglis began to yell.

"Wait, Chris! It's fine. Let them go!" Rafinha insisted.

Suddenly, something moved within the ward at the knights' academy. It was as bright as the sun and filled the ward with a dazzling light.

"Wh—?! That... That's the same light we saw when the hieral menace transformed into a weapon, isn't it, Chris?!"

Inglis knew Rafinha was right. "Looks like it."

"Meaning, Ripple probably returned to normal and turned into a weapon! Hooray!" Rafinha cheered. "They might be able to beat that Prismer! All right. Then we can capture these two—"

"No! Not allowed! We need to get back to the knights' academy. It's dangerous!" Inglis yelled. True, that light had resembled the light from Sistia's transformation, but it had still been different somehow. Completely different.

"Right, right. The real danger is that they might defeat the Prismer, right? And you want to fight it first?"

"You're not quite wrong, that's fine, but we need to hurry to the knights' academy!"

The man in the black mask spoke up as if he could see straight into Inglis's thoughts. "That's for the best. If you don't hurry, you may not make it in time."

"It's a shame," she responded. "I wasn't able to fight you as much as I wanted—then, until we meet again. Pardon us."

"Just as well. There's no gain for us in fighting you—only a great threat."

There seemed to be no more time for conversation.

"Come on, Rani, let's go! Hurry!"

"G-Got it!"

The Flygear carrying the two flew off at full speed toward the knights' academy.

Chapter VIII: Inglis, Age 15—Orders to Defend the Hieral Menace (8)

Shortly before Inglis and Rafinha encountered the leader of the Steelblood Front, the battle against the horde of magicite beasts was reaching a fever pitch. The knights' academy students and Principal Miriela had contained the chaos to the sub-dimension they had created to keep the fight against the creatures that Ripple had summoned away from the outside world.

"C'mon!" Yua yelled.

Whoosh!

Some powerful magicite beasts had meant to attack her from either side, but Yua's swift karate chops slashed them in half vertically.

"Wow, you really are amazing, Yua!" Liselotte had seen the attack up close, and she couldn't help feeling astonished. Even Inglis couldn't take down a magicite beast bare-handed. *Just how does Yua do it?* she wondered.

Liselotte didn't know, but Yua's strength was a clear boon. The group had defeated many magicite beasts, probably dozens, but they'd never have been able to do so without Yua's help.

"Thanks, Spike," Yua said.

"You're, ah, welcome..." Liselotte did wish Yua would ease off on the strange nicknames, though.

"I'm getting a bit tired," Yua said.

"Yes, and I as well." Liselotte had been fighting while using her Gift at full power repeatedly without a break.

Yua and Liselotte weren't the only ones tired; everyone was starting to feel worn out, including Principal Miriela and Silva, who were supplying Ripple with mana so that she could continue to summon more magicite beasts.

"Silva, how are you holding up?" Miriela asked.

"It's tough," Silva answered. "But Lady Ripple's still absorbing power from us, isn't she?"

"Yes. That she is…"

They still had more beasts to summon; Principal Miriela and Silva had a strong sense of that.

"So we can't stop yet! Let's keep going!"

"Yes… Everyone! There's more coming! Be careful!"

Despite their exhaustion, Principal Miriela and Silva sent more of their mana to Ripple. Once again, the vortex-like twists in space opened up. This time, three of the stronger magicite beasts appeared.

"Everyone, please—!" Miriela said as encouragement to her students while she and Silva focused on their own duty, but as they focused, they noticed something was very wrong.

Vreeeee!

The dark globe covering Ripple was suddenly changing. Various colors swirled and shimmered, becoming seven distinct colors. Miriela and Silva felt Ripple pulling at their mana with a greater intensity than before.

"Ugh?! Wh-What's going on?!" Silva gasped.

"Ripple's absorption has gotten much stronger for some reason…!" Principal Miriela managed to say. *At this rate, it will be hard to give her any more!*

While the two of them did their best to keep going, the others were already in the process of wiping out the three magicite beasts that had appeared. Yua went for one head-on, and Liselotte distracted another. That left the third magicite beast, which was gathering its power to use its wide-hitting heat rays.

Chapter VIII: Inglis, Age 15—Orders to Defend the Hieral Menace (8)

Liselotte noticed what it was doing. "I won't let you do that!" she shouted as she pulled out her wings.

However, with a *poof*, her Gift's white wings faded away. She'd reached the limits of her endurance. "Someone must attack this one for me, please!"

"I'll do it!" Leone's greatsword Artifact extended, sending the magicite beast flying.

"Thank you, Leone!"

"Nice, Also Boobies," Yua said as she took on her own target.

Without paying that comment any mind, Leone let out a grunt. "But sorry, I'm at my limits!"

The separate dimension faded away, replaced with their original scene: the lecture hall at the knights' academy. The other students whose Artifacts had been sequestering the group away were drenched in sweat as they called out.

"Sorry, no way I can keep this up anymore!" one said.

"Me neither!" another said.

With everyone exhausted, it was hard to continue on as a vanguard in the other dimension. "Everyone's at their limit… It's going to be hard to fight for much longer!" Leone said.

"For now, let's defeat the magicite beasts already on our doorstep!" Principal Miriela ordered.

Yua did exactly that, quickly delivering a karate chop. "There." The head of the magicite beast she faced fell to the ground.

But the magicite beast Liselotte was fighting was still in action, and the one Leone had sent flying clambered to its feet and began to build power again.

"Here they come again!" Liselotte announced.

"All right, then I'll—" Silva stood to lend a hand, but he couldn't see as he got to his feet quickly. He felt dizzy and swayed. The late-stage transfer of mana to Ripple had been more of a strain on him than he'd expected. "Ugh!"

He wasn't in time, and the magicite beast fired a blast of heat rays at the students' circular formation. They'd managed to prevent all of those destructive attacks—until now.

"Ahh!"

"Oh no!"

As shouts arose, a four-legged form that glowed a deep blue placed itself in the path of the heat rays meant for the students. It took the impact and exploded with an intense flash.

Boooooom!

The explosion and the force canceled each other out. The magicite beast's heat rays disappeared.

Leone gasped. "A lightning beast?!"

As if responding to her, four more of them appeared and surrounded the magicite beast all at once. As their opponent swiped at the new creatures...

Boooooom!

The lightning beast exploded, blowing off the magicite beast's arm.

"Gwohhhh?!"

As it staggered backward, the remaining lightning beasts crashed into it, adding more explosions. Once the destruction cleared, the magicite beast was no more.

"Hey, Lady Arcia! Get back now!" a voice called. The lightning beasts reappeared and faced the last remaining magicite beast, the one that Liselotte was fighting.

"Ah?!"

As if to replace her as she leaped backward, the lightning beasts charged in. The magicite beast suffered the same fate as the previous one, disappearing in an explosion. The flash of light which swept over the lecture hall faded, revealing a young man at the entrance.

Leone gasped. "Brother!"

"Yo. Well, uhh. I'm sure there's a lot to talk about, but for now I'm

Chapter VIII: Inglis, Age 15—Orders to Defend the Hieral Menace (8)

just gonna help out." Embarrassed, Leon scratched the back of his head and smiled.

The students began to buzz. "Hey, is that—"

"Y-Yeah. I've seen him before!"

Leon was a former holy knight. He'd once been considered this country's hero. More than a few of the students knew his face.

"Brother! What are you doing here?!" Leone yelled, and then everyone in the room grasped the situation. It was well known that she was the sister of Leon, the traitor who had abandoned his rank as a holy knight to turn to the Steelblood Front.

"So the Steelblood Front is here to interfere too?!"

"Of all the times to—!"

"Are we going to have to fight an ex-holy knight?!"

The students were furious.

"Hey, hey, hold it," Leon protested. "You saw what just happened, right? I get that it's probably hard to believe, but I'm here to help out. Hey, Miriela, say something to your students."

"You've made your bed, now you have to lie in it. I can't protect you from the consequences of your own actions." Principal Miriela maintained a stern expression.

"Well, that much is true, ha ha ha."

"It's nothing to laugh about! Do you realize how hard things were for Leone when you left her behind? I understand you have your own beliefs, but I can't stand behind them. Leone is one of my students—and I don't forgive anyone who hurts my students, even if they are their flesh and blood."

Leon's expression turned serious. He paused to bow his head slightly to Miriela. "I'm grateful for that much. Take good care of Leone, will you?"

She sighed. "Do you think you'll be forgiven just for helping here?"

"Of course not. I know being forgiven just for this is too good to be true. But hey, I'm just following orders."

However, when giving the order, the black-masked man had said to Leon, "No matter what others think, one should not abandon one's cause. If there's something you want to protect, you should protect it. And if that results in us walking the same path, so much the better."

"Principal Miriela, we need any assistance we can get! And a former holy knight's strength is formidable!" Silva said.

"Ooh! Sharp one, ain'tcha? Not bad. You've got potential," Leon remarked.

"Do not misunderstand me!" Silva shot back. "As someone else with a special-class Rune, I can't forgive someone who fled from their duties! When this is over, I'll have you bound immediately and brought to justice! Leone, you're fine with that, right?!"

"Y-Yes, Silva!" Leone replied.

"Sheesh... Ah well, guess I'll just have to make my escape before that." With a shrug, Leon pushed his way into the midst of the circle of students. Approaching Leone and Silva in the center, he produced a sphere from his pocket. It had a mottled pattern, with black and white intertwining. "Here ya go!" Leon threw the sphere at his feet.

Crrrackkk!

As the sphere shattered, the area was filled with a gray mist.

"Wh-What was that?!"

"A smoke bomb?!"

"Be careful, everyone!"

Leon responded to the raised voices with a sigh. "C'mon, have a little faith. You kids are supposed to be the elite! The ones with the future of this country riding on your shoulders! Don't panic, pay attention to what's happening in front of you." But even without his words, some were noticing the effect.

"My strength! It's returning?!"

"It really is! How did—"

"My body feels lighter!"

"Yeah, with this..."

They could use their Gifts at full power again.

"This is mana mist. You've all felt its effects now. Not too shabby, huh? I don't know how the boss does it, but he sure does have some interesting things." Then, he gave orders to Leone.

Chapter VIII: Inglis, Age 15—Orders to Defend the Hieral Menace (8)

"Leone, bring us back into that dimension."

She did not respond.

"C'mon, it's fine. I'm not going to spring some trap on you at this point, right?"

"Understood." Leone tried her best to be blunt. If she said what she was really thinking, she'd regret it. She was relieved that Leon had shown up to save her in this situation. As he'd bowed to Principal Miriela, asking her to take good care of his sister, Leone's feelings of kinship had begun to rush back—even though they shouldn't have. In a critical situation like this, she had to cooperate with him, but she also had to see him as an enemy who happened to share the same goals at the moment. Her heart shouted in distress, not wanting to view him that way. It frustrated her, but she told herself not to let that show.

In any case, with her power back, Leone reactivated her Gift. The scenery around her shifted to a dark, empty space.

"Okay, I'll lend a hand over here. We're feeding Ripple mana so she can summon magicite beasts, right?" Leon knelt down beside Ripple, who was still unconscious, and brushed her with his Artifact gauntlets. "Ugh! Wow, she sure is hungry for it…"

"Silva, we need to do the same!" Miriela said.

"Yes!"

The three each poured mana into Ripple from their Artifacts. As they did, the light shrouding her swelled, becoming brighter and brighter. Exhaustion racked their bodies from the rate and quantity of mana that Ripple absorbed.

"C'mon! All this mana and she's not coming up with anything?" Leon remarked.

"Up until now, they came quickly!" Principal Miriela noted.

Silva agreed. "This is completely different from before!"

Before long, a gigantic distortion suddenly appeared outside the circle.

Booooom!

* * *

A moment later, a huge pillar of light shot up toward the sky. In its aftermath, the dimension created by Leone was destroyed, and the group of students found themselves back at the knights' academy.

"What?! The dimension—?!"

"It was destroyed?!"

Meaning, the pillar of light had considerable power. It pierced the ceiling, then the roof, of the school building, and the shockwave that followed blew away the walls.

"Whoaaaa!"

"Eeeek!"

The other students there were scattered and blown away. All that was left was the rubble of the building—and a mountainous form looming in the middle.

Leone was blown away, but someone caught her, saving her from serious injury.

"Yo. You okay?"

"Brother…" It seemed Leon had caught her. He smiled at her, but she turned away. "What was that?!"

"Yeah. Just look at that thing. Ripple sure did fish up a hell of a beast." Leon pointed to a magicite beast glimmering in seven colors—a Prismer.

"Gwohhhh!"

The roar of the Prismer shook the air around them, gusts striking at their cheeks.

"Th-This is a live Prismer?!" Leone gasped.

It had tremendous power and presence. She had seen the frozen Prismer of Ahlemin many times. But a living, moving one was completely different—by an order of magnitude. An instinctive fear washed over her, and she shivered involuntarily.

"I get it now," Leon said. "Ripple's condition is a punishment on this country from the Highlanders. Seeing a Prismer come from it, it's so obvious now."

A Prismer could destroy an entire country. Leone knew her brother was right—it was an effective way to pass judgment on an entire people.

Chapter VIII: Inglis, Age 15—Orders to Defend the Hieral Menace (8)

"We need to do something... Something! B-But—" What could they even do against such a beast?

"Leone, get that thing back in the dimension!"

"Yes, brother!" Leon's orders snapped her back to attention, and she focused on her Gift. Her Artifact responded, and for a moment their surroundings began to change with a *vo-voom!*

But then her power weakened, and they returned to where they'd been. "It's no good! The Prismer's too strong! I can't restrain it!"

"Gotcha. Then we've got to fight it here!" Almost a dozen lightning monsters spread out around Leon. "Leone, gather everyone who was knocked out and get them somewhere safe! They're going to get caught up in this mess!"

"But I want to fight too!"

A familiar voice called from overhead. "Leone! Are you all right?!" Liselotte was carrying three unconscious students.

"Liselotte! Yes, I'm fine!"

From another direction, Principal Miriela gave orders. "Leone, Liselotte, you two get the unconscious to safety! We'll hold off the Prismer!"

"Got it!" Leone responded.

"Yua! You and Leon, keep drawing its attention!"

"Err... That big beefy thing's scary, though..." Yua protested.

"No back talk! Do it!"

Yua grumbled in shock before she acquiesced, shuddering and nodding nervously. "Y-Yes, ma'am... Guess I have to... Even though it's scary..." She slowly, smoothly, approached the Prismer, gradually trying to work her way behind it—

As if offended by this, the Prismer turned toward Yua and roared. "Gwohhh!"

"Eeek." Yua was afraid, but her face was still expressionless.

"Hey, don't get nervous. But I guess that does make you a good decoy!" The lightning beasts, driven by Leon's will, rushed toward the gigantic Prismer, exploding in its face.

Blammm!

* * *

There was an intense flash of light, and a few scrapes appeared on the incomplete parts of the Prismer—the patches of its hide that were not yet iridescent.

"Wow, you're good," Yua said, impressed.

"Oh? That's good to hear."

"Yeah. Nice, Pops." Yua gave a firm thumbs-up.

"Hey, c'mon, I'm still in my twenties! But I guess I may as well seem old to a kid like you. Hmm... Ah, whatever! Let's do this!"

One by one, the lightning beasts leaped at the Prismer, relentlessly targeting its head with explosions, but they weren't making any progress. Any time they wounded the Prismer, it immediately began to regenerate. The Prismer's durability was fearsome. But the flashes of the explosions blinding its vision were enough to bring it to a halt.

As Miriela watched the pair's attacks, she waved her Artifact staff. "It's working! Keep going! Let's take shelter while we can!" Wards extended in a dome around the Prismer. Because they could not isolate it in another dimension, this was the only way they could keep damage to their surroundings to a minimum. "Prioritize getting the wounded to shelter while we look for a way to take it down! Silva, how's Ripple holding up?!"

"The light's faded, and she's not absorbing our mana anymore!" Silva answered. "I think this is the last demihuman magicite beast!"

"I see—so we just need to hold out!"

"Isn't Lady Ripple going to awaken soon? If we can hold out until then, I can borrow her power and—!"

Leon shook his head and interrupted. "Don't count on it."

"Yes, he's right!" Principal Miriela agreed.

"But why?" Silva argued back. "At times like this, we need a hieral menace's power!"

"That Prismer doesn't seem to be complete yet. We should be able to make do without calling on Ripple."

"Yeah, Miriela's right. Ripple's probably not in the best shape after being sick. We can't force it," Leon agreed.

As Leon and the others discussed things, Yua approached the legs of the Prismer. She swung her arms in wide circles, like she was winding

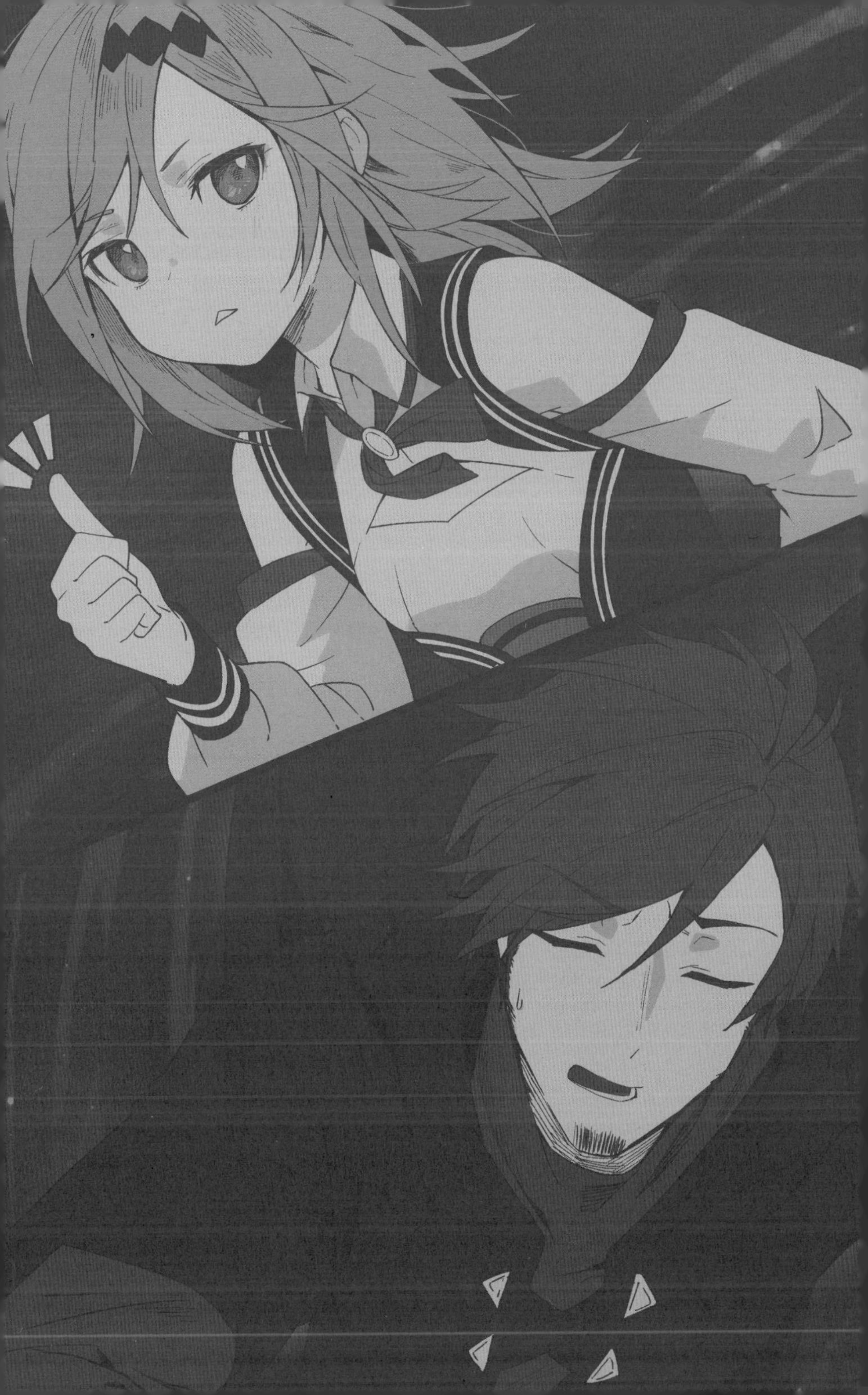

up to gather her strength. Her fists shone faintly from within. "Let's just get this over with…"

She launched from the ground with a powerful *thud*, kicking her knees high. She was near its solar plexus.

Thump!

With a loud, dull impact, Yua's fist pierced its body. It shuddered to a halt. Her punch seemed to have done the trick.

Leon whistled. "Nice punch! It's working! That reminds me of Inglis!"

"No, something is wrong." Yua's expression remained blank.

"Wh—?! What do you mean? You punched through it!"

"No. I'm stuck. It's squishy." Yua was right. Her hand—no, her whole body was being pulled into the Prismer.

Leon gasped. "No! It's trying to absorb her and gain strength that way?! Hold on, I'll get you out of there!"

"Cast a ward on Yua!" Silva called out.

Principal Miriela pointed the ring on her finger at Yua. As she did, Yua's body was enveloped in a pale green light. "This way, the rest of you can make flashy attacks, and Yua will be fine!"

"All right, Yua! This may hurt a little, but try to bear it!" Leon sent his lightning beasts at the Prismer's torso all at once.

The explosions would cut its flesh and free Yua, who would be fine thanks to Miriela's defensive wall around her—or maybe not exactly *fine*, but it was better than the alternative of the Prismer absorbing her. This situation called for drastic measures.

The lightning beasts rushed at the Prismer's legs.

Whoosh!

The Prismer brushed them away with a swipe of its long tail. The fierce blow knocked away the lightning beasts from its torso. They all exploded far away and disappeared. As for the Prismer's tail, it was also

Chapter VIII: Inglis, Age 15—Orders to Defend the Hieral Menace (8)

a bit scorched, but it quickly began to regenerate. Leon's lightning beasts wouldn't be enough like that.

"Tch! You were eating those straight-on before, but now that you've got your hands on your prey, you decide to counterattack?! Were you just playing dumb at first?!" Leon grumbled.

This foe had originally been a sapient demihuman. Now that it was a gigantic Prismer, everyone had assumed it operated solely on instincts, but it was capable of tactics. They had mistakenly judged a book by its cover.

"I'll help!" At Ripple's side, Silva raised his red long gun.

Bang! Bang! Bang!

As the shots rang out, a barrage of fireballs sprang from the barrel of his gun. They transformed as they flew toward the Prismer, becoming a bird of red flames. It traced a complex path toward the Prismer at high speed. In response, the former demihuman held its fingers together in a spear-hand position and thrust it precisely at Silva's bird. His attack couldn't get close to the beast's torso, where Yua was being sucked in.

"Ugh...! So this is the power a Prismer has..." Silva bemoaned.

"A focused strike, maybe?!" Leon suggested. "If we can't slip through, let's push through with brute force!"

Forming in front of him was something many times bigger than the previous lightning beasts. Instead of dispersing and creating many beasts, it was focused on a single point. With mastery of an Artifact, wielders could do impressive things.

"Of course! At the ready!" Silva answered back. A ball of flame several times larger than before formed at the muzzle of his gun.

Yua listened to them in shock. "Are you trying to kill me?"

"Have you ever seen yourself?! You'll be fine! Just be ready!" Silva answered.

"We don't have any other choice!" Leon said.

The large lightning beast and flaming bird rushed toward the Prismer as if one. It was a straight-on offense with no awkward confusion.

When the Prismer saw this, it snapped its mouth open. A thick beam of light shining in seven colors erupted forth from its mouth, easily sweeping away the attack.

"What?!" Silva and Leon gasped. Some of the power was canceled out, but the rest of the light swept toward Leon.

"Ngh?!" He couldn't dodge it. Behind him, Leone and Liselotte had gathered the injured. "Grahhhh!" He crossed his Artifact gauntlets in front of himself to shoulder the blow. The impact pushed him back quite a bit, but somehow he held himself together. Nonetheless, his gauntlets were a wreck. The damage was too severe; they crumbled apart. "You bastard! I've had those things forever!"

"Ahh! Yua?!" Principal Miriela gasped.

"W-We didn't make it in time?!" Silva cried out. Yua's body had been completely absorbed into the Prismer.

"Gwohhhh!"

The Prismer's roar seemed to indicate it was pleased about having absorbed Yua. Its body glowed even brighter, and its skin looked even more prismatic.

"Don't give up! We'll cut her out of there somehow!" Leon yelled.

The protective membrane of light that covered Yua's body was still shining, visible through the Prismer.

The monster gave them no time to move, though. Countless points of light emanated from its surface. The light was reminiscent of the beam that had come from its mouth earlier, except now it was coming from all over its body. Each and every beam appeared to have as much power as the original. Had its absorption of Yua granted it additional strength?

"Oh no! It's going to let those loose through this whole area! Leone, you and all the students must escape into the other dimension! Leon, Silva, fetch Ripple and join them!" Miriela instructed.

"Principal Miriela, what are you going to do?!" Leone asked in worry.

Miriela smiled. "I'll figure out something for myself! If I go into the other dimension, this ward will disappear. Now hurry! I'll be fine!"

Guilt stabbed at Leone's heart, but she knew that if no one was here

Chapter VIII: Inglis, Age 15—Orders to Defend the Hieral Menace (8)

to isolate the Prismer somehow, many students would die. She had no choice but to follow orders.

"Here goes!" Leaving Principal Miriela behind, she separated herself and those near her into another dimension.

The scenery transformed into a dark, shapeless space.

"Mm... I..." Ripple opened her eyes.

As Silva cradled her body, a chorus of voices rose up at once. "Ripple!"

"Ah, everyone... Thank goodness you're okay..." Ripple's face softened into relief as she saw everyone present.

"Don't get ahead of yourself. We're not out of the woods yet. It's getting pretty crazy out there," Leon said.

Ripple's eyes went wide. "L-Leon?! What are you doing here?!"

"This isn't really the time to catch up, y'know?" he replied.

Silva cut in to explain. "This is a serious emergency, so he's lending his support. I apologize; as soon as this is over, we'll have him in chains immediately."

"Hey, hey, what the hell?" Leon objected. "I'm here helping you out, you know!"

"There, there," Ripple said to ease the tension. "That makes sense, but... Hmm. We're in a pretty tight spot, huh? What's happening?"

"Lady Ripple, could you try touching this?" Silva extended the barrel of his charged Artifact to Ripple.

"Mm-hmm." Ripple brushed her hand across it. They had their confirmation immediately. "Oh, hey! I'm not absorbing your mana! So that must mean..."

"Indeed, it seems you've summoned the last of the magicite beasts."

That Ripple's condition no longer attracted demihuman magicite beasts through the sixth sense that they shared proved that demihumans as a species were nearly extinct. They had reached her limit of how many of them she could summon.

"I-I see... That's good," Ripple said, crying. "Then I won't have to cause trouble anymore... I can go back to being your hieral menace..."

Seeing her tears of relief, those close to her could allow themselves to be proud. Not just Silva, but Leone and Liselotte also took pride in their hard work. The risks had paid off.

"But Ripple, we can't celebrate yet," Silva continued.

"Oh, right. You said this is an emergency... Did something happen?"

"Yes. The last magicite beast to be summoned...was a Prismer."

"Whaaaaat?! A demihuman like me turned into a Prismer?! That's crazy!"

"It's still not complete, but it's the beefiest magicite beast I've ever seen. Prismers are on a totally different level from normal monsters," Leon said.

"Where is it?!" Ripple asked. "We need to stop it!"

"Right now it's outside of this dimension, rampaging through the knights' academy. The principal cast a ward to keep it from getting out into the city, but it was about to use an attack that would have hit all of us," Silva explained.

Liselotte continued, "Leone used the power of her Artifact to send us to safety in another dimension. The principal's alone out there to keep the ward up."

"Miriela did *that*?!" Ripple gasped. "But that's so risky... All right, we need to get back out there for her!"

Silva nodded intently in response. "Yes, Lady Ripple! The only thing that can defeat a Prismer is a holy knight wielding a hieral menace in weapon form! I'm still in training, but if you lend me your strength, I'll give it my all! Please!"

"Silva... I... I still can't."

"B-But why?! Do you mean I'm not strong enough?"

"Nuh-uh, that's not it. Leon said that it wasn't complete yet, right? So there could be another way to defeat it. We've gotta try everything we can."

"You agree with the principal, then."

Leon cut in. "The combination of a holy knight and a hieral menace is the last hope for humans on the surface—and last means *last*. When you grow up a bit more, you'll understand."

"As if a man who abandoned his post as a holy knight has room to talk!" Silva fired back.

"Ha ha! I mean, you're not wrong."

Chapter VIII: Inglis, Age 15—Orders to Defend the Hieral Menace (8)

"Anyway," Ripple said, bringing people back to the point. "Let's go, everyone! Leone, can you bring us back out?"

"Yes! Here goes!" Leone released her Gift, and the scenery around them changed. They returned to the ruins of the knights' academy surrounded by wards. The school building was in an even worse state now. Rooms were practically rubble. The ground was covered in holes and large cracks.

"Miriela! Are you okay?"

"Yes, Ripple! Good timing! I'm fine, but I could really use your help!" Principal Miriela was mostly fine, but she had picked up a number of shallow scratches, and she was breathing heavily. The battle had taken a lot out of her, but it was impressive that she'd managed to hold out against the Prismer so well.

"Sure, leave it to me! I've been causing trouble for everyone for so long, now it's my turn to protect you—as a hieral menace!" Twin golden guns appeared in Ripple's hands. She moved nimbly in front of Principal Miriela to protect her before settling her gaze on the Prismer.

She recognized this demihuman.

"What?! No, no... That's... That's too—" She couldn't hold back the tears welling up. She stared in shock.

"Ripple? What's wrong?" Miriela asked.

"My dad... That's my dad! When our village was destroyed by the Prism Flow, he became a magicite beast! And now he's here!"

That was a far-off memory from long before Ripple had even become a hieral menace. It all came rushing back to her now.

Her father, the demihuman chieftain, had been struck by the Prism Flow and became a magicite beast. The village had been wiped out, and Ripple was the only survivor. Since then, her father had lived on as a magicite beast, evidently becoming a Prismer.

"Wh-What?!" Principal Miriela gasped.

"That's your father, Lady Ripple?!" Silva repeated in complete surprise.

"Yes, I'm sure of it! So much time has passed since then... He survived somewhere in the world..."

Over those long years, how many people had he hurt? How many

169

lives had he taken? Just how far had he deepened his sins? Ripple found herself asking those painful questions.

Principal Miriela winced. "Ripple, I'm sorry... That's terrible..."

"Then allow us to shoulder this burden, Lady Ripple! We can't ask you to fight your own family!" Silva said.

"Gwohhh!"

But the Prismer showed no mercy. Stomping the ground, it moved with a quickness that belied its size, pointing its spear-hand gesture directly at Ripple again.

"N-No! That doesn't mean I want to sit this one out!" Ripple somersaulted high, dodging the Prismer's strike. At the same time, she rained down gunfire on its hand. Its rainbow-colored skin repelled her shots, but she pierced the parts that had not completed the Prismer transformation process. The force of her attack thrust its hand into the ground.

"Now!" Ripple ran up the Prismer's arm to its shoulder as nimble as a cat. "*Because* you're my father, I have to do this! Before you're too far gone!"

Pointing the muzzles of her guns at its neck, she fired a burst of bullets made of light. The still-incomplete skin at the base of its neck opened as deep wounds formed—only to begin healing and closing up. Before long, it would be as if nothing had happened.

"You can heal already?! But if I attack harder—!" Ripple hastened her fire rate, putting her all into an onslaught.

"Gwohhh!"

The demihuman Prismer's free hand reached up toward Ripple to swat her away.

"I don't think so!" She gracefully dodged the extended hand without pulling away from the Prismer's neck. Dodging left and right, she kept up her focused fire, not letting the regeneration outpace her assault. The wounds deepened and widened.

Chapter VIII: Inglis, Age 15—Orders to Defend the Hieral Menace (8)

Silva watched, transfixed by the sight. "Beautiful! A true hieral menace!"

Ripple's rapid fire was gouging out more and more of its neck. She started to have hope that she could take off its head. "It's not too late! This is working! Everyone else, attack too! Focus on its neck, and cut off its head!" Ripple yelled.

"Yes, Lady Ripple!" Silva said.

"Leave it to me!" Leon called.

Both Silva and Leon readied their Artifacts to support Ripple, Leon now using a dagger to replace his broken gauntlets. But before they could make an all-out attack, the surface of the magicite beast's body lit up once more. Bright points of light shone in all directions from its body, signaling it was charging the same destructive rays it had used earlier.

"Lady Ripple, this is the attack we took shelter from earlier!" Silva warned.

Ripple pulled herself together after a moment of alarm. "Everyone but Miriela and me, take shelter! Leone, if you will!"

"Of course!" Leone nodded to Ripple and focused her power into her Artifact. "All right, here goes!" Leaving Miriela and Ripple behind, the others disappeared into the other dimension.

"Miriela, try to hold up through it rather than following me!"

"Yes! I'll do my best!"

The magicite beast fired its beams of light in all directions within the wards Principal Miriela had set up. Closest to the Prismer, Ripple would almost certainly take the brunt of the onslaught.

"I can't let those hit me!" she told herself. Focusing her efforts only on dodging would give the Prismer time to heal. She needed to keep up her rate of fire as she evaded.

To the right and the left, ahead and behind—every direction was lit up like firecrackers. And as the Prismer moved, the beams' trajectory changed.

Ripple twisted, leaped, always finding a place where the beams wouldn't hit. Of course, the aim of her twin guns would be off, but that wasn't a problem. Even in human form, hieral menaces had an Artifact-like power to twist dimensions. Eris could unleash a slash from a distance. Ripple could change the path of her bullets. She couldn't keep it up for long, but it was a powerful skill.

While continuing to evade, she kept the bullets coming through different dimensions toward the Prismer's wounded neck. Finally, its storm of light stopped.

"All right! At this rate—" *I can switch to firing directly and keep going!* Or so Ripple thought.

Suddenly, there was an explosion of light in various colors all along the magicite beast's wounds. Its injuries closed instantly.

"Wh—?! No way! It healed?!" Ripple gasped.

Its former wounds had the iridescence of a rainbow; it was nearing the end of its transformation into a full Prismer.

"It's getting stronger during this! It's nearly complete!" Principal Miriela warned.

"But...! But it's not done yet!" Ripple, not giving up, kept up her fire.

"Gwohhh!" it roared, lunging at Ripple. It was even faster than before.

"Ugh...!" Still dodging, she tried to leap onto the Prismer's arm again, but as if it had known she'd do that, its other hand quickly grabbed her and tried to crush her with all its strength.

"Aaaaaagh!" she screamed. Its massive body was too strong. Her bones were about to crack.

"Ripple?!" Miriela was busy dealing with the rays of light.

"M-Miriela, you need to focus on your wards! I'll be fine—ugh!" Ripple knew their priority was to keep the Prismer from escaping.

"But—!"

"It's okay! Hieral menaces aren't that soft!"

A hieral menace's body was completely different from that of a normal human; given enough time, they could always regenerate. She could heal wounds that would be fatal for a normal human. Ripple had even lost both of her arms in the past, but she'd recovered nonetheless.

Rather than people who could take the form of Artifacts, they were more properly Artifacts which could take the form of people. So the standard rules of the human body did not apply. Even Ripple didn't know for sure how hard of an attack it would take to kill her. Even if every bone in her body was crushed, she would probably heal over time. Over her long history as a hieral menace, she had experienced quite a bit of pain. She was used to it. After all, there were things that left scars far worse than what she got from physical pain. This wasn't enough to bring her down!

"Damn you!" she growled.

Splrrrch!

Even as the Prismer crushed Ripple and beams of light leaked forth, she hadn't let go of her guns. Instead, she had been gathering her power; it took time to ready, but she could unleash a single powerful shot. Once it was charged enough, she blew apart the Prismer's hand with it. She didn't go unscathed, but she could rely on her hieral menace hardiness.

"Gwohhh!"

Shocked by the attack, the Prismer's grip loosened.

"Good fathers don't try to crush their daughters!" Ripple yelled. She slipped out through the gap that opened and flew backwards, but something was off. She felt a stabbing pain in her legs. Not sticking the landing, she tumbled to the ground with a wince.

"Ripple!" Miriela cried.

"Ugh... Something's not right with my legs... This isn't good..." Ripple wasn't quick on her feet anymore.

At that moment, a dimension popped up from which Leone and the others returned. As soon as Silva saw Ripple injured, he rushed over to her, his face red with concern and anger. "Lady Ripple! Your legs! Are you all right?!" He reached out a hand to help her up.

Leon gasped. "Be careful! It's still—!"

His warning rang out sharply. The Prismer was charging forward to seize Ripple again.

"Ugh...! I won't allow you to touch Lady Ripple when she's wounded!" Silva stood before Ripple, trying to defend her.

"No! Silva, get out of the way!" Ripple pushed him to the side and faced the Prismer's attack herself. She knew that attack from before would almost definitely kill him. As a cadet holy knight and the holder of a special-class Rune, Silva was strong, but he was still a flesh-and-blood human. He couldn't survive what a hieral menace could endure.

"Ah! Nghhhh...!" Ripple grunted as the Prismer grabbed her again with a tight grip. This time, she endured without screaming. If it bought the others time to think of a plan, she could hang on.

"You bastard! Let go of Lady Ripple!" Panicking, Silva shot a flaming blast from his Artifact at the Prismer's hand around Ripple, but the Prismer swatted it away with its other hand. "Ugh...!"

From behind Silva, the rest of the group decided on their course of action.

"Hey, Miriela! What do we do now? Even if it's incomplete, this Prismer's a hell of a foe!" Leon said.

"That it is... Let's leave destroying it for later. For now, we'll lead it away from the city! If we draw it far enough away from a settlement, it may decide to go somewhere else!" Principal Miriela said.

"Okay! By the way, where's Inglis?! If she were here, she might be able to come up with something!"

"She's at the palace, protecting His Majesty. When things calm down there, I'm sure she'll be right back."

"I see! So that makes buying time an even better plan!"

Silva couldn't agree with that, though. "Please wait! If we do that, the city will be destroyed along the Prismer's path! Our best chance would be for Ripple to transform and finish it off here! Plus, why are you just standing there talking?! We need to hurry and save her!"

"Hieral menaces are tougher than you think! She's still okay!" Leon insisted.

"I understand, but someone that slender, that delicate—"

Splrrrch!

Again, Ripple fired off an explosive shot in the Prismer's hand with stored-up power. Her body slipped from its hand as it loosened. This time, she smashed directly into the ground, unable to land gracefully.

"Lady Ripple!" Silva rushed to her side and tried to help her up.

Chapter VIII: Inglis, Age 15—Orders to Defend the Hieral Menace (8)

"I—I'm okay, I'm okay..." As Ripple strained to speak, she coughed up blood.

"Ah, Lady Ripple! Is that blood?!"

"Ugh... I think I broke a rib... But I'm fine. It takes more than this to defeat a hieral menace."

"But you're...! Please don't do anything so risky!" Silva protested.

"No! We want to lure him out of the city, right?" Ripple asked. "So I have to be the bait!"

As Ripple staggered to her feet, Leon stepped past her and stood in front. "You should sit back. I'll draw it away!"

"Please...! Once I get a little rest, I'll—!" Ripple fell to her knees again.

Silva placed a hand on her shoulder. "Lady Ripple, please! Transform into a weapon, and lend me your strength! Leading it out of the capital is nonsense! The only way to deal with this situation is for me to borrow your true power!"

Ripple immediately shook her head. "No! We can't do that! We can still try to stop him without resorting to that!"

"I don't want to see you get hurt like this!" Silva insisted. "Ever since you saved my life as a child, I've been training to fight alongside you! I've grown strong, just like you said! Isn't this the time to use that strength?!"

Surprised, Ripple paused. "Silva... Time sure does fly, huh? For a little boy like that to grow up into a man... I'm getting older too."

"Then lend me your strength! I want to repay you for saving my life by protecting your heart! I'll save you from having to fight your father because of Highland!"

"Silva... But, but— Agh!" From within Ripple's body, a light began to shine like the sun—the sign that a hieral menace was transforming into a weapon. "N-No way! I didn't mean for this to happen!"

A hieral menace could only transform if her own will and that of a holy knight with a special-class Rune aligned. No matter how Silva felt, Ripple shouldn't be able to transform if she didn't want to do so. However, it was clear that she was transforming into her weapon form, as if Silva's will was driving her.

This was an immediate cause for panic in Leon's mind. "C'mon, Ripple, stop! It's too early to give up! And he's so young…!"

"I… I can't! I'm not doing this! He's dragging me along!"

This was unheard of for Ripple as well. The hearts of a hieral menace and holy knight had to be as one; it required unity. In that case, if Ripple didn't want it to happen, why was it happening?

Did Silva not know what was happening and just genuinely want to use her strength for her sake? Did the combination of Silva's deep respect for Ripple and her warm thoughts of him mean their hearts were close enough? Did Ripple deep down want to free her father, who had become a Prismer, as soon as possible? It seemed like a combination of many things that allowed Silva to push her into transforming.

"Ahhhhh!" she yelled, frightened. *I can't stop!*

Ripple's body glowed brighter and brighter, and when it reached its peak, her body was no longer that of a girl—but a golden, gleaming double-barreled long gun.

"I can feel it… This is incredible! This can defeat anything—even a Prismer!" Silva said.

With excitement on his face, Silva gripped the golden gun that Ripple had transformed into.

"No! C'mon, stop! Put her down!" Leon barked.

Principal Miriela was equally tense. "Silva, calm down! Don't give in to the power!"

Leone watched her elders yell and had no idea why they were upset. If they could take down the Prismer with Ripple transformed into a weapon, wasn't that fine? She agreed with Silva wholeheartedly; it would be hard to lead the Prismer out of the capital and would probably cause a lot of damage. If they had time to lead the residents to safety, that could minimize casualties, but that wouldn't save the houses, shops, and other buildings on the route from being destroyed along the way. In her mind, a knight also had a duty to protect where people lived and worked.

Liselotte said, "What a beautiful light, fitting of the true power of the hieral menaces who watch over us…" She was genuinely riveted to the scene.

"Y-Yes…but…" Leone still found it somehow unsettling. The light

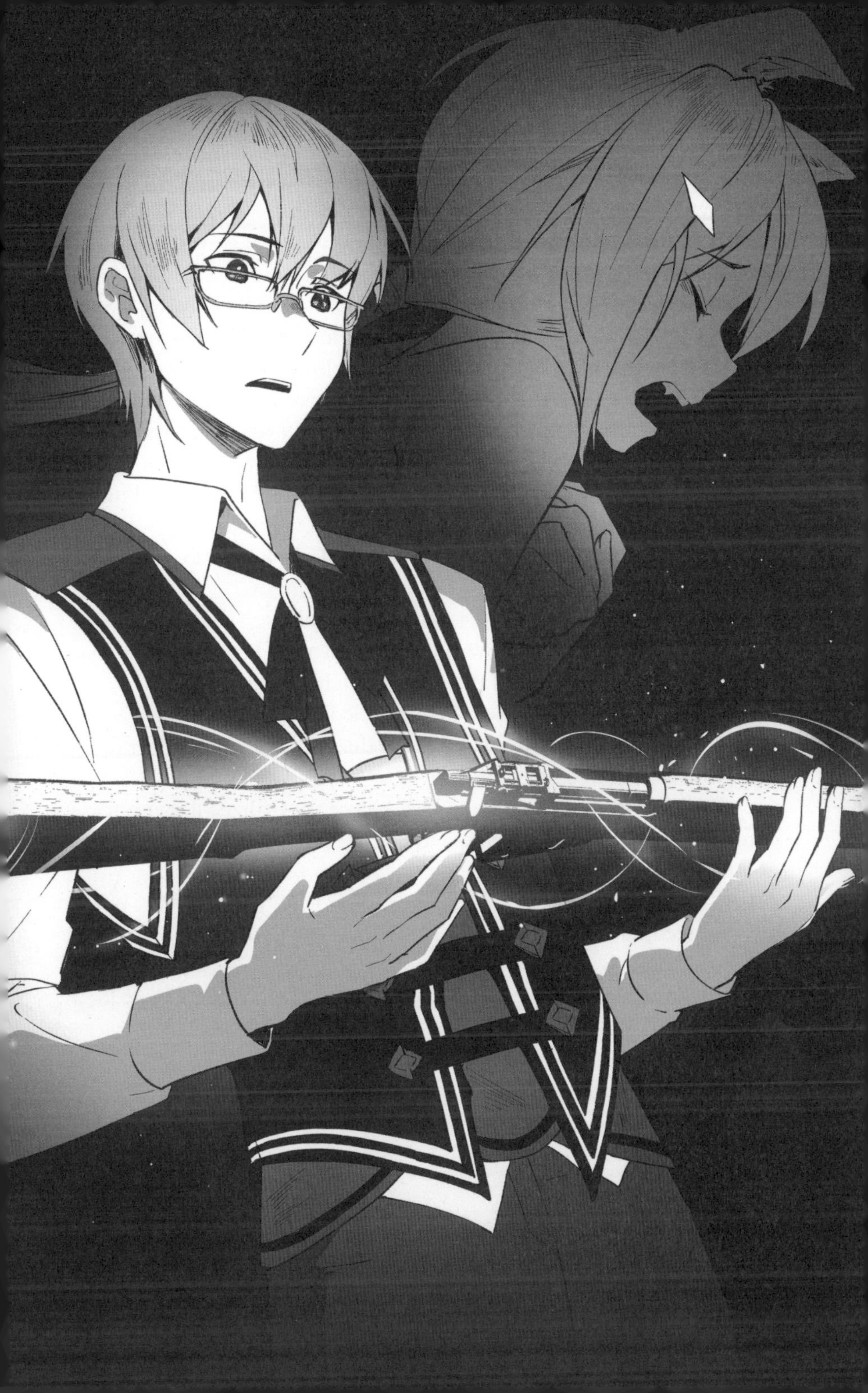

was so divine, so beautiful, but it scared her nonetheless. She couldn't explain why, but her fear was real.

"Get a hold of yourself! You're still not ready!" Leon tried to grab the gun that Ripple had become.

"Lady Ripple responded to my will! I'll do this! Out of my way!" Silva merely brushed Leon and effortlessly sent him flying. "A-Amazing... Hieral menaces really are like goddesses watching over us! This strength is unlike anything else!" Nodding confidently, he pointed the barrel of the gun at the Prismer. "Lady Ripple's father—I have pity for you... But with Lady Ripple's power, I'll shoot you down!"

"Tch! I'm telling you, stop!" Leon rose to his feet, and stood in the line of fire toward the Prismer.

"Are you a fool?! Get out of the way or I'll fire at you along with the Prismer!"

"Not gonna happen! So put down that gun!"

"I can't do that! So I'll take you both down!" A huge ball of intense light formed at the muzzle of the gun, as bright as the sun.

"Ah! No, Silva!" Principal Miriela called out.

"Why?! Taking down this traitor at the same time would be killing two birds with one stone!"

"W-Wait, Silva!" Leone called out before she realized it, her unease compelling her. Leon was their enemy, but he must have had a reason for going so far to try to stop Silva.

"Gwohhh!"

The Prismer let out a roar as the light spread out over its body for a third time. Its large ray attack was charging.

"Look out! Leone, get back!" Principal Miriela called out.

"Y-Yes!"

But at the moment that Leone responded, a louder sound overlapped with her voice.

Crrrack!

* * *

Chapter VIII: Inglis, Age 15—Orders to Defend the Hieral Menace (8)

The ward Principal Miriela had placed shattered with a high-pitched noise. At the same time, a blur of a shape slipped close to Silva.

Blam!

"Gah…?!" Silva's eyes rolled back. He collapsed. The golden gun slipped from his hands and returned to her form as a demihuman girl.

Her eyes were wide with surprise. Reflected in them was the person who had knocked Silva unconscious.

Inglis had just landed a beautiful elbow strike.

Chapter IX: Inglis, Age 15—Orders to Defend the Hieral Menace (9)

"I-Inglis?!" Ripple said, surprised.

"Looks like I made it in time," Inglis said with a grin.

Rafinha, who'd stayed in the Flygear hovering above, gaped at the sight. "Wait, how…?! What?! It looks more like you just attacked someone on your own side so you could steal their turn!" Even she hadn't expected Inglis to knock Silva unconscious.

"Aha ha ha. Poor Silva," Leone said with a quiet but startled chuckle.

"Indeed," Liselotte agreed.

"Don't worry about it! Well done!" Ripple exclaimed.

Their principal wasn't so pleased. "*Well done?!* Pleaaase don't break my waaards!"

"Dammit, the shots will get through!" Leon barked. "Miriela, cast another ward!"

"I can't! I need more time!"

The Prismer would wreak havoc on the city if its rays scattered—and it was just about to fire.

"Then I'll take responsibility!" Inglis said. In no time at all, she was cloaked in the pale blue glow of Aether Shell, already close to the Prismer. "Haaaah!"

Thuddd!

* * *

Her kick, containing all her might behind it, sent out an unusually loud echo. The mountain-like body of the Prismer flew up and over the altitude of Rafinha's Flygear. But unlike Ivel, whom she had blasted out of sight during their skirmish, the Prismer didn't travel any great distance. In fact, even while soaring through the air, it kept its stance, staring down at Inglis. Clearly, it hadn't suffered any serious damage. Incomplete or no, this was a Prismer, the strongest kind of magicite beast. It lived up to Inglis's expectations.

"Whoa! She sent the Prismer flying with a kick?!" Leon remarked in surprise.

"I-I can't believe it! Her strength is immense!" Miriela gasped.

"But it's not over! He's gonna shoot!" Ripple cried.

The lights flitting over the body of the Prismer hadn't dissipated; its attack was still oncoming.

"Interesting! All right, show me what you've got!" Inglis beckoned to the Prismer. She couldn't tell if it understood, but nonetheless it let loose rainbow-colored lights from all over its body.

"I-It fired!"

"Th-The city!"

"Th-This is bad!"

As her comrades raised their voices in panic, they stared at the Prismer in the sky. They had failed to notice that Inglis was gone. They only noticed something was different when a beam fired by the Prismer suddenly changed its trajectory. It should have struck the ground and torn the streets apart, but it had shot straight upward.

"Oh! The light changed directions!" Leon said.

It wasn't just one beam, but two, then three, then more and more.

"S-Something's moving them!" Principal Miriela exclaimed.

"It's Inglis! Inglis is punching away its light beams!" Ripple announced.

Precisely—Inglis was moving at full speed and getting ahead of each beam, using her fists to bash away the Prismer's attacks, deflecting them into the sky.

That was why she'd kicked the Prismer into the air. If it was above the city and shot off an attack that fired in all directions, half of those

Chapter IX: Inglis, Age 15—Orders to Defend the Hieral Menace (9)

shots would fly off into the sky and be wasted. If she focused only on the remaining half, it would be possible to deal with all of them. That was Inglis's intuition, at least.

"Disappear into the sky!" she yelled.

Rrrumble! Rrrrrrumble!

The Prismer's beams became a rainbow fireworks display above the city before ultimately disappearing into the sky.

"Good job, Chris! That's the stuff!" Rafinha cheered.

"She's so fast... I didn't even see her move!" Leone remarked.

Liselotte chuckled in amazement. "Aha ha ha... It's so amazing. I can't hold my laughter back... Ahh, the sky's so beautiful."

But Inglis's actions weren't as easy as they looked. Each and every one of the beams of light was *heavy* in a way that even Inglis could feel. She had needed to put her all into repelling them, and it was hard for her to change their course. After repelling a number of them, her hands and feet were numb.

But that numbness, that resistance... It felt good. It was proof of her foe's strength. That meant there was value in this fight.

She breathed in calmly. "Wonderful! This means..."

I've found a fitting foe to try my new technique on!

Now that the Prismer had finished its attack, it continued falling downward on an easy-to-predict path. Even a Prismer couldn't avoid gravity.

And it probably can't avoid an attack aimed at it in the air either. This is my chance! Inglis thought.

She released Aether Shell, focusing the aether swirling around her into a single point. She was preparing an Aether Strike. The mass of pale blue aether began to swell into a gigantic bullet.

Principal Miriela called out to her at that moment. "Inglis! Do you see the green light in its abdomen? Yua's trapped in there! Please, get her out somehow!"

"That's Yua? Understood!" *I can't lose a valuable sparring opponent here!* "Go!"

Blammmmmm!

A blast of aether raced through the sky and caught the Prismer. It crossed its arms in a defensive posture, trying to withstand the Aether Strike. It was neither vaporized in an instant like a lesser magicite beast nor deflecting her attack with an unheard-of technique like the black-masked man had done. It was taking Inglis's power head-on—which was exactly what she had been waiting for!

"Heh heh heh heh!" Inglis's eyes gleamed brightly. She was already crouching, preparing to strike again, but she still needed to gather aether. While she didn't need to do this for small attacks like Aether Pierce, it was hard to fire off major attacks like Aether Strike repeatedly. A short pause was needed before the next aether technique could be used. Inglis focused as hard as she could to hasten the process.

Supportive voices rose up around her.

"W-Wow... It's working!" Leon gasped.

"Y-Yes! Inglis hurt even the iridescent parts of its skin!" Principal Miriela said.

"This is so weird! It's amazing, but I don't really understand where Inglis gets her strength!" Ripple said.

"Gooooooo! Blow that thing away!" Rafinha cheered.

"You can do it! You can take that thing!" Leone called out.

"Indeed, you can triumph, Inglis!" Liselotte shouted.

But Inglis responded to their encouragement differently. "No! C'mon, Prismer! Hang in there! Endure it!"

"Whaaa?!" the others yelled in unison. They all gawked at Inglis in confusion.

As Aether Shell wrapped her body in pale blue, she became able to use her next aether technique. "All right! With this..."

She quickly leaped into the air toward the Prismer and traced the same path that her Aether Strike had taken, following behind it with immense speed. She put her all into a full-force punch, hitting her opponent as it was still blocking the Aether Strike. So much had happened in such a short span of time.

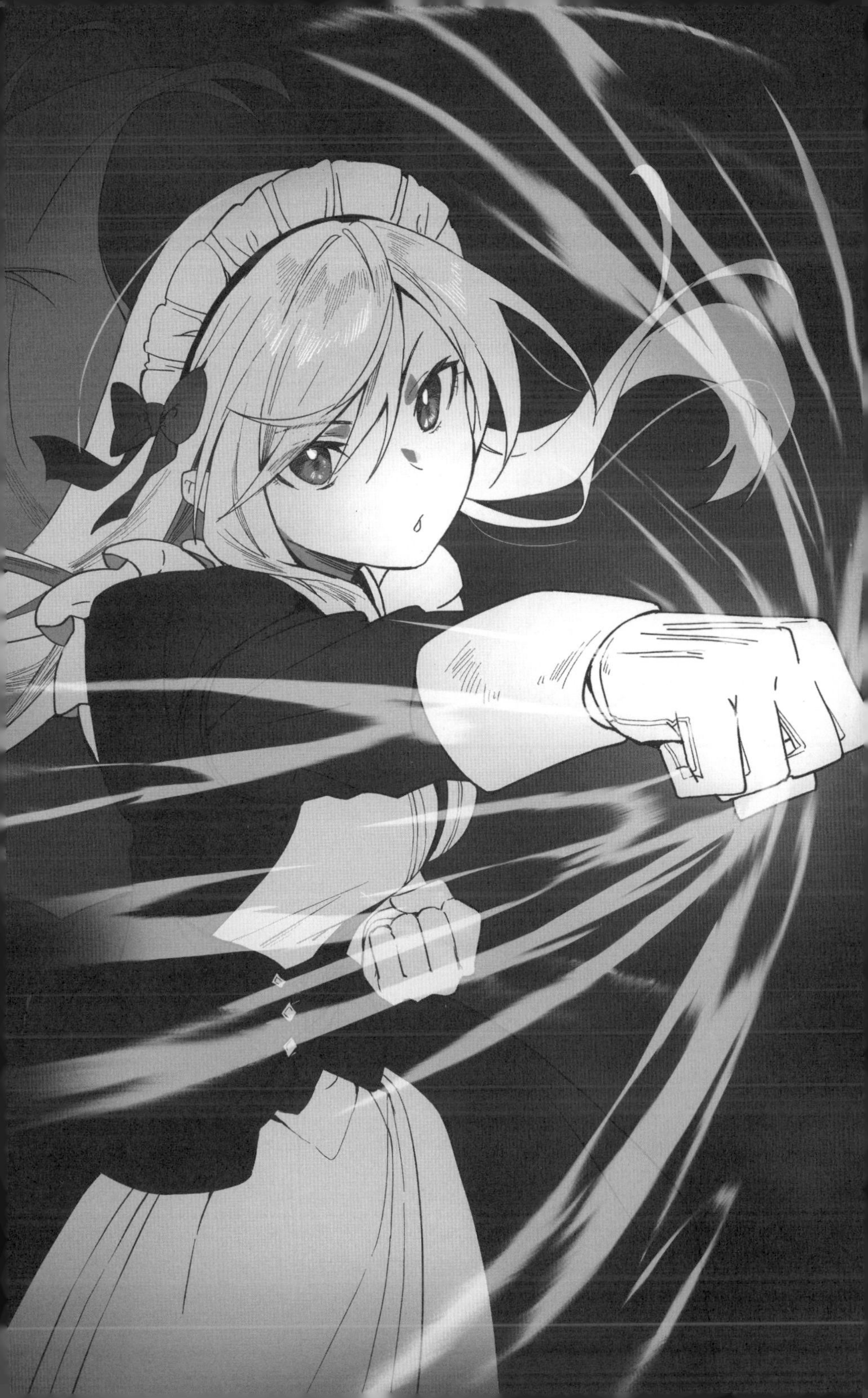

"Take thiiis!" she yelled. Her fist smashed through the Prismer's arms and pierced its body, leaving a gaping hole.

Boooooooooom!

A gigantic explosion of aether lit up the city like a supernova.

This was the new technique she'd been researching; she considered naming it Aether Breaker, perhaps. The technique required her to activate Aether Shell and deliver a blow just as an Aether Strike hit, causing a synergistic effect that raised the destructive power to an explosive level. It must have been several times more powerful than a normal Aether Strike. It was the most powerful technique she'd ever used, even including her experiences in her past life as Hero-King Inglis.

However, there was a drawback: the target had to survive long enough for her to fire an Aether Strike, and then she had to accurately time her Aether Shell-powered punch. She needed to wait a short time after firing Aether Strike in order to activate Aether Shell. However, as she became more practiced with the use of aether, her timing would become more precise.

Regardless, with this technique, Inglis Eucus's power now surpassed that of the old Hero-King Inglis.

Her attack's explosion had created an intense light that blinded the others. When the light faded, everyone was stunned, staring up at the empty sky.

Miriela was the first to speak. "Umm... There's nothing there..."

"Y-Yeah... There isn't even a trace of the Prismer. I know it wasn't fully transformed yet, but still... Wow..." Ripple trailed off.

Rafinha cheered, "Whoa, amazing, Chris! So *that's* the new technique you were talking about. It really is the most powerful ever!"

"B-But what about Yua?!" Leone asked, worried.

"She's fine, Leone," Principal Miriela reassured her. "The barrier covering her is still intact."

"Really?! Then—"

"Yua's okay?!" Rafinha interjected.

"Yes, I'm sure she is," Principal Miriela said, relieved.

Chapter IX: Inglis, Age 15—Orders to Defend the Hieral Menace (9)

At that moment, Inglis returned, a pleasant smile on her face and an unconscious Yua in her arms. "Phew... I sure worked up a good sweat today."

"Inglis!" Principal Miriela cheered. "Ah, thank goodness... Well done!"

"Nice, Inglis! You're the best!" Ripple added.

"What a relief!" Leone said. "For a moment I thought she might have been caught up in Inglis's attacks..."

"But you saved her!" Liselotte finished.

"Yeah. I pulled her out of the Prismer while piercing through it," Inglis replied.

"Good job, Chris! This means we get to keep having our meals covered at the cafeteria!" Rafinha said, delighted.

"Is that correct, Principal Miriela?" Inglis asked.

"Yes, yes, of course!" Principal Miriela nodded.

"All right! Mission accomplished, Chris!" Inglis and Rafinha high-fived.

"My stomach's empty after all those battles. Let's hurry and get something to eat."

"Yeah! Let's!"

It was then that Inglis and Rafinha noticed one crucial detail missing. "Huh...? Where's the cafeteria?" they asked together.

"It was blown away. Once it's rebuilt, you're welcome to eat your fill!" Principal Miriela answered.

"Aaaaaaaaaaaah!" They were screams of terror and despair deeper than that which would come from facing any foe, no matter how powerful. And by the time Inglis and Rafinha had calmed down, Leon had already disappeared.

◆◇◆

Several days later, the repairs to the knights' academy were proceeding at a breakneck pace. Inglis and her classmates took off during a break to give their farewells at the gates. They were seeing off Ripple and Ambassador Theodore, who were returning to the battle against Venefic.

Ambassador Theodore had rushed back to the capital after Principal Miriela's messengers, Lahti and Pullum, informed him of the situation, only for the ambassador to arrive late in the night after the battle had ended. However, his trip had not been a waste, as he had been able to pronounce with clear authority that Ripple would show no more abnormalities.

He had also negotiated with King Carlias to accept Ripple remaining as one of the kingdom's hieral menaces. King Carlias never really had a choice, as Highland's Papal League had refused his offerings and decided against improving their working relationship. The actions of the knights' academy had also gone unquestioned thanks to Ambassador Theodore. He'd smoothed over everything in the aftermath of the events there.

As a result, Inglis and the others were able to focus on rebuilding the academy as they continued to train. The dorms, untouched, afforded them a place to sleep, but the destruction of the cafeteria was an extreme emergency. If it wasn't quickly rebuilt, they wouldn't be able to fill their stomachs. Therefore, Inglis and Rafinha made a proactive effort to help in the rebuilding.

"Thanks, everyone. Thanks to your help, I can go back to the Paladins. Thank you so much." Ripple bowed deeply to those who had come to see her off.

"But isn't it a bit soon for you to return to active duty? Maybe you should recover for a little while first," Silva said with a conflicted expression.

As a hieral menace, Ripple's body was different from a human's, which meant Rafinha's healing Gift wouldn't work on her. Ripple's wounds had to heal naturally. It was true that she had superhuman recovery, but...

"It's fine, it's fine! See?" Ripple thumped herself on the chest. "Ugh! Owww... That did still hurt a bit."

Silva continued insisting, "Please don't push yourself too hard! You should stay here a little bit longer and recuperate—"

"Nah," Ripple interrupted. "It's gonna take a few days to get to the border, and I'll be all healed up by then. Plus, Lord Theodore needs an escort back to the front, right?"

"I'm terribly sorry that I couldn't aid you. My inexperience pains me."

As Silva stared at the ground, Rafinha comforted him. "No, that was just Chris hitting you out of nowhere to steal the show. It wasn't your fault."

"No, no. A holy knight wielding a transformed hieral menace should be invincible... Getting knocked out can't be anything but the result of my own inexperience. I must assert that the fault is mine; I cannot let it reflect poorly on Ripple."

"Nooo, it's Chris's fault for giving someone on her own side an elbow strike! I'm really sorry, and I apologize on her behalf. She just can't stop herself when she sees a powerful foe."

"No, no, no, I must take the blame."

As Inglis watched the rather unproductive exchange, Ripple unobtrusively tugged at her sleeves.

"Inglis, Inglis..."

"Yes, what is it?"

"Did you notice? When I transformed into a weapon..." Ripple whispered, not wanting anyone else to overhear.

"Yes. That was alarming. But I understand—when thinking about why something so powerful would be granted to the surface..."

"Yeah. Agreed. Thanks for stopping it."

"No, don't thank me. I already had reasons to step in." Meaning, she'd wanted to steal the Prismer from Silva so she could fight it herself.

"Ha ha ha... That's just like you, Inglis."

"But there's one thing I don't understand. When I saw the Steelblood Front's hieral menace transform, I didn't sense anything from Sistia like I did from you. It seemed to have no side effects at all..."

"Huhhhh?!" Ripple was so startled that she forgot she was trying to be quiet.

"What's wrong, Chris?" Rafinha asked, turning to them.

Silva did the same. "Is anything the matter, Lady Ripple?"

"Ah, no, it's nothing, nothing at all..." Ripple said, brushing his concerns aside. "By the way, Silva, how are you doing?"

"Fine. No major problems to report."

"I see. That's nice. Your health always comes first! If you're healthy, you can get stronger, and become the image of yourself that you want to be."

"Yes! I'll continue training, and I will become a full-fledged holy knight!"

"I bet. But don't push yourself too hard, okay?" As she clapped a hand on Silva's shoulder, Ripple again whispered to Inglis, "What we talked about... Don't tell them, okay? When he really becomes a holy knight, he'll learn."

"Yes, understood."

Theodore finished his conversation with Miriela and beckoned Ripple over. "Then, let's go, Lady Ripple. I'd like to see how Wayne and the others are doing on the front lines."

"Okay! Goodbye, everyone! When I return to the capital, I'll come see you!"

Ripple and Ambassador Theodore made their way to the ambassadorial large Flygear.

"Everyone, I truly thank you for your actions during this crisis. With knights-to-be like you, this country's future is sure to be bright." Ambassador Theodore bowed his head to the retinue from the knights' academy. "Leave the rest to me while you focus on your studies. Someday, the time will come when the burden of this country's future rests on you. Now, if I may take my leave..."

His affectionate smile seemed to be directed at Rafinha personally, so Inglis deftly stepped in front.

"Hey, Chris. I can't see."

"That shouldn't be seen by children."

"What are you talking about? It didn't seem obscene to me."

"How would you know?!"

As she watched Inglis and Rafinha squabble, Ripple giggled. "See you later, everyone! Bye-bye!" As Ripple waved from the Flygear, her smile receded into the sky with the aircraft's departure.

Extra: The Artistic Count

Rrrumble!
Grrrgggl!

"Haaah..."

Inglis and Rafinha let out deep sighs at the same time while they carried construction materials. Currently, all students were helping to rebuild the destroyed buildings of the knights' academy.

"So hungryyy! Can't go on..." After lamenting together, they dropped off the mountainous loads of lumber at the stockpile.

Thump! Thump! Thump! Thump!

Even in her current state, Inglis could do the work of ten.

Leone watched with a bemused expression. "Regardless, if you can lift that much, I think you're doing well enough..."

"But that's all I've got in me. I can't move anymore," Inglis protested.

"Me too..." Rafinha agreed.

The two slumped down.

"Ha ha ha. Then let's take a quick break." Leone sat down next to Inglis and Rafinha.

"Ha ha… We're stuck like this until the cafeteria reopens, aren't we…?" Inglis bemoaned.

"Yeah. The rations the principal's supplying aren't nearly enough…" Rafinha agreed.

Rafael, whom the pair normally counted on when it came to financial matters, was away at the front lines. Little remained of Inglis and Rafinha's allowances—definitely not enough to feed their appetites.

"We haven't been hungry like this since the year before last…" Rafinha rolled over and rested her head in Inglis's lap.

"You're right." Inglis didn't mind Rafinha's being there. It was just like Inglis was spoiling a grandchild.

"Did something happen?" Leone asked.

"The harvest in our hometown of Ymir failed that year…" Rafinha began to explain.

"And because the citizens were tightening their belts because of the lack of food, we did the same in solidarity," Inglis continued.

"Back then, I acted like my dad was a monster."

"But isn't leading by example a part of being a good lord?" Inglis replied.

"Mm-hmm. It was the right thing to do. But it still sucked!"

"If I remember right, you even tried eating a magicite beast."

"Whaaat?!" Leone gasped.

"You tried too, Chris!" Rafinha shot back.

"I'm your squire, Rani, I'm supposed to do whatever you do," Inglis offered as an excuse.

"You always blame other people when something inconvenient comes up." Rafinha pouted, sulking.

"So, uh… Did you end up eating it?" Leone asked.

"Nope. The knights got really mad and stopped us," Rafinha said.

"We never did eat one," Inglis said.

"So back then you endured it, right? That should mean you can do the same now," Leone prompted.

"Well, not exactly. We got something to eat right after that," Rafinha explained.

"How?" Leone asked.

"A part-time job with benefits," Inglis answered.
"Oh...? Doing what?"
"Well..."

◆◇◆

The year before last, when their hometown of Ymir was struck by famine...

Inglis and Rafinha, even though they had been as hungry as they were now, regularly accompanied the knights of Ymir on hunts for magicite beasts. By then, at the age of thirteen, Rafinha had already become the best of Ymir's knights with her upper-class Rune and Artifact, and Inglis was seen as a martial-arts prodigy even while hiding her aether abilities. The knights had come to rely on their power. They couldn't slack off simply because they were hungry.

During one hungry excursion, Inglis and Rafinha spotted a group of people under attack by magicite beasts in the forest near Ymir. There were dozens of people, all carrying ample amounts of luggage. Since they were aware that magicite beasts could attack at any time, they were naturally armed to defend themselves. Still, they seemed to be having a hard time due to the large number of magicite beasts.

Inglis and Rafinha immediately moved to rescue them.

"Chris! If this goes on for long, we'll feel even hungrier, so let's take them out in one shot like normal!"

"Okay—got it!" Inglis led the way, plunging into the pack of magicite beasts. She prioritized the ones that were attacking the group's guards and sent them flying.

A guard gasped in awe. "She's beating magicite beasts with her bare hands?!"

"Wh-What?! How can she do that?!"

"A-Amazing! A girl that cute..."

The guardsmen stopped, their eyes glued to Inglis's movements.

Inglis urged them to clear the area. "Get back! There's a big attack coming from above!"

"Okay!"

"Got it!"

"But what about you?!"

"I'll—" Just as Inglis began to respond, a rain of Rafinha's arrows of light began to fall from overhead. It was an unrelenting wide-scale attack meant for when the guards had fully retreated, but Rafinha was a bit impatient today—perhaps her empty stomach was to blame.

"Aaaaagh!"

The guards screamed in terror at the sight. Their worry was unwarranted, because a few moments later, all that was left in the area was a wiped-out pack of magicite beasts and a scratchless Inglis.

"It may be a bit late to say so, but I'm fine. Thanks for being concerned, though," Inglis said.

"S-Sure..."

"You're amazing..."

"Th-There's no way you're an ordinary person!"

Then Rafinha rushed over. "Chriiis! Are you okay? I didn't hit you?"

"No worries, Rani. I'm fine."

"Okay. Well, I figured it would take more than that to hit you." Rafinha nodded, and called out to the guards. "Hello! We're knights of Ymir. Be careful on your journey!"

"Safe travels," Inglis added. "Now, if you'll excuse us."

The two smiled, and were about to leave, but—

"Simply *incredible*! What a lovely sight you young ladies are! You've set my heart aflaaame!" A slender middle-aged man hopped up and down as he called out in a crazed voice. With a proud strut, he approached the two girls.

The two recoiled. They had to admit—he was a bit creepy.

"Ah, I simply must have forgotten to introduce myself! I'm none other than Count Weismar, the leader of this grand troupe! But please, you must listen!"

"Uhh...?" they both said.

Grrrgggl!

Inglis and Rafinha's stomachs rumbled at the same time.

"My, my, do you happen to be hungry? Have no fear, I'll have something right out! We can converse as we eat."

Inglis and Rafinha nodded without hesitation. "Yes! Absolutely!"

◆◇◆

The Bilford ducal residence in the fortress city of Ymir had a visitor the next day.

"Hmm... So the famed 'Artistic Count,' Lord Weismar, seeks to put on a performance in my city of Ymir..." Duke Bilford said.

"Yes, indeeeed!" the count said. "I've heard of your failed harvest and the resulting famine! In times like these, the people's hearts must surely be troubled, yes? Buuut the power of art can heal them! Or, perhaps not to go too far, at least provide a distraction. Please, grant your permission for me to perform!" Count Weismar spoke in a high-pitched voice and with gestures that were perhaps a bit *too* exaggerated, but that seemed to be normal for him. His clothing—his everything, really—was eccentric.

But despite his strange appearance, he was quite well known. He led a theatrical troupe that traveled from place to place, performing plays, songs, and dances. Originally his family was noble, but they had lost their holdings in his grandfather's generation, and he was the third to lead a traveling troupe. The Weismar Troupe had been performing for decades.

"Very well. I suppose it will be enjoyed by the people. I'd wanted to ask that of you anyway—but about putting Rafinha and Inglis on stage..."

"Yes, yes, *of course*! When those young ladies appeared before me, I thought angels had come down from heaven! Their existence alone is art! Please, I beg of you! Allow me to have them on stage! They're the daughters of the local lord and the captain of the knights, so surely the people will recognize them? For them to appear on stage would only make the smiles of the audience shine brighter!"

"Well... I understand your reasoning, but...Rafinha..."

Duke Bilford was still uncomfortable with the idea of his daughter being on stage. Inglis could understand that feeling. Rafinha would probably be made into a spectacle.

"Yes! This performance will include a song and a dance! And I'm sure her beautiful appearance will charm the people!"

"Well..."

Rafinha, though, was eager. "Father, I want to participate! It'll cheer up everyone in town!"

That was true, but Rafinha's interest seemed to come more from a maidenly whim of curiosity. She also couldn't forget Count Weismar's promise of all-they-could-eat food during rehearsals and the performance—that was possibly the most persuasive part. The troupe had traveled with plenty of food for themselves and had enough to spare. They wouldn't go hungry if they shared it with two more people. Plus, if it sounded like fun, Rafinha was sure to be on board.

"Hey, Chris! You wanna join too, right?!" Rafinha asked.

"Huh...? Well..." Inglis was extremely conflicted. On the one hand, she didn't like the idea of singing or dancing in front of people. After having a hard time with the curious stares when she dressed up for the party, she didn't think she'd take appearing before an even larger crowd well. If that had been all there was to it, she'd decline...but then she'd be hungry.

"Hmm... I'm not sure."

"C'mon, Chris, you know you wanna!"

"Listen, I at least need to ask my parents first."

Her father, Luke, was likely to have the same reaction as Duke Bilford, and her mother, Serena, was modest and proper. Inglis couldn't see her smiling on the idea. Irina, Rafinha's mother and Inglis's aunt, had a personality much like Rafinha's, so she might be okay with Rafinha being in the performance.

"Very well. It's not a decision for me to make myself. I must ask Irina and Serena, and Luke will be back later tonight. Lord Weismar, let us come to a conclusion in the morning," the Duke intoned.

"Oho ho! Understood, my good man!" With another strange flourish, Count Weismar smiled.

Once evening arrived, as everyone gathered for dinner at the castle, the subject came up.

Extra: The Artistic Count

As Inglis's mother heard the story, her face was stern. Then she said with the utmost sincerity, "Chris... This is a great opportunity. You absolutely should do it!"

"Whaaat?!" Inglis, not expecting that response, was uncharacteristically shocked.

"Come on, Serena, are you serious? Inglis doesn't even seem that excited about it." Luke was surprised too.

"Yes. She *must!*"

"Umm..." Inglis began, at a loss for what to say next. *This isn't like my mother, who's always calm and composed*, she thought.

"I knew it! I knew you'd understand, Aunt Serena! C'mon, mom. Let me go too!" Rafinha said.

"Well, if Chris is..." Irina chuckled. "That's every girl's dream, isn't it? It might be better than just fighting magicite beasts all the time."

Duke Bilford had a troubled expression. "Come now... Fighting magicite beasts is a knight's noble duty to protect their people."

"That much is true. But as a mother, I'd like to see my daughter shine on the stage."

"Well... I suppose if Inglis is along too, I don't object..."

It seemed that the decision rested on Inglis.

Her father turned to her. "Now, Inglis, your mother seems to like the idea, but you can decline the offer if that's what you want. What would you like to do?"

"W-Well... I'd like a little time to think." Even with what her mother had said, she still wasn't convinced.

Late that night at home, Inglis opened the window of her room and gazed at the stars. As she did, the voices of her parents drifted to her from the next room over.

"Serena, it wasn't like you to be so insistent with Inglis."

"Sorry, dear. But Inglis... She's always wanted to be a squire, and the people of Ymir are kind to her. However, when she leaves for the knights' academy in the capital, she might have unhappy or painful experiences because she doesn't have a Rune."

"You're right. That could be a problem. She's able to live a carefree life here in Ymir, but..."

"Yes. Just in case terrible things happen in the future, I think she needs to know that she has other options open, so I think this is a good opportunity. That's why I was so insistent."

"I see. That's a really good way of putting it. Tomorrow, I'll recommend to Inglis that she give it a try."

"Yes. Thank you, dear."

Hearing that much, Inglis softly closed her window. It seemed she should accept the offer. Standing on stage would definitely be embarrassing, though.

In the end, Inglis ate her fill while practicing singing and dancing, and her time on stage was a huge success. Her mother watched over her with joy in her eyes. Thanks to that, Inglis was okay enough with the stares that washed over her.

Rafinha later said that she'd matured as a girl; whether that was a good thing or a bad thing was a bit complicated.

◆◇◆

"Huh, so you met Count Weismar? I suppose if you're as good looking as Inglis, you're bound to catch his eye," Leone commented.

"It's such a nice memory! Chris was so cute, and the food was tasty too! Though I guess I was just up there next to her to make her look better." Rafinha pouted.

"That's not true. You were very cute, Rani. I remember it well," Inglis said.

Rafinha giggled. "Ahh, I really wish Count Weismar would conveniently show up with food again..."

"Yeah. I wonder where he is now."

"Inglis! Rafinha!" Just then, Principal Miriela came jogging over.

"Yes, Principal?" Rafinha asked.

"What is it?" Inglis followed.

"A summons from the palace! His Majesty King Carlias would like to speak with you!"

Inglis and Rafinha gasped, thinking the same thing.

It was lunchtime. He wanted a conversation. Of course, there'd be refreshments—supplied by the palace's cooks, no less.

Delicious food!

"All right! I'm sure there'll be stuff for us to eat there, Chris!"

"Yeah, Rani, and it's probably tasty too!"

"Off we go!" the two shouted happily, immediately setting off for the palace.

Afterword

First, thank you very much for picking up this book!

So, that's the third volume of *Reborn to Master the Blade: From Hero-King to Extraordinary Squire* ♀. I hope you enjoyed it.

Things have been a mess lately, but the part of it that's affected my family the most is the kids staying home from school. My daughter loves playing games just like her parents, so at least she's happy to have more time to play. I happened to have bought her a Switch before schools closed, and that turned out to be a good decision. I've heard there were shortages after everyone started to stay home to quarantine.

I was surprised to find out that she built up a pretty impressive island in *Animal Crossing* before I realized it. It's amazing that a six-year-old kid can pick up decorating and building tips from YouTube videos and put them into practice for her own island...

Finally, I'd like to thank my editor N, the illustrator Nagu, and everyone else involved for their hard work and dedication. The illustrations for this volume were great as usual. Moto Kuromura's manga version is great too! If you haven't seen it yet, check it out! Goodbye for now!

HEY/////////
▶ HAVE YOU HEARD OF
J-Novel Club?

It's the digital publishing company that brings you the latest novels and manga from Japan!

Subscribe today at
▶▶▶▶j-novel.club◀◀◀◀

and read the latest volumes as they're translated, or become a premium member to get a *FREE* ebook every month!

Check Out The Latest Volume Of
**Reborn to Master the Blade:
From Hero-King to Extraordinary Squire** ♀

Plus Our Other Hit Series Like:

- ▶ Min-Maxing My TRPG Build in Another World
- ▶ Campfire Cooking in Another World with My Absurd Skill
- ▶ I Shall Survive Using Potions!
- ▶ Black Summoner
- ▶ Knight's & Magic
- ▶ My Quiet Blacksmith Life in Another World

- ▶ The Invincible Little Lady
- ▶ The Retired Demon of the Maxed-Out Village
- ▶ Now I'm a Demon Lord! Happily Ever After with Monster Girls in My Dungeon
- ▶ Back to the Battlefield: The Veteran Heroes Return to the Fray!

...and many more!

In Another World With My Smartphone, Illustration © Eiji Usatsuka   Arifureta: From Commonplace to World's Strongest, Illustration © Takayaki